THE
SECOND SUN

THE SECOND SUN

P. T. Deutermann

ST. MARTIN'S PRESS
NEW YORK

First published in the United States by St. Martin's Press,
an imprint of St. Martin's Publishing Group

www.stmartins.com

Library of Congress Cataloging-in-Publication Data

Names: Deutermann, P. T. (Peter T.), 1941– author.
Title: The second sun / P.T. Deutermann.
Description: First edition. | New York : St. Martin's Press, 2025.
Identifiers: LCCN 2024043469 | ISBN 9781250360977 (hardcover) |
    ISBN 9781250360984 (ebook)
Subjects: LCSH: World War, 1939–1945—Naval operations, American—Fiction. |
    Manhattan Project (U.S.)—Fiction. | LCGFT: Historical fiction. | Thrillers
    (Fiction). | Novels.
Classification: LCC PS3554.E887 S43 2025 | DDC 813/.54—dc23/eng/20241011
LC record available at https://lccn.loc.gov/2024043469

Our books may be purchased in bulk for promotional, educational,
or business use. Please contact your local bookseller or the Macmillan
Corporate and Premium Sales Department at 1-800-221-7945, extension
5442, or by email at MacmillanSpecialMarkets@macmillan.com.

First Edition: 2025

10 9 8 7 6 5 4 3 2 1

This book is dedicated to all the American families who lost sons and daughters, husbands, and fathers to the cauldron that was the Second World War, and then had to watch as Germany and Japan were rehabilitated in pursuit of a necessary strategy to keep America safe in the postwar world. Even though they could see the logic, it must have been extremely difficult to suppress their fury at our new allies.

THE
SECOND SUN

ONE

STRAHLUNG

My desk intercom buzzed. "Captain Bowen," my secretary said, "there's a call from the commander of the Portsmouth Naval Shipyard on line one."

"Which one?" I said.

"Sir?"

"There's a Portsmouth Naval Shipyard in Maine, and then there's the naval shipyard in Portsmouth, Virginia."

"That's the Norfolk Navy Yard, sir," she reminded me. "This will be New Hampshire."

"Smart aleck."

"I'll take that as a compliment. Sir," she said tartly. Marianne was my civilian secretary and a real crackerjack. I couldn't survive without her, and she well knew that. She was a war widow. Her husband had been killed on the USS *Vincennes* back in those first bloody weeks of the naval campaign for Guadalcanal. That always seemed to me to have just happened, but it had been three years ago. Three long years.

"Okay, okay," I said, and picked up the line. "CNO's office, Captain Bowen speaking."

"Captain, this is Admiral Tommy Carter, CEC. I'm the Commander, Portsmouth Naval Shipyard."

Instinctively, I straightened up in my office chair. "Yes, sir. How can I help you, sir?"

"I've got a situation up here involving a surrendered German U-boat. I called my bosses in BuShips, and they specifically told me to call the CNO's office. They told me to call you."

Aw shit, I thought. Here comes another can of worms. German U-boat?

"Yes, sir?" I said.

"You remember that after the Germans surrendered, Admiral Doenitz ordered all their U-boats to go find an Allied warship, wherever they could, surface, and then surrender to it?"

"Correct, sir."

"Five days ago, a U-boat surfaced in the Atlantic and surrendered to a small Canadian corvette that was transiting alone back from the UK to her home port in Halifax. This happened about five hundred miles northeast of here. This corvette is small, with a max speed of eighteen knots. They reported to their operational commander in Halifax that this sub was big—really big. They sent a prize crew aboard and then discovered there were civilians aboard as well. *Japanese* civilians."

That got my attention. Japanese on a U-boat?

The admiral continued. "There was no way a corvette could take the U-boat's crew aboard, so Halifax went to our ComEasternSeaFrontier in New York and asked if we could send a destroyer to help out and then escort the U-boat here, to Portsmouth, which is the US base nearest to their position. Eastern Sea Frontier said yes. Tugs are mustering right now to go bring the boat alongside one of our piers at 1100 this morning."

"Okay," I said. "This won't be the first one. I think Norfolk's got three of them so far. Nazi U-boat skippers don't want to surrender to a British ship, so they're making the transit west to surrender to us instead."

"Can't hardly blame them," the admiral said. "After what they did to England. But: I sent a liaison officer from my staff out on the destroyer to rendezvous with the corvette and take over the escort. He's a line officer, but his billet here is as my intel officer. He went aboard the sub, made a quick tour while it was underway, and then sent me a message from the destroyer. He says the sub is much bigger than our *Balao* class and that there's something 'off' about this sub."

"Such as?"

"Well, no torpedo tubes, for one. And he thinks there's a second deck. We build subs here at Portsmouth, as you know. Never heard of one with two decks. He confirmed the civilians were two Japanese nationals who were carrying Third Reich papers, complete with the logo of the SS. He said nobody aboard the ship would or could—he's not sure which—speak to him except the captain, who kept asking him, in broken English, if they could please be taken to an American base."

"What did he tell them?" I asked.

"He told them with a perfectly straight face that there was an excellent naval prison where they were going."

I laughed. Of course, there was—the Portsmouth Naval Prison, where the Navy sent officers and enlisted men who'd been convicted of prison-worthy serious crimes at a court-martial. It was like the Army's Fort Leavenworth pen, but scarier, I thought. I'd seen pictures—a massive, alabaster-white pile built in the last century, with fifty-foot stone walls and turreted towers, all of it looming above a fast-flowing river that acted like a moat.

"But here's the thing," the admiral went on. "I thought someone from ONI ought to come up here to check this thing out, so I called them, too. They told me the same thing that BuShips did, that the CNO's direct staff—OpNav—was running the surrender program for German ships, and that they, ONI, had their hands full with matters much farther east of here."

"I understand, Admiral," I said. Boy, did I. The Office of Naval Intelligence was infamous in Washington naval circles for executing a bureaucratic lateral arabesque when anything sounded like a real problem. I reminded myself to find a way to pay those smug phonies back for this one. But now:

"Let me suggest you get the U-boat alongside an empty pier," I said. "Put armed guards on its weather decks and around the pier, and close that entire pier to everybody. Remove the entire ship's company, including their guests, to the penitentiary, but keep them separate from the main population. Separate the officers and those two mystery civilians from the crewmen if you can. Do all this the moment she lands and shuts down so they can't scuttle it. I'll go find the right guy here in DC to get up there and deal with this. May I have your secure number, please?"

He gave it to me with obvious relief.

OpNav is the Navy's abbreviation for the Navy's headquarters staff. The head of the Navy is the chief of naval operations, a four-star admiral. OpNav: operations, naval. There is a vice chief, and then several deputy chiefs of naval operations for specific policy areas: naval air, surface ships, submarines, the Navy's budget, logistics, public affairs, strategic plans and policy, etc. The vice chief is a four-star. The deputies are three-stars, or vice admirals. Within their directorates are division directors—usually two-stars, or rear admirals.

I'm a surface ship captain who'd spent 1942–43 as captain of a destroyer in the Guadalcanal campaign, then as captain of a heavy cruiser from 1943 into early 1945. After that I'd been pulled back to Washington, supposedly to the Plans and Policy Directorate, which dealt with war plans, strategy, and most importantly, relations with the Army, Marines, and the Army Air Forces, which were often fraught with bureaucratic conflict. In early 1945, while I was awaiting actual orders and still hoping hard for another command at sea, I was informed that I was going instead to the small, personal executive staff of the CNO himself. I would have no title, nor any office staff other than a secretary. The assignment officer had told me that I was going to join the CNO's so-called Strategic Planning Committee. There were only four of us, and our job was to solve thorny Navy headquarters problems by going around, through, over, and even under the increasingly large naval bureaucracy that had grown up in Washington to run and, presumably, win this goddamned war against Germany and Japan. One down, one to go.

To say that there was interservice competition for roles, missions, and most importantly, budgetary money in Washington by 1945 would be the gross understatement of the year. The Army and Navy headquarters staffs had grown exponentially since Pearl Harbor, but the Army staff was twice the size of ours because it incorporated the explosive growth of the Army Air Forces arm, which had grown in size and importance. Even with the war in Europe officially over, the Army Air Forces were quickly becoming an equal to the entire naval air effort in the Pacific as we closed in on Japan. While almost the entire US Navy was preparing for the invasion of *Okinawa* and, ultimately, Japan itself, the Army Air Forces were actually bombing the Japanese homeland. In the constant bureaucratic maneuvering between the two military departments, Army and Navy, that fact carried a lot of weight.

The war with Japan was most definitely not over, and in fact was getting bloodier by the day. The invasion of Japan had been seen as the *Götterdämmerung* of America's war effort ever since Pearl Harbor. Recently the Joint Chiefs had formally ordered the invasion of *Okinawa*. That meant that forces—*huge* forces—would soon go in motion to assemble off the home islands. Ultimate victory was pretty much assured, but at what cost? If the recent *Iwo Jima* invasion was any indication, the human cost of going into the home islands would be beyond belief.

We'd "won" in Europe, although the nagging suspicion, Washington-wide, was that the Soviet Union was going to be the Next Big Problem. Because Mother Russia had been absorbing and thus holding down several German armies, its government claimed that America owed them a debt of material, money, manpower, and food. Ironically, Hitler's blunder in invading Russia had ultimately made the Normandy invasion possible because so much of his army was locked in a battle to the death on the eastern front.

President Roosevelt had quickly seen the value of Russian armies tying down German armies, even as the Russian people suffered terribly. He'd made sure that the United States did its best to send relief to them, even as the realization dawned across Washington that the Soviets had much bigger ambitions in postwar Europe. The problem now was that, by all "insider accounts," Roosevelt was dying in office. He had been such a stalwart, oversize, totally involved, often prescient and equally often tyrannical player in this titanic game of total world war that his absence would create a crisis of its own. Everybody knew it, probably even his vice president, a somewhat unknown factor named Harry S. Truman. I'd been to several high-level briefings at the White House, mostly as a minor horseholder, but I had never once even *seen* the vice president.

Hitler's Germany had been utterly defeated, and only now were the Allies and their populations beginning to understand the full depth of Hitler's Final Solution. Far-seeing elements of the Allied governments were making the argument that Germany would have to be reconstituted if the Russians were ever to be checked, but the international outrage at what the Germans had been doing in their euphemistically called "labor camps" was making that entire effort extremely difficult.

I went down the hall to the CNO's office and asked for a minute with his executive assistant, a rear admiral named Henry Carlstein. He was a newly promoted flag officer but absolutely *not* new to Washington and its many intrigues. I liked working for him because I rarely had to explain the antecedents of any problem. He'd seen it all before. I told him about the Portsmouth situation. He seemed a bit underwhelmed until I mentioned the Japanese passengers with German SS papers.

"Say that again?" he said, suddenly looking up.

"Two Japanese nationals—officers, civilians, we don't know, but they had Third Reich identification papers, issued by the SS HQ in Berlin."

"*You* go up there," he said immediately. "Right now. Tonight. Contact me on my secure line when you find out who or what *they* are. And, and this is important: you, personally, go aboard that boat, find out what she's carrying. Take the CO of the boat with you. Make him show you. If he balks, tell him he'll be hanged that very day if he doesn't. Nazi-style. In a basement. With piano wire."

"Seems extreme," I said. "He did surrender, pretty much as ordered."

"He's a German, and a Nazi," Carlstein spat. "I'm no longer certain there's any difference between the two, but he'd expect nothing less in different circumstances. Go. I'll brief the Boss."

TWO

PORTSMOUTH NAVY YARD

Admiral Carter graciously sent a Navy staff car for me when I got off the train in Portsmouth the next day. I was shown into his office twenty minutes later. Rear Admiral Tommy Carter was at least ten years older than me, with gray hair and a pleasant aspect. He was CEC: Civil Engineering Corps, the Navy's shipbuilders, maintainers, naval architects, and fixit corps. He exhibited none of the *I'm an admiral, you're just a captain* mannerisms I'd often encounter in Washington. He seemed relieved that I was there.

"This boat is definitely something different," he said after coffee had been passed around. His young lieutenant intelligence officer was present for our meeting, as was his chief of staff, one Captain Jarrel Gray, also a CEC officer.

"I saw the crew," the admiral said. "They're arrogant, as if they're special, but they're also maybe scared of what we're going to find aboard that boat that might get them killed."

"And the two Japanese?"

"They're calm, silent, and of course, inscrutable. They gave me the impression that they expect to be executed quite soon."

Uh-oh, I thought. "Admiral, if you will, sir, call that prison," I said. "Put those two under isolation and twenty-four-hour surveillance, right now. They are likely to try to kill themselves if they get the chance. They may not have surrendered, but they'll feel dishonored. In fact, transfer them to the naval hospital here into a suicide-prevention clinic with twenty-four-hour, in-person surveillance. Restrained."

The admiral nodded at his chief of staff, who left the room to see to my "requests." If the admiral was upset with my giving orders, he made no sign of it. I always tried to be polite, but my role on the CNO's executive staff was to defuse problems before they had a chance to grow. The people I talked to in that tone of voice tended to recognize that. It wasn't personal arrogance on my part, even if it might look that way. An admiral is an admiral, whether he's line, engineering, supply, or medical corps, and I was just another captain. Aboard a ship, a captain was somebody. In Washington, Navy captains and their Army counterparts, colonels, were a dime a dozen. Within the Navy, the fact that my phone number was listed as a part of the CNO's executive office carried weight. It didn't hurt that I was also six one and had been a hobby weightlifter for years. I typically did not enter an office. I mostly loomed in the doorway for a moment until all conversation stopped.

The train trip had taken all night from Washington to Portsmouth with lots of delays because wartime freight traffic always took precedence over the passenger trains. We didn't get in until the next morning. The admiral offered to have me over for dinner at his quarters that evening but I respectfully declined. I was tired from a diet of seven-day weeks and the high pressures of working at the four-star level at headquarters. My briefcase was full of problem papers, none of them classified but no less complex. The CNO often wanted his small brain trust's candid opinion on just about everything to balance what his enormous staff was telling him in great volume. Two of our small group handled operational problems; the other two handled the equally important snarls of the eternal budgetary and influence competition between the two services. This one sounded quasi-operational, but when the CNO's executive assistant says go, we go. Right now, my plan was to hit the O'Club for a drink and dinner, then go back to the BOQ and on to bed. I needed to be clearheaded and rested for this U-boat mystery bright and early tomorrow morning.

Japanese in Germany, I thought, as I enjoyed a small brandy after dinner in the nearly empty O'Club. What in the world had they been doing in Germany? True, what we had called the Axis powers during the war had been Germany, Japan, and, to a lesser extent, Italy. Nobody in Washington who'd seen news films of Mussolini's theatrical antics took Italy all that seriously, except perhaps the British convoys that had suffered under Italian air attack in the Mediterranean. But the Germany–Japan Axis was something else altogether. Germany, under Hitler, had wanted domination of the Western world; Japan, suzerainty of Asia. That said, though we'd been using that term, Axis powers, since 1941, it was hard to imagine that there was much detailed cooperation between the two, if only because there were twelve thousand physical miles between them. This strange submarine might shed a light on that assumption, I thought. But what?

THREE
A REALLY BIG SUBMARINE

A Navy Yard staff car picked me up at 0700 the next morning and delivered me to the end pier at the Navy Yard's shoreline, Pier 5. I wasn't in uniform, but rather was wearing a set of Navy-blue overalls with no insignia. I'd been aboard some operational submarines in the Pacific, and they were necessarily hostile to expensive uniforms. I could see the U-boat, alone at the pier, distinctive in its pinkish-gray warpaint. It was indeed big, maybe twice the size of some of the captured attack boats down in Norfolk. There was no gun on the foredeck, and no antiaircraft guns on the conning tower. The lieutenant had said that there were no torpedo tubes, either.

Not an attack boat, then. Maybe she was what the Germans called an Atlantic *milch* cow, a resupply ship for the attack boats. They'd go out to sea and loiter in an area away from the convoy routes. The attack boats would go alongside for fuel, water, torpedoes, mail, and food. That way they didn't have to go back all the way to Germany to replenish. Except, as I studied her, she had no visible refueling fittings, either. I also thought

her conning tower was smaller than it should be for such a large submarine. She just looked "off," as the lieutenant had observed.

Admiral Carter was already there, and together we went aboard. He
was dressed as I was—shipyard coveralls with no rank insignia. He could
have been a shop foreman, except for the deference being shown by all
around him. There was a hatch on the boat's weather deck that led into
the conning tower. From there we proceeded down into the boat's interior. I was surprised to see a German officer waiting for us, accompanied
by three grim-looking Marines from the penitentiary. The admiral introduced him to me as *Kapitänleutnant* Eric Groff, the skipper of the boat.
He did not look happy to be there. I made sure to let him see that I was
devastated. The admiral had brought along a German-speaking officer,
who explained to Groff that we wanted a thorough tour of his boat. I
don't speak German, but it appeared to me that Groff said something
along the lines of, help yourself, *amerikanischer* dolts. I checked with our
interpreter, who said that was about right.

"Tell the captain that I am from the headquarters of the national security intelligence office in Washington. He will give us a personally
led tour or there will be consequences. Extreme consequences, *Prinz-
Albrecht-Straße*-style."

Groff gave me a hard stare once that message—including the address
of SS headquarters in Berlin—was delivered. I gave him one back. For a
moment, he did nothing, but then his shoulders slumped and he agreed.

We began at the back end, where normally there would have been
the after-torpedo room, which turned out to be just a storage area. We
progressed forward through some crew quarters, the engine room, gen-
erator room, galley and messing, the control center, officers' quarters, the
sonar sound-shack, the radio room, more berthing, and finally the compartment that normally would have been the forward torpedo room, but
was more crew accommodations. No torpedo tubes. Groff stopped and
gave us a look that said: satisfied?

"No," the admiral said. "I want to see the second deck."

The interpreter spoke and then turned to Admiral Carter. He said the captain had told him there was no second deck. I'd had enough of his bullshit. The admiral had said the captain spoke broken English. I turned to the admiral and said that the captain was being uncooperative. He should be taken back to Portsmouth Naval Prison and hanged forthwith. I turned on my heel and started aft. The captain called out: "Vait!" I kept going. A second call: "Vait, please!" I turned around. The admiral had been playing along, beckoning to his Marines.

"Well?" I said.

"*Hier,*" the captain said, pointing to an unobtrusive hatch in the deck, almost concealed between two storage lockers. I made him open the hatch, which produced a strange smell almost immediately. Chlorine? Some other halogen? Hydrogen-something? I looked down into the hatchway. Darkness.

"Lights," I ordered. Groff found a switch.

I looked again. There certainly *was* a second deck, and it consisted of two rows of what looked like vertical torpedo tubes. Big, heavy, round hatches with compressed air connections and brass operating wheels that stretched in each direction for what looked like the length of the boat. There was an overhead gantry track for loading the vertical tubes.

Now I knew what this boat was for—she was a minelayer. An advanced minelayer, at that. Instead of the usual method, by which a sub would deploy mines out of her after torpedo tubes, this boat had been designed to maneuver to precise undersea locations for the minefield and then fire the mines straight down to their programmed positions. Much more accurate. The sub would take time to nail down her exact position, and then lay the field array. But what was that strange smell? Acidic. Metallic. Chemical, too. Like acid vapors. I couldn't place it.

I told the captain to lead the way down there. He refused. He then made it clear there was no way he was going down there. Hanging threats or no. He sat down on the deckplates like a sulking child and wouldn't look at any of us.

The Marines were armed with .45 sidearms. I summoned one, asked for his .45, and then bent down over the captain. He shook his head. *Nein. Nein. Nein.*

"Why not?"

He shook his head again.

I pointed the .45 at his head.

"*Nein, nein, nein!*"

"Why not?"

"*Warum nicht!*" the interpreter shouted from behind me.

"*Strahlung!*" the captain yelled. I looked at the interpreter, who seemed to be trying to dredge up what that word meant. Then he got it.

"Radiation," he said. "He's saying there's radiation down there."

The admiral spoke up. "Captain, if that's true, we need to close this hatch and get everybody off this boat, right now."

There was no doubt about who was giving orders now. I had the Marines secure the hatch to the lower compartment, but told them to leave the light on. We then followed the admiral and the German skipper up and out of the boat. I told the Marines to get the shipyard guards down from the weather deck and then to post two armed sentries on the pier by the brow leading to the sub. The very unhappy-looking skipper was dispatched back to the penitentiary.

Back in the admiral's office, we were met by the head of quality control in the shipyard, a CEC commander. Admiral Carter had called him in to explain to me about radiation, about which I knew not much, other than that certain elements from the periodic table naturally emitted radiation. And the fact that X-ray techs wore lead aprons. The QA officer went into lecture mode.

"Here at Portsmouth Yard, we build submarines, which have welded joints in their hulls in addition to rivets and other fastening techniques," the commander began. "Where we do use welds, they must be perfect. No voids, no cracks, no discontinuities in the fused metal. Zero. You may have seen a regular welder hammer on a fresh bead to see if a part of it collapses because there was a bubble in the steel, but that's not good enough for subs going deep underwater. So, we X-ray them."

"You X-ray steel?" I asked in disbelief.

"Yes, sir. Let's say the weld is joining two sections of pipe together that will never need to be opened at that point in the line. We use bolted flanges with gaskets wherever the sub's crew might have to open that line for maintenance purposes, but for a long run of piping, we weld sections together. To X-ray it, we have a machine that can encircle the welded pipe joint. We put a long band of X-ray film down the pipe, and then we mount a radiation source in the machine. It then revolves all the way around the joint. We then pull the band and 'read' the X-ray, which will show any defects in the weld."

"What's the source of the X-rays?" I asked.

"The object of the game is to produce a stream of high-velocity electrons that can penetrate really dense materials, such as steel, or even lead—which is very dense—and then capture that stream on a recording material, such as a special film. These electrons can be produced by specially designed vacuum tubes, but that requires extremely high voltages. There are also natural materials that are fundamentally unstable and thus called radioactive—such as uranium or several of its isotopes. One of these is called cesium 137. Our source for high-velocity electrons is cesium 137. It naturally emits what's called ionizing radiation."

"And why do I care?"

"In simplest terms, because if you stand in the way of cesium-generated ionizing radiation, it will cook the cells of your body in pretty short order. Have you ever had an X-ray?"

"Yes, I have," I said, suddenly alarmed. Cook the cells?

"They put you on a table, point the snout of a large, weird-looking machine at your whatever, drape a lead apron over your vitals, and then the techs leave the room. They told you to hold still, and then the machine made a noise, right?"

"Yes."

"How long was the noise—in seconds?"

"Not even that," I said. "Barely a blink."

"Exactly," he said. "Barely a blink. Like Speedy Gonzales—this won't hurt, will it? Right?"

I nodded, smiling at his off-color analogy.

"An X-ray of the human body is deliberately as short as we can make it. We want to see the bone, but not fry it, or the marrow within. Minimize the exposure to ionizing radiation, while getting it to print the interior picture onto some film. Now: If something in that boat is producing *ionizing* radiation, I would say it's probably uranium or one of its isotopes. Until you know which one, you can't go down there and expect to live very long afterward."

"Damn."

"If that boat was transporting a radioactive material, it's probably *not* a high-energy isotope, otherwise nobody would be alive when they got to wherever they were going. It might be just uranium oxide, or even uranium ore, unprocessed. But before you or anyone else can go down there, you need to know what stuff is in those mining tubes."

"The boat's captain wouldn't even go down there," the admiral pointed out. "Even with a .45 pointed to his head, courtesy of our Washington visitor here."

The commander gave me a strange look.

"I have a low threshold of patience when it comes to Nazi U-boat skippers," I said.

"Um, okay, I guess, Captain. But what I said stands—you need some expert help to determine exactly what you've got here."

I nodded, thanked him, and the commander left.

"Uranium," I said. "I need a drink."

"You read my mind, young man," the admiral said, opening a lower drawer in his desk. He produced a bottle of some good Scotch and poured out a generous measure for us both. We tipped glasses in a traditional *salud* and then just sat there for a few minutes.

"What's significant about uranium?" he asked, finally.

"At the moment, it's a dangerous word," I replied. "If certain people hear you say it in Washington, some scary guys will come around."

"It's a word," the admiral protested. "Just another element from the periodic table, albeit a pretty heavy one. What the hell, over?"

"Sir, are those two Japanese suitably restrained?" I asked, ducking his question for a moment.

"The hospital CO says they are. At least so they can't open their bellies and make a big mess in the ward. And he knows that this is important."

"I know someone," I said. "And if this is about what I think it might be, two things: first, don't even mention that word, officially or unofficially, and make sure you caution the QA officer not to mention that word. And, second, you should expect a crowd here in a few days."

He gave me a raised eyebrows look.

I shook my head. "Admiral, this goes way, way above your pay grade *and* mine, assuming I'm right. The less you know, sir, the safer you are. Me, well, situations like this come with the territory, I'm afraid. May I please use your secure line?"

FOUR
VAN RENSSELAER

I first called my office in Washington on the nonsecure line and asked Marianne to put a call in to one Captain Van Rensselaer at the Old Executive Office Building. I then gave her the shipyard's secure phone drop number and told her to ask him to call me, secure. ASAP. The admiral, overhearing my call, suddenly developed an urgent appointment and told me to make use of his office while he was out. I think he'd heeded my warning, and now that I was contacting someone in the National Security Office, he probably knew he shouldn't be hanging around. Smart. Probably why he was an admiral.

Captain Villem Amherst Van Rensselaer came from an interesting New York family that went way back. A long time ago that name would have been Wilhelm Horst Van Rensselaer, but he'd anglicized it when he entered the naval academy. Not that that fooled anyone. The Van Rensselaer family had once been the third-richest in the nation back in the 1700s, owning an estate of more than a million acres with a large manor house near the present city of Albany. He was in the class of

1925, one year ahead of mine, and known to be a blisteringly smart, somewhat aloof, and unusually tall Dutchman. So tall, in fact, that he'd required a waiver just to graduate, as he exceeded the academy's height maximum. Through what many in the military assumed to be family connections, he'd been selected upon graduation for a Rhodes Scholarship at Oxford, to study physical sciences and languages. Family connections notwithstanding, no one who knew him quibbled with his academic qualifications to go to Oxford.

He never did go to sea or serve in the usual sea and shore billets assigned to almost all recently graduated naval officers. He came back from Oxford with a PhD in physics and the ability to converse comfortably in German and Russian in addition to the French and Dutch he'd brought to Annapolis. He'd subsequently done assignments as a White House aide, a desk officer at the State Department, a professor at the Navy's postgraduate school at the naval academy, and then at the Naval War College in Newport. After that he'd sort of fallen off the radar, reappearing in Washington the week after Pearl Harbor as a lieutenant commander. Six weeks later he was a full captain working on some secret project committee in the Executive Office Building, or EOB, of which there were rumored to be many during the war.

I'd worked with him a couple of times since coming to the CNO's inner sanctum staff, so I was assuming he remembered my name. Having been at the top levels of government for so many years, he might well not, but this radiation business smacked of a new physics discipline called nuclear physics. Not to mention rumors of an extremely secret project, so secret that at least one officer I'd known who had stuck his nose in had literally disappeared. If Van Rensselaer couldn't tell me what to do, he might know someone who could. I fervently hoped.

In the event, he called me back in Portsmouth, and to my surprise, he was immediately interested when I told him I had a captured German U-boat here at the shipyard that was showing signs of radioactivity. He fired off a couple of technical questions that I couldn't answer, but when

I told him we also had two Japanese civilians who'd been aboard the sub in custody he went silent for a moment. I thought he'd hung up.

"Do you *know* they are civilians?" he asked finally.

"I know they're Japanese," I replied. "That's all. I've taken precautions to make sure they can't commit suicide, because I figured someone in your world might want a word."

He laughed quietly at that, and then said, "You'd be positively *amazed* at who would want a word with them, my friend. Good work, Wolfe Bowen. *Very* good work. Now: speak of this call to no one, especially in the shipyard. You may inform Admiral Carter that Washington will take this problem for action. You wait there at Portsmouth. I will be there in two days or less, with some, um, reinforcements. Keep everyone away from the U-boat, but don't make such a big deal about it that the local press gets wind of something going on, understood?"

"Understood," I said. "I'm staying at the BOQ. I did plan to go visit the prisoners and reassure them that we weren't planning to cook and eat them."

"Don't make promises you may not be able to keep, Captain," he said, and then hung up.

Okay, I thought, as I signed off the secure link. What the hell did that mean? Time to see if the shipyard had a gym. I was definitely feeling the need. What the *hell* was this all about?

One day later, not two, I found out. Admiral Carter's duty officer called me in my BOQ room at 0530 and informed me that a "special military train" had entered the shipyard at 0330 that morning and had proceeded to Pier 5, where it had deployed an entire company of Marines. The officer in charge, one Captain Van Rensselaer, USN, had ordered that all shipyard personnel must remain clear of the waterfront and its adjacent buildings because it was possible the enemy submarine had been rigged with a large amount of explosives. Shift workers arriving at 0730 to relieve the night shift would be told to take the day off until tomorrow morning. These measures were precautionary only. No one should be unduly alarmed. Not to worry, I thought. No one in a naval shipyard would bitch about a day off.

On the other hand, don't make a big deal out of it? All those measures would bring press jackals from three states on the run. Villem Van Rensselaer, you've been in Washington too long, I thought. Nobody's gonna believe that bullshit.

Pier 5 was only a half mile from the BOQ. I got dressed in my anonymous jumpsuit, grabbed some coffee from the BOQ office, and walked over there. A conference seemed to be going on at the head of the pier. Admiral Carter was there, along with his chief of staff. Captain Van Rensselaer, distinguishable by just his height alone, six foot plus too much, was explaining to the admiral that he, and some civilian scientists he'd brought with him, needed to go aboard to inspect whatever was secreted aboard this strange-looking submarine. He said that there might be a need for some of his train cars to come down onto the pier so that material could be offloaded. *His* train, I marveled; now that was real juice. Admiral Carter told him the yard had a pusher engine that could manage that. He asked if Van Rensselaer needed the German captain. To my surprise, Van Rensselaer said, "No, but I do want Captain Bowen to accompany us aboard."

Minutes later we were at the hatch to the lower, minelaying deck. Van Rensselaer's two civilians unpacked some test equipment. They then donned white jumpsuits that I would have sworn were made of thick paper, respirators, gloves, and visored hoods. They each pinned on what looked like an oversize domino with a thin, lighted window and then climbed awkwardly down the ladder into the lower deck compartment. We went back up and waited on the main deck of the submarine. They came back up in two minutes. One of them debriefed us.

"There is radiation, but it's within established limits. In my opinion, there's uranium in those tubes. Quite a lot of it, actually. But not refined, and definitely not in a metallic form. Yellowcake, pitchblende, perhaps, or one step past that. But definitely just U-238."

Van Rensselaer nodded. "Activate the removal team," he told them. He turned to me. "Ask Admiral Carter to summon that pusher engine.

We'll need to push my entire train onto the pier, and position the two boxcars just abeam of the brow. Have you spoken to the Japanese?"

"No," I said. "I was supposed to meet with them this morning. You said two days."

"Good," he said, ignoring my small jibe. "I'll go with you. I've brought an interpreter."

FIVE
REVELATION

The two Japanese looked small in their American hospital beds. One of them was older and visibly angry. The other one seemed mostly resigned. They were physically restrained—arms and legs—and lying on their backs, heads propped up on pillows, in adjacent hospital beds. Nurses lingered outside the room, terribly interested in what was going on. Van Rensselaer closed the door on them and then nodded to his interpreter, an Asian woman whose nationality wasn't obvious to me. I thought she was much too tall to be Japanese, but I knew little about the various ethnic physical differences in Asia. I'd shot at Japanese ships and aircraft often enough and experienced their return fire much too often. But I'd never seen an actual enemy human being. What we'd seen were burning, sinking ships and flaming aircraft. If we were lucky, not ours. If we'd been unlucky, we thought about the Japanese often and with great malice.

The woman approached the prisoners and there was a brief conversation in what I assumed was Japanese, after which the interpreter shook her head.

"They will not give me their names," she reported. "By the way, they are insulted to be questioned by a woman. They say only that they are scientists who were being returned to Japan once the Germans surrendered."

"Ask them what's in the second-deck tubes," Van Rensselaer said.

More Japanese. The older man clamped his mouth shut and turned his face away, but the younger one did respond.

"He says it's uranium from the German weapons program."

"Why was this material being sent to Japan?"

This time it was the older man who spat out some more words, still not looking at us. The interpreter's eyes widened as she turned to Van Rensselaer and dutifully translated. "For *our* weapons program, of course, you idiot."

I knew that the interpreter was translating literally, but those words hung in the hospital room like silent, blazing thunderclouds. From the horrified expression spreading across Van Rensselaer's face, I realized that my presence in this room might have been a big mistake. Weapons program? Uranium? What the in the name of God was *this*?

Van Rensselaer suspended the interview, and nodded at me to leave the room. "Wait outside, please," he said.

I did as he asked and joined the small crowd of nurses and now a few doctors hovering in the corridor. One of the docs asked me what was going on, and I said that I couldn't talk about it. Another doc asked why there were Marines with guns all over the shipyard right now. I shook my head, trying to communicate that if I did know, I couldn't tell them. The truth was, I didn't know, so it wasn't much of an act, but that cold feeling in my gut was getting bigger.

Captain Van Rensselaer popped out of the hospital room with his interpreter and announced that he needed an outside phone line right now. One of the docs took him down the hall to an office. He was back in two minutes, indicating that I was to stay right here until guards arrived. One of the remaining docs asked who the hell are you, mister? Van Rensselaer turned to stare at the young doctor from up there in the clouds, his large Dutch visage rigid with anger.

"I would strongly advise every one of you to move along right now," he growled in the coldest voice I'd ever heard. He didn't make any threats. He didn't have to. I wanted to move along with them. This guy was becoming scarier by the moment. The corridor cleared almost by magic. I was left standing alone next to the hospital room door. Then Van Rensselaer spoke. "Captain Bowen," he said, "once the guard detail arrives, I'll ask you to return to Admiral Carter's office. When he gets back from his appointment, I want the both of you to come back down to Pier 5 to witness the unloading. After that, you and I need to have a little chat before I go back to Washington."

"Got it," I said. No more first names, I noticed. Suspicions confirmed. I felt like an ensign on his first ship being told that the XO wants to speak to him. No ensign ever forgot that feeling. My mind was trying to recover what I knew about uranium. Not much.

Uranium. U-238. Weapons program. "Our" weapons program. The look on Van Rensselaer's face when he heard that, and then the look he'd given me, as in, *you* should not have heard that, I'm afraid. My graduate degree was in chemistry, specifically the chemistry of military explosives. How they were made. How they had to be stored. The various forms. The difference between detonation and deflagration. Why dynamite wouldn't work in a gun barrel. Lots of organic chemistry formulae and calculations regarding the mechanics by which six silk bags of gunpowder could reliably propel a 2,600-pound, sixteen-inch battleship projectile twenty-one miles. How zinc and sulfur when properly combined turned into rocket fuel. Chemistry for gunnery officers. Uranium was on the periodic table, but only as an exotic element that went through as many as twelve different shapes—"isotopes"—as it underwent natural decay. Interesting to academics, chemists, and physicists, but of no practical use because it was radioactive, which made it somehow bad. Now we had a Nazi U-boat, filled with uranium, and carrying two Japanese—what? Engineers? Scientists?

I wanted to call back to OpNav and ask the CNO's office to recall me forthwith for some emergency tasking. My game, when not at sea, was to break up bureaucratic logjams, the problems that the everyday bureaucracy was afraid to get into because careers could get hurt, enemies could be made, admirals with long memories offended. In other words, the lively political games played at every military headquarters in the whole world, ours and our enemies', especially in wartime. Encountering a Japanese cruiser squadron rising up out of the hot dark of The Slot was dangerous stuff. Tripping up an Army budgeteer at a congressional hearing was—fun, but certainly not dangerous.

But uranium?

SIX

TOUCH THE TAR BABY

Once the guards arrived, I left the hospital and went for a walk through the mostly deserted shipyard. I was still in my coveralls jumpsuit, augmented by a white safety hat. No one was allowed to walk around in a shipyard without a hard hat. White indicated a commissioned officer or senior supervisor. Other colors denoted trade skills or management/worker bee. I'd called Admiral Carter's office and told his secretary that Captain Van Rensselaer requested the admiral's presence on Pier 5 when convenient. I went to the pier directly, not wanting to just hang out in the admiral's office.

The removal was in full swing when I got there. Figures in bulky white hazard suits and filtered breathing masks were wheeling small drums about half the size of standard 55-gallon barrel tanks down the sub's brow and directly up a ramp into one of those unmarked boxcars. It took one man to roll the drum down, but two to push it up the railcar ramp, and they both were leaning into the effort. I remembered from grad school that uranium had an atomic weight of 92 or thereabouts, one of the heaviest elements on the periodic table. There were metal plates, some four by four feet square, stacked like dishes on either side of the ramp. For every three drums that went aboard, a dull gray metal plate followed them in. It took four men to move one plate. Also very heavy. Lead, maybe?

I mentally tried to square uranium with that term "weapons program" I'd been so privileged to hear about in the hospital room, but there'd been no mistaking the horror that had spread across Van Rensselaer's face. Could this have something to do with the supersecret program that occasionally raised its head and steamrollered the entire Washington war-making establishment before subsiding again behind a maze of security precautions? Maybe Van Rensselaer was going to fill me in later today. Or maybe I was going on a long voyage. Like my weight lifting buddy Billy Peterson.

Billy was an Army colonel who had worked in the political-military division of the Army headquarters staff. He was a lifter like me, so we'd often pump iron together at a local military gym at one end of the Tempo-infested Mall. I'd once asked him what he did over there at HQ, but all he'd say was that he was a country specialist and one of the Army chief of staff's principal briefers. We would usually make a run to the other end of the Mall, which at one time had been a lovely swath of green space stretching from the Lincoln Memorial to Capitol Hill but was now entirely covered in those hideous-looking buildings called Tempos, meaning they were temporary. Two- and three-storied, white plywood-sided, they'd been put up after World War I. Bigger additions were added in early 1942, right after Pearl. They were an unpleasant contrast to all the dignified marble monuments and granite-sided permanent buildings lining the Mall, but putting a few million men under arms and overseas cried out for much bigger headquarters staffs, or so the theory went. "Tempo" was another word for "ugly."

One day Billy told me he'd heard about some big and super hush-hush research project that had been going on since 1942 and was now so big it was eating hundreds of millions of federal budget dollars—a month!

The Army was in charge of it, but there were also hundreds if not thousands of people involved all around the country. I'd cautioned him to not go poking his nose in—if it was that big and that secret, somebody might chop it off for him. I'd never heard of anything like that, but the problems I dealt with were much more organizational and logistical than research. Billy, however, was a bit of an adventurer, and he said he was gonna find out what this was all about.

Two weeks later while I was acting as his safety guy while he pressed a pretty big set of plates, six men in suits and sunglasses came into the gym, asked for Colonel Peterson, and escorted him out of the gym, protesting loudly, still in his shorts and T-shirt. They looked like FBI or Secret Service types, both of which I'd seen at some of my White House meetings. I called his office the next morning and his secretary said he'd been "unexpectedly" transferred. To where, no one knew, even including his wife, who'd called several times. His general had come out at noon and told everybody in the office to stop asking questions about Colonel Peterson. He'd hinted that there were slots open for the invasion of Japan if anyone was really all that interested in Colonel Peterson's sudden departure. Amazingly, interest in Colonel Peterson's whereabouts had quickly evaporated, his secretary admitted. Is there anything else I can help you with, Captain?

Nope, I told her, and hung up. I'd been to dinner at their home over in Alexandria a couple of times, so eventually his wife reached out to me. I'd told her I was as mystified as she was, but that it might pertain to a national security issue for which they suddenly needed his services. The Army will tell you when they can, I said, but I'm pretty sure he's okay. I could tell she wasn't all that convinced, so I also told her that if she persisted in asking questions, it would be Billy who might bear the brunt of any repercussions. I think she folded after that.

The two dark-colored freight cars were still attached to the Yard's donkey engine, a half-size diesel locomotive. The rest of the train had been pushed back to the base of the pier. It was a weird lash-up for a train. One full-size locomotive, three passenger cars with normal windows,

what was probably a dining car, a passenger car with several radio antennae on its roof and blanked-out windows, and finally what looked like
an oversize caboose, painted Army green instead of red, with the words
"US Army" painted on both sides.

The caboose had sidearmed and helmeted Army military police posted,
while the rest of the train was being protected by Marines in combat
utilities and field helmets carrying carbines. At that moment, there didn't
seem to be anybody aboard the pusher engine. A fully crewed shipyard
fire engine was posted at the head of the pier, and there were two obviously armed patrol craft loitering out in the shipyard's harbor. Four men
in white suits were patrolling the pier and studying some kind of test
equipment each time they stopped. Looking for some *strahlung*? I wondered. The technical guys had said there was radiation, but not enough
to be harmful. So why had the sub's skipper been so blatantly terrified?
Did he know something our guys didn't?

I checked in at a temporary table set up at the head of the pier and was
directed to the next to last car before the caboose on the main train, where
one of the sentries asked to see my ID card and then went up the stairs to
see if I could be admitted. He came back in a minute, saluted, pointed to
what he called the command car, and told me to go on up. The inside of
the command car was nothing like I'd imagined. It looked more like a
miniature version of the combat information center on my cruiser. All
that was missing was radar screens, although there was a wall-size map
of what looked like the entire train system of the US East Coast, with
small colored lights indicating I knew not what scattered all over it. Two
railroad company civilians wearing telephone headsets were manning the
big board. Other personnel were manning radio desks and camera mon-
itoring equipment. The entire ops room took up the back half of the car.

I was escorted through one metal door, through a small kitchen/
pantry area, and on into the next car, which was a much better-appointed
bedroom-cum-office suite where Van Rensselaer sat at one end of a conference table, which also served as his desk. He was talking on a red handset.
This room was carpeted and had windows with permanent drapes, what

had to be a bathroom in one corner, and some straight-backed chairs around the table. His bedroom was at the front of the car. He waved me to a chair and kept talking. Remarkably, there were five—count 'em: *five*—other telephone instruments on the desk. The CNO himself only had three.

He finally quit the call and leaned back in his armchair. I realized it had been made to accommodate his outsize frame.

"Where's the admiral?" he asked, peremptorily.

"I don't know. I told his secretary that you wanted a meeting down here but then came direct to the pier. I wanted to see what was going on."

"Yes, I can well imagine," he said. "What's going on is that my people are removing a fair amount of uranium in as yet unknown form from that boat. I'm told we'll be here until around two, maybe three in the morning. There are twenty-four mine tubes. We've emptied six so far. It'll start going faster now that they've moved one of the yard cranes down to this pier. We also formed a working party made up of the German crew from the prison. Now: you want to know what this is all about, don't you."

"Not if you say I don't," I said. "Wartime secrets have their uses. Most of my day-to-day work concerns process matters within the Navy. Bureaucratic logjams. Admirals getting in the way of progress. I report directly to the CNO, so it's high-level stuff, but I have nothing to do with operational matters, war plans, secret projects, etc. My wars these days are the ones being fought in Washington. Political. Bureaucratic. Roles and missions. Budgetary, above all else."

"Which are just as important as what's going on in the far Pacific," he said. "If not more so."

He paused to gather his thoughts.

"As I think we all know, Japan's fabled Greater East Asia Co-Prosperity Sphere is no more. We're in the endgame, as far as that's concerned. We know it. They know it. *We* Westerners would find a way to bring it all to an end if *we* faced what they face, proportionately. That's what the Germans did. The Japanese will *not* do that. They've made it clear that they will literally fight to the last man, woman, and child even if it means their extinction. We will necessarily have to invade and kill them all to put a stop to this war. Most recently, *Iwo Jima* confirmed that. Saipan, Tinian, Guam, Peleliu also telegraphed that proposition. *Okinawa* is in progress and is confirming that the results will surely be the same, if not worse. And then come the so-called home islands. The current war plan, called Operation Olympic, is to put one million troops into the invasion of Japan, proper. One *million*. And we'll probably lose half of them in the process."

"I've heard talk like that," I said. "If it were me, I wouldn't invade the home islands. I'd starve them to death. Total, crushing, absolute blockade. No oil, no coal, ruin every rice paddy with salt-bombs. No fishing fleets. Once the offshore winds got to smelling really bad, then I'd invade and make fish sauce."

For the first time, he laughed. "I like how you think," he said. "You're not alone in considering that option, either. Or the use of some heavy-duty biologics, either. Are you married?"

That kind of threw me for a moment. Grand strategy, then this?

"No," I said. "Almost, way back when, but then I was called back to sea duty. By the time I came back, she was gone."

"Gone?" he said. "As in—"

"No. A few letters, then: I've met someone. We're going to be married. I'm sorry."

"I see," he said.

No, you don't, I thought, but it's none of your concern. I wondered what he would say if I asked him the same question. I was suddenly tempted. Wisdom prevailed.

"I'm content," I said instead. "I'm a professional naval officer. I don't know how the ones who are married contend with all the separations. The loneliness. The wanting. The: where's Daddy? Doesn't he like us? Endless questions. The never-enough money. The constant struggle to make ends meet. And in wartime, the ever-present threat of a black Navy sedan showing up out front one day with a chaplain and an officer of your husband's rank. Your husband has been killed in action or is missing in action. We regret to inform you. The president and a grateful nation, etc. . . . I decided I couldn't do that to a woman I loved. Maybe when I retire from active duty. But not now, with one half of the world still in flames. Now, then, Captain: either tell me what's this all about or I'll take my leave."

He nodded. "Fair enough. But once I tell you, taking your leave, as you so quaintly put it, won't be an option. And I wouldn't tell you except for what I heard at the hospital. More importantly, what *you* heard. Remember what that prisoner said?"

I thought back. Weapons program. *Our* weapons program. The Germans had been doing something with uranium, but then the world fell in on them. That older one had implied, no, he'd outright said it: *our* weapons program. That meant the Japanese were doing something with uranium.

Van Rensselaer watched me work it out, his face inscrutable.

"You're telling me," I said, "that we're trying to make some kind of a weapon out of uranium? And, secondly, that the Germans and the Japanese have also been trying to accomplish this? And, third, that the bit about Japan having such a program was news to you?"

He gave me an unfathomable look. "They told me you were smart *and* quick," he said, finally. "First off, you, personally, face new circumstances. You no longer work for the CNO, by the way. My boss spoke to him this morning. You work for me now, for the moment, anyway. Go get your stuff from the BOQ and be back aboard this train by midnight. And then I'll tell you about something called the Manhattan Project."

"May I ask where are we going?" I asked, when I couldn't think of anything else to say.

"A middle of nowhere place in deepest, darkest Tennessee called Oak Ridge," he replied. "Nice, small Appalachian town with a prewar population of around two thousand people. It's grown somewhat since this project got going, but more on that later. Lots of rules, but the main one is never to say or write the words Manhattan Project. When I show you what it's all about you will completely understand. Now: enough cryptic conversation. This train will be going straight through to Oak Ridge with this uranium. We'll give you some time in a week or so to close out your lodgings in Washington and settle all local accounts, bills, and so on. Anyone close to you who might get upset if you just vanish?"

Vanish. I momentarily conjured up an image of Billy Peterson. Then a second image of six men in suits and sunglasses escorting him out of the gym.

Okay, this was definitely serious, I thought. So I shook my head. My parents had both passed away. I had no siblings. I was the original solitary man, even in the Navy.

"Good," he said. "That helps."

He paused for a moment. Van Rensselaer was a man who thought before speaking, something I admired. I'd been trying to adopt that habit for years.

"This project—this Manhattan Project—will, if it succeeds, put the power of the sun itself into the hands of man. Everything we know and think about weapons will change forever. War, itself, will be changed forever. The news that the Japanese are also attempting to do what we're attempting to do is—shattering.

"We. Had. No. Fucking. Idea.

"It was the Germans we were worried about. They've surprised the Allies time and again with new, horrendous weapons we never thought possible. Giant ballistic missiles coming silently straight down out of the sky with two-thousand-pound warheads that flatten whole towns, jet-engine-powered fighters, height-finding radars. Two years ago, the Brits discovered the Nazis were making something called heavy water up in Norway. They asked their scientists what the hell heavy water was, and their guys told them to bomb that plant immediately if not sooner. You've heard of Albert Einstein?"

I nodded. Who hadn't, although exactly what he did or thought about was still a mystery to regular humans. Strange-looking German guy with a big mop of hair and a disarming, almost childish grin.

"Well, back in 1942, Dr. Einstein wrote FDR a letter warning him that the German scientific community was trying to develop a bomb using atomic science. And uranium. FDR called him in and they talked. FDR then called in some of our top physicists, mathematicians, chemists, and metallurgists. That's when he found out that research into getting vast quantities of energy out of purified uranium had been going on for over a decade, all over the world. This was news. The president's reaction was to initiate a wartime program here to catch up. That's the Manhattan Project nobody's ever heard of. Or speaks about.

"Now Germany, facing the endgame and certain defeat, has thrown in the towel. We needed to defeat the Germans first, before we turned *all* our military strength against the Japanese. A cornered Nazi Germany with a weapon that could draw on the almost unlimited energy from an atomic device of some kind would certainly use it, unless they simply ran out of time. Which, thank the gods, they did. Our whole focus has been on that possibility; everyone just assumed that the Japanese, whose weapons have not advanced like the Germans' stuff, and whose industrial base has been bled white by American submarine warfare, couldn't begin to develop such a capability. Now all those assumptions have been undone by our little discussion in that hospital and the presence of a captured, large U-boat, bound for Japan, filled with uranium. The shock to the thousands of people we have working on this project in complete secrecy will be profound, magnified by the common knowledge that Japan will never, ever surrender."

This was a lot to take in at such short notice; my expression must have revealed that I was simply stunned. Van Rensselaer was staring at me like an eagle about to grab its prey. Thousands of people? Since 1942? Where were they? Who were they?

"Of necessity, I'm going to pull you into the project, which I will explain later. From here on out, every day of your life will seem like GQ, day and night, just like mine. Especially now. If Japan succeeds before we do at what we're now *both* trying to achieve, our casualties during an invasion will be one hundred percent, not the fifty being projected."

Not surprisingly, I was speechless, because I didn't know either what he was talking about regarding uranium or how I ever could be of use in what seemed like a galactic effort. Putting the best face on it, I told him I'd help in any way I could. As soon as I understood what the *hell* he was talking about.

"Go make preparations to get underway, Captain," he said with total authority. "As I said, we're going to Tennessee."

SEVEN
THE NIGHT TRAIN

I'd come to New Hampshire expecting only a one-day stay, so I went straightaway to the shipyard's Navy uniform shop and stocked up on extra work khakis, underwear, socks, and toiletries. I then went to the package store and purchased two bottles of Scotch.

Everything else that I owned—the rest of my uniforms, civvies, and a car—was in Washington. My parents had both been government bureaucrats. They'd owned a house in the Chevy Chase area of Washington, up at the northern end of Connecticut Avenue. It was no mansion but still a nice 1920s vintage two-story house on a half-acre lot, one block south of Military Avenue. My father had suffered a heart attack back in 1938, and my mother, unable or unwilling to cope, had turned her face to the wall one night a year later and died. As the only child, I'd inherited the house. I was at sea at the time, so I considered selling it, but another CO had advised me to hang on to it against the day when I had to go back to Washington for my post-command tour. I had no intentions of getting anywhere near Washington headquarters duty, but he'd just smiled. Wiggle as you might,

Wolfe, that will happen sooner rather than later. So, when the hammer fell, I fortunately had a ready-made, fully furnished home. When I did go back to Washington and found out what a house like that cost in the capital in 1945, I'd been more than grateful to my friend.

I dropped my purchases in my BOQ room and went down to the BOQ office to use a telephone to call the admiral's office. I felt as if I owed him some kind of back brief, having invaded his command on such short notice. Interestingly, he was "presently unavailable" and did I want to leave a message? I told his chief yeoman to thank him for all his help and say that I'd be leaving late tonight. The chief took that down, and then said: actually, Captain, I think he's been informed about that. He'll appreciate the courtesy. Have a good trip, sir.

Ah, I thought, the long arm of Captain Van Rensselaer at work, no doubt. Still, I thought it was only polite to make my manners. I told the desk I'd be checking out later that night (yessir, we know, they said) then went to my room for a nap. Afterward, I had dinner at the club and then, with bags in hand, went down to Pier 5 and checked in with the train staff. They took me to a sleeper room in one of the passenger cars. I worked on paperwork for a few hours, had a nightcap, and then went to bed. I'd looked out the window and seen that the unloading operation was still ongoing up on the pier. The crane with its spotlights lit up the pier as men in white protective gear struggled to bring those short, heavy barrels of— what, exactly?—aboard.

Uranium, I thought. That's what. Advancing technology and scientific wonders had characterized my time in actual at-sea naval service since Pearl Harbor. New and better radars. Better sonars. Gun projectiles that no longer had to hit an airplane to bring it down. Air-conditioning aboard ship. Antibiotic medicines. UHF radios. And now an odd element from the exotic and large-atomic-weight end of the periodic table was suddenly center stage in some supersecret research project or weapons program. How could that be? Were they going to drop some on someone's head?

I woke up late the next morning—eight o'clock. That notorious sleeping drug called clickety-clack had put me down for a good night's sleep. I glanced out the window and saw what looked like the industrial backyard area of a major city flashing by. Drab warehouses. Small and large factories. Grimy neighborhoods. Sludge-filled canals. One startlingly large power plant with four brick smokestacks. A river, crisscrossed with different kinds of bridges. A prison or penitentiary. A real urban beauty pageant.

Ah, I thought. This must be New Jersey.

I put on working khakis and made my way to the dining car, which was full. A waiter pointed me to an empty seat where three enlisted Marines were having breakfast. They tried to stand up when they saw the silver eagles on my shirt collars but I waved them down.

"Morning, gentlemen," I said. "What's good for breakfast?"

"Morning, sir," they replied in a respectful chorus. "Coffee's not bad."

I got some coffee, then eggs and bacon. They finished up and I had to get up to let them out, but then I had the four-seat dining table to myself. For about one minute. Captain Van Rensselaer showed up. He, too, was in working uniform. He sat down opposite, and I got the impression from the waiters that we wouldn't be joined by anybody else, even though I could see there were several soldiers still waiting for tables.

Van Rensselaer looked tired. I could guess why—the unloading operation had been going strong when I'd gone to bed and I'm sure he'd been there, supervising. I had a million questions, but decided to let him tell me things when he was ready. And besides, this was a rather public venue, with dozens of undoubtedly straining ears all around us.

He got coffee and asked for a donut. The waiter said they were all out, but he could rustle up some toast and marmalade. Van Rensselaer shook his head and stuck with just coffee.

"As I said, what we heard yesterday came as a real surprise," he said. I was a bit surprised myself. Here? I thought. You're gonna talk about this *here*?

"This project is an Army show," he continued. "There are two chains of command, ending at the White House. One chain involves just about every university in the country with a strong scientific and engineering reputation. The other involves the Army and its air forces."

I leaned forward. "Shouldn't we do this in your office?" I asked.

His tired eyes looked up. I think he was so tired he didn't know where he was, but then he realized. "Absolutely," he said, shaking his head. "*Damn!* Thank you."

"You should eat something," I said. "You need fuel."

"I don't eat much," he said, starting to get up. Then he swayed a bit and sat back down. That unnaturally tall body had just reminded him that, yes, it needed fuel. I signaled the waiter and told him to bring us some bacon, eggs, toast, marmalade, and whatever else he had. He was back in five minutes, and Van Rensselaer tucked in with sudden enthusiasm.

I'd seen guys like this before. The entire weight of the world on their shoulders. No sense of how to pace themselves. I wasn't an athlete, but I did know something about calories out and calories in. If you did a full set of weights and then didn't rehydrate and refuel, you could pass out in the gym's parking lot. And I knew what was coming next. A full load of carbohydrates and protein after eating very little would have him asleep in about ten minutes. I knew he had a suite in that command car, but I hadn't seen any connections to that car from the rest of the train. I took him back to my room and then told him I needed to hit the head. When I came back, he was sound asleep in the cabin's one reclining chair.

I left him to it and went back to the now almost empty dining car with my briefcase. I took up residence at one of the corner tables while the staff cleaned up after breakfast. I realized as I sat down that this paperwork was probably no longer mine to work, but old habits die hard. Once we got to Washington, I'd go back to Main Navy and perhaps turn over my duties to—whom? That was assuming we were going to stop in Washington. Of course we were. Washington had this great suction effect on any govvie getting near it. Everybody official who came near Washington always stopped, if only to kiss a few rings and otherwise get a little visibility.

Except—we didn't. We went through the maze of tracks and switches around Union Station at a sedate pace with lots of clicking and clacking and whistle blowing, but we never stopped moving. In fact, I noticed that our train was the *only* train moving in that ordinarily bustling rail hub. Every other visible train was stopped. I even saw some military personnel along the tracks. Armed soldiers posted next to panting steam locomotives or one of the new, rumbling diesels. High-priority military train coming through; everybody freeze in place, please. Wow.

We did stop on a gated siding just outside of Richmond to add six more boxcars that looked like general freight and one more of these newfangled long-haul diesel engines, positioned at the back of the train. I took the opportunity to get off and stretch my legs, as did many others. The Army guys set up a cordon around the two unmarked freight cars. Typical Army move. The two cars had been totally inconspicuous. Now, of course, they weren't.

A steady stream of trucks came and went, loading "stuff" into the additional boxcars. After about an hour the farthest forward engine, which was now a steamer, sounded a long blast on her whistle and the crowd on the landing scurried to get back aboard. I went back to my compartment and found Van Rensselaer gone. My turn for a nap.

That evening we stopped again, I wasn't sure where, so I stayed aboard. I'd missed lunch so I went back to the dining car and took up residence at "my" corner table, determined to be in place before the hordes arrived. There a messenger found me and asked me to accompany him back to the command car. I discovered there was a way to get from the main train to his car, through a canvas-covered tunnel that required me to step over the open-air coupling and the ties flashing below. The messenger delivered me to Van Rensselaer's private suite at the front end, where he offered me a Scotch-rocks and then we sat down at the conference table.

He sat there for a few minutes while we enjoyed the whiskey and he gathered his thoughts. He'd been one year ahead of me at the academy, but as the late afternoon sunlight came through the windows, his face was that of an old man. I suppose I looked old, too, but his face showed the wear and tear of four years of war*time,* not warfare. Not shooting war, but the perhaps even more insidious grinding down that came with endless political, diplomatic, and bureaucratic pressures, combined with the notion that everything depended on *his* not screwing something up. These were the pressures that forged energetic, outgoing, full-of-life, national election–winning presidents of the United States into quiet-speaking, hollow-eyed human ingots of case-hardened, gray-haired steel. In the federal bureaucracy, there was rarely if ever a clear winner. They just shape-shifted and came back at you through another door.

Van Rensselaer had never had the opportunity to experience the rush of battle, where you put the intellectual side of your brain into a corner and let the lizard brain cry: havoc! If you live through it, as I had, you find yourself weirdly refreshed, renewed, and with rising confidence moderated by a sudden, keen understanding of what a huge role luck plays in actual combat when you finally compile your casualty list. He'd missed all that, so I did not prod. Finally, with his eyes now closed, he resumed his lecture.

"The Manhattan Project is about creating a weapon of such unbelievable power that one such weapon, detonated over a large modern city, will reduce that city to blackened ashes in one-thousandth of a second and burn every living being in that city into a bleak carbon stain on whatever ground they stood on when it detonated."

I gulped. That was clear enough, if more than a little scary. One weapon? He went on.

"This weapon," he said, "will summon the fires of the sun itself for just long enough to utterly destroy anything and everything within its sight. It draws its power from the energy contained in atoms, the smallest things in the physical universe. I'm talking about the energy required to hold together each individual atom, with its nucleus and with a varying number of electrons and other particles orbiting about that nucleus. It is a mysterious force the physicists call *atomic* energy. It is minuscule, when measured atom by atom. But the physicists discovered that in every physical substance on earth: iron, hydrogen, oxygen, carbon, gold, chlorine, uranium—all those arcane symbols on the periodic table of the elements—there are billions and *billions* of these atoms. Then some genius realized that there must be some kind of energy present that is strong enough that you can hold a solid ounce of, say iron, in your hand and feel it, see it, weigh it, work it, forge it, melt it, hammer it—do all of those things and yet still have a piece of iron in your hand—and, secondly, that the *sum* of all that energy sitting in your hand must be enormous. Beyond enormous."

He paused to sip some Scotch and then continued. "Finally, one of the scientists asked the big question: what if you could tap some of that energy? That question set off another whole realm of research, ending in the conclusion that you *could* tap it, but if you did, the process of getting at some of that atomic energy would change what it was you were holding in your hand. It wouldn't be a piece of iron anymore, would it? It would have been transmuted into something else, because iron is, by definition, made up of atoms with a specific number of atomic particles spinning about a nucleus with specific mass. If the energy is robbed in the form of electrons, which turned out to be the most convenient way of taking energy from an atom, then it's not iron anymore. Needless to say, the means by which one robs atoms of electrons, the machinery and the chemistry that can do that, if you will, is unbelievably complex. So, it all took time, decades in fact. Dozens of geniuses, dozens of Nobel Prize winners, too. And lots and lots of collaboration, worldwide collaboration, with each major discovery, theorem, and fascinating experiment being shared with all the other scientists who were studying how to move energy from the infinitely small to the enormous."

He fixed me with an acolyte's fanatic glare. "Energy on the move," he repeated. "You're an MIT chemistry grad. Do you follow?"

"I'm not really a chemist," I said. "My master's degree in chemical engineering specialized in explosives, the kind that makes Navy guns, bombs, and torpedoes work."

"I know that," he said. "Okay: visualize a sixteen-inch shell rammed into a waiting gun barrel. Behind it come six silk bags of gunpowder, all locked into a massive steel tube called the gun. An ignition device energizes the first powder bag, the one at the back of the chamber, which begins to burn—I think deflagrate is the term of art. It burns incredibly fast and sets off all the other bags in one-hundredth of a second. The burning powder produces titanic amounts of pressurized gas. The shell, which might weigh three thousand pounds, is lying between all that gas and the escape route, namely the muzzle. The pressure created by all that hot gas is strong enough to push that shell out of its way, accelerating the projectile to a velocity of just under a half mile per second by the time it leaves the barrel.

"That acceleration imparts enough kinetic energy to that big chunk of steel that it will travel up to forty thousand yards—twenty miles—before all that kinetic energy is converted into *potential* energy at the top of its trajectory arc. Then it begins to descend along the arc, a three-thousand-pound lump of steel going twenty-six hundred feet per second. At the bottom of the arc, with any luck, it strikes the side of its target. All that potential energy built up at the top of the trajectory has once again been converted back into kinetic energy. When that shell hits and decelerates to a momentary stop, all that kinetic energy is transferred into the target ship's side, blowing a significant hole into all that steel."

"The energy is always conserved, then," I said, vaguely remembering that there was a theorem about the conservation of energy. I think I was trying to impress him.

"The energy is not only conserved, but once again changed, this time into a huge force that penetrates into the target ship's innards and allows the powder inside the shell to explode, causing an even bigger explosion inside the target ship.

"Consider now a single grain of the powder in those silk propellant bags. As you know, in battleship ammunition, that grain is the size of a thin cigar. In that grain are chemicals. In those chemicals are atoms. Each has a nucleus and some protons and electrons held in orbit around that nucleus by atomic energy. At the most fundamental level, that's what gets loose when these reactions are initiated, causing a three-thousand-pound shell to fly twenty miles and then tear up the target ship. Pure energy, on the move, and changing state.

"Now here's the thing: the energy that's released when all that powder catches fire in a single instant moves the shell, and by doing so, transmutes itself from potential energy to kinetic energy, until the shell hits the target. Then all that kinetic energy transmutes itself back to instantaneous *potential* energy until the ship's side gives way and the shell moves again, this time inside the target's vitals. To an observer, the explosion is the energy. To an atomic scientist, the explosion is just a process by which electrons are being forced off of a zillion nuclei, releasing visible and invisible heat, light, physical force, noise, smoke, fire, and dead people. It's ultimately a process happening at the atomic level. Now: what if one could control that atomic process?"

"You mean like some kind of slow-motion, but contained, explosion?"

"Very good—precisely like that. Control it at the atomic level, so that the process produces a *predictable* amount of controlled energy in its most elemental form—heat. You could then boil water with that heat, change it into steam, and run electrical generators with that steam."

"Well," I said, "if that's all you're doing, why all this hugger-mugger?"

"Why indeed?" he replied, staring at me with suddenly unfathomable interest.

I had to think for a moment. "Unless, of course," I said, slowly, "that's not the process you're trying to control. You guys are after an *un*controllable, runaway process."

And then it hit me. "At the atomic level. You don't want some electrons to be stripped off a nucleus. You want them all. By the zillion. You're making a really big bomb."

He gave me an appreciative look. "That's *exactly* what we're doing. I shouldn't say 'we.' I'm a minor cog in a huge program, an unbelievably huge, secret military program. Thousands of people working on this, all across the country, but doing so in such a way that no two organizations, labs, universities, chemists, physicists, mathematicians, construction companies, hydroelectric plants know what the other ones are doing. Only a few senior scientists, about six senior military officers, and the president of the United States know that it's all about a bomb. Now you understand about that uranium?"

I thought for a moment. Uranium. "Atomic number 238," I said. "Many electrons. Many, many, many electrons. The basic currency of heat in the universe."

"Correct. Now, many other particles besides that are involved in this process. I've oversimplified this a great deal. The trickiest trick is to make that runaway reaction happen without two things happening: one, it goes off in your face when you put it together; two, we can keep number one from happening, but then it goes off before we are able to get *all* the goodies to cooperate and make what happens a real crowd-pleaser.

"That's the stage we're in now in this year of our Lord 1945. We've come up with two ways to assemble an atomic bomb, which are being carefully put together, and soon we're going to test all these amazing theories. July is the target month. Now: I'm gonna stop right here. We're headed to Oak Ridge, Tennessee. That's one of the places where uranium is converted into a purer state, to put it simply. There's another, but Oak Ridge is the main production center right now. Look—I've simplified this to an incredible degree. I've left out decades of research in describing all this, from atomic theory to the actual fabrication of such a weapon."

"Okay, I understand what you've told me so far, and that's probably all I need to know. But you seem to be in a great hurry. Germany's finished. What's the hurry now?"

He nodded. "Yes, we're in a huge hurry. This program has been running for years. The problems have been and remain formidable. But, since we began, we've also gained a far better appreciation of what it's going to cost America to invade and destroy Japan's ability to make war, courtesy of the recent island campaigns. The closer we've moved toward the actual home islands of Japan, the bigger the butcher's bill. Thus, FDR wants this thing ready to use *before* we have to invade Japan. He feels, as most of us do, too, that when Japan is confronted with an atomic bomb, they'll give up, despite all their *bushido* and never-surrender beliefs. The whole strategic objective of this entire program has been to get one before Germany, and afterward, to *make* Japan surrender, and thus obviate the need for an invasion."

I sighed. Make the Japanese surrender. A tall order indeed. I'd heard all the talk in Washington about the frightening prospects of putting American troops on the ground in the home islands, which is why I liked my starve-them-to-extinction theory. But no one had been asking me.

"One final question," I said. "And then I'm gonna have to do a lot of thinking. Why me? Yes, I know I was working at a high level in the Navy, but I was anything but important. A high-priced bureaucratic hit-man is more like it. What would you want me to contribute to this, well, somewhat incredible scenario?"

"Because of what you and I overheard in that hospital. Normally I would have had you picked up by the Secret Service and transferred to a, let's call it, secure location that very day. But that one-liner from the prisoner in the hospital has upended the whole dynamic. We had no idea, *zero* idea, that the Japanese military might be working on a similar program. I think now I'm going to need the Navy's help to do two things. One, to verify if that's true, that Japan also has an atomic weapons program, and, two, to get to it and destroy it before they fly one out over the ten-thousand-ship Pacific invasion fleet and melt it."

For a couple of seconds, I thought I was in the presence of a madman. One bomb? Destroy a fleet? He saw my incredulity. I'd never have made a good poker player.

"It's that big, Wolfe Bowen. Not the Bomb, although it's going to weigh on the order of three to ten tons, all by itself. I'm talking about what happens when it goes off. It will create a shock wave on the order of thousands of pounds of force per square inch with temperatures in the millions of degrees, which will travel outward in all directions at twice the speed of sound. Over a city or land there would be attenuation. At sea? Nothing to slow it down for miles. And radiation—ionizing radiation that will both fry a human's soft innards and irradiate his bones like a persistent X-ray would, only worse. That radiation would linger for a long time, making cities or surviving ships unviable. We can't assemble and then concentrate a huge invasion fleet off the coast of mainland Japan if they have such a weapon, too. We *must* know whether or not they do, and where they are with their project, because, as I said, such a project takes years to bring to fruition."

"Did the Germans have a viable program?" I asked.

"The Germans were trying hard, and, as I told you, they were the ones we were all worried about. Remember, the theoretical underpinnings of atomic energy were developed over decades by scientists all over the world, and they shared what they'd learned. So, yes, the Germans certainly had a program. So did the Brits, and so do the Russians. As we speak, the Allies have intelligence teams crawling over the wreckage of industrial Germany, sniffing around to see how far they got before Hitler's maniacal blunders caught up with them. They've found more stashes of uranium and some labs with the right equipment to enrich it. We did think about Japan, because they'd been part of the prewar international exchange of discoveries, but we knew that our submarine campaign, and now the B-29 bombing program, had stripped them of so many fundamental resources—oil, primarily, but also electricity, coal, iron ore, copper, and even food, not to mention the daily destruction of their physical industrial plant. Such a program should no longer be feasible in Japan, if it ever was. Or so we thought until that day in the hospital."

"What do our intelligence assets say about this?" I asked. "If our program is as big as you say it is, surely one of our spies—ONI, the OSS, embassy naval attachés all over the world—would have gotten wind of a similar Japanese effort?"

He leaned back in his chair. "We have *no* intelligence assets in the Japanese homeland," he said. "What few we did, given the difficulty posed by the Japanese language and a culture of deep secrecy and xenophobia, were rolled up long ago by the *Kempeitai*. We do have assets in China and Korea, but that's as close as it gets. Both are occupied by Japan. Korea is a slave state, and China is both occupied and now increasingly entangled in a civil war between nationalists and communists. Plus, there's the matter of physical distance. England and Germany are separated by only six or seven hundred miles. America and Japan are separated by almost ten thousand miles. Which brings me back to the Navy; the Navy specializes in getting things done at very long distances."

I was still trying to get my mind around what the Navy could possibly contribute to this sudden and uniquely urgent problem. He got up and poured us both a heeltap.

"Yesterday," he said, "we found out from that younger prisoner from the U-boat that the Japanese and the Nazis have been exchanging technology and actual military supplies ever since 1941. Initially by covert air routes flown over southern Russia and Manchuria, until Hitler attacked Russia in June of 1941. After that, the exchanges have been from German Atlantic ports down the coasts of Africa, and thence through the Indian Ocean to *Tokyo*—by fucking submarine! That boat sitting up there in Portsmouth was on its way to Japan when the Nazis surrendered. With a full load of goddamned uranium! And, by the way, at the front end was an entire disassembled German fighter *jet*, of all things."

By then he was almost shouting. I was in disbelief mode again. A submarine trip from Hamburg to *Tokyo* must have taken weeks, if not months.

Unbelievable. "Why the Navy?" I asked, finally. "The Army is already bombing Japan. Tell them to find it, smash it."

"Where would you suggest we start?" he asked. "Did you know that there are sixty-eight *hundred* islands in the Japanese archipelago? Besides, there's a reason not to involve the rest of the Army just now. An excellent reason."

I couldn't think of one.

He took a deep breath. "I know this is a lot to absorb," he said. "But for now, like I said earlier, you're working directly for me and not the Manhattan Project. I will have to brief the president, of course, but he's given me a lot of leeway to do what I have to do to protect the project."

"You do work directly for the president?"

He smiled. "I've been working at or for the White House my entire naval career," he said. "Remember, the Roosevelts and the Van Rensselaers go way back."

Of course they did, I realized, feeling a bit stupid for not having understood that before. FDR's family estate, Hyde Park, was up on a hill overlooking miles of the Hudson River. The Van Rensselaers had owned *all* the land above the Hudson River since Revolutionary War times.

Then the gray telephone rang. He answered it, and then his face darkened. "Dammit," he spat. "When? Where?" He listened some more. "Oh, shit and goddamnit. Okay. Thank you."

He hung up. "The president has died," he announced. "Mr. Truman has been sworn in. Now I'll probably have to go back to Washington." He banged his hand on the table and spilled his drink. "*Fuck!*" he shouted.

I felt it as well. Franklin Delano Roosevelt. The big, tall, seemingly invincible man with the huge head. The giant in the wheelchair. The flywheel of the Second World War. America's center of gravity.

All of informed Washington would now claim to have seen this coming. Still, I personally could feel a moment of great sadness. Van Rensselaer was already regrouping.

"I'll catch a fast passenger train in Charlotte in the morning. *This* train must continue to Oak Ridge. Dammit. Dammit. Dammit. We didn't need this right now."

"If I'm being brought onboard your program," I said, "I need to go wrap things up at Navy headquarters and at home. May I come with you, back to Washington?"

He stared into the middle distance as if he had not heard me. Everybody in Washington who'd seen Roosevelt lately knew that he wasn't long for this world. The blotched face. The halting speech. I'd been amazed he'd made it this far. He'd be missed, though. Like most naval officers, I had no political affiliation with any party. I hardly ever even voted, so I wasn't a Republican or a Democrat, but FDR had been such a big part of the national landscape for so long that it would take some time for people to accept that he was gone.

"Yes," he replied, finally. "That's a good idea. You come with me when I go to the White House to meet with President Truman."

He saw my surprise. He grunted. "I told you that the president knew about this program," he said with a sigh. "But this might surprise you: FDR directed us *not* to inform the vice president. Mr. Truman doesn't know anything about the Manhattan Project. I have a feeling General Groves is going to make me do the honors, because Truman's going to be pissed."

I was astonished. The vice president hadn't been given access? And I had? A small warning voice crawled out from under a mental rock and said: watch yourself, Sonny Boy.

"Who is General Groves?" I had to ask.

"The head of the Manhattan Project. Shit and hellfire. Let's have dinner. It's gonna be a long goddamned night."

EIGHT
TRUMAN

We got to Charlotte early in the morning. Two Army colonels came aboard to confer with Van Rensselaer. He gave them detailed instructions about the uranium cars, and then told them he had to go back to Washington. One of them asked who I was, almost as if I wasn't there and listening. Van Rensselaer simply said that I would be accompanying him back to Washington, and if they had no further questions, they could go. Suitably chastised, they both left the car.

"Get your stuff, meet me in the station in fifteen minutes."

I did as he ordered, and then we boarded a passenger train that was headed for Washington, DC, and points north, which had been held at the station. We got seats like ordinary passengers, and the train left ten minutes later. I still had a million questions, but this wasn't the place. I sat back and went to sleep. Anyone who'd ever had command at sea knew to grab rest whenever you could. My new friend, the clickety-clack, made it easier.

An Army sedan met us at Union Station and took us to the Parker Place hotel, where we had already been reserved rooms. I got breakfast and then changed into my dress khakis—coat, shoulder boards, black tie, shirt collar insignia. I made a mental note to get over to Main Navy and turn over my current projects. To whom, I still wasn't sure. I called my next-door neighbor, a retired civil servant, who'd been looking after my house in Chevy Chase whenever I expected to be away for long periods of time. I told him I'd be stopping by briefly that afternoon.

Damn, I thought, as that little voice started up. I ignored it.

Then I called Marianne at my office and told her I had some paperwork to turn in. To my surprise, she asked me where I was. I told her the Parker Place hotel, downtown.

"It's all unclass, right? This paperwork?" she asked. I said yes.

"Please leave it with the hotel's front desk, then, Captain," she said. "A Main Navy driver will come pick it up in an hour."

"Everything okay, Marianne?" I asked. She was being uncharacteristically formal.

There was a tiny pause on the line. "Yes, sir, everything's okay. I guess. Our office is being disestablished. The other officers are being reassigned. I, myself, need to find a new position. It's all been rather sudden."

"Well, damn," I said. "I didn't know. Look—you need a recommendation, you let me know. You want to stay in OpNav?"

Another pause. "I don't think so, sir," she said. Now I was getting concerned. When Marianne and I spoke on the phone, there were no "sirs." An exchange of faux insults, a dirty joke, but this was all wrong.

"Somebody right there?" I asked.

"Yes, sir, and thank you. I'll send someone for those papers right away."

"Got it, my friend," I said. "Later, okay?"

"Yes, sir, and thank you again, Captain." Click.

I hung up. What the hell was going on there? Admiral King was disbanding his insider posse? That didn't sound like him, not at all. We'd had meetings twice a week in his inner office, usually after hours. We'd tell him what we'd been doing, individually, and he'd fire questions back at us.

The vice CNO was usually in attendance, but none of the other staff. This was us-to-him information. Officially, we didn't exist. We were not listed on the OpNav organization chart, and more importantly, we weren't in the OpNav phone book. And, as I'd told Van Rensselaer, we weren't involved in operational, win-the-war matters. Our remit was bureaucratic: the Army Air Forces wanted to become a separate service. How would this affect the Navy? OpNav's carrier division was doing an end-around of the Navy staff, direct to certain congressmen, to get more carriers. There'd been rumors that the OpNav budget division had two budgets in play—one for consumption within the OpNav staff, another the fruit of quiet, back-channel negotiations with certain congressional committees, whose interest in steering Navy budget money to their districts was intense. Helpful stuff like that. Stuff the CNO needed to know without his entire staff knowing that he *did* know. When it came to bureaucratic power games, Admiral Ernest J. King was the consummate insider knife-fighter who took no prisoners.

The problem was that the Chief of Naval Operations was double-hatted, as the term went. He was also the commander in chief of the Navy. In wartime, that was a full-time job, especially now that the war in the Pacific was rising to a climax. Interservice competition for resources, influence, roles, and missions was also rising to a climax. Once Japan was defeated, as it surely would be, who was going to get what? Careers and commands were in play, not to mention vast sums of federal budget money. The senior officers who'd won the war in Europe and who were about to win the war in the Pacific would be given suitable honors, titles, and ranks—and then they'd be retired with the thanks of a grateful nation. It was the upcoming crop of generals and admirals who were positioning themselves for postwar power, and that would be a vicious competition indeed. That was the milieu in which I'd been working. But now I was enmeshed in something else altogether, something beyond huge, if Van Rensselaer were to be entirely believed. I was also clearly way out of my depth, sworn to serious silence, but, of course, more than a little bit intrigued.

My little inner voice squeaked.

"What?"

"You, sir, are getting out of your depth," it said.

"So?"

"Run."

NINE
ONI

Van Rensselaer called and said to meet him down in the lobby. I took a deep breath and went downstairs. There was yet another Army staff car waiting. A driver and an armed guard were in the front. We got in. Van Rensselaer sat in the right rear seat—the senior officer's seat. I sat beside him. I was one year junior to him, so technically I was his subordinate. But as one Navy captain to another, I'd made a point of not recognizing that in our discussions. He was what we called a Washington ballerina. I was a combat-proven fleet officer, and people like me did not look up to officers who'd made their way entirely in Washington or other headquarters but who'd never faced and fought the actual enemy. It was petty, I realized, but that's how I felt.

"We're going to brief the president on the project," he said.

I looked at the driver, who was pretending to be totally absorbed in his driving. All drivers eavesdropped. You wanted to find out what a general or an admiral was up to on any given day, ask his driver. The guard in the right front seat was scanning the raucous Washington traffic, looking for I knew not what.

"We?" I asked, being just a tad sarcastic.

He gave me a sideways look of impatience. I pretended that it had been an innocent question.

"We're going to the EOB, not the White House," he continued. "When we get there, I need you to get small and stay small. The project director is one Major General Leslie Groves, US Army. Between you and me, he's a prick, but a brainy prick. Hundred percent Army green, all the way. Hates the Navy and all its works. Of the ramrod school of leadership. Brilliant at herding cats. Try not to attract his attention. Move quietly away when we get to the briefing room. Keep walking down the hall, but come back once the principals go in. There'll be Secret Service there. When the president shows up, pretend you're there for something else. I just need you to be kinda invisible, but available."

"Well, hell, why don't I just stay in the car, then," I said.

He hesitated for a few moments. "Because I just might have to call you into the briefing."

"You better tell me what for, so I can at least make some mental preparations."

He nodded. "Fair enough. Start thinking about this: if the Japanese indeed have a 'program' underway, where is it? How close to fruition are they? Who could find that out? The Navy, perhaps? How would they do that? Where would *they* look? Like that. Driver, the west entrance, please. Then we'll need you to wait."

"Piece o' cake," I muttered. He smiled, but it was a condescending smile, as in we're on my turf now, Oh Captain of the Ocean Seas. After that we stopped talking.

We arrived at the Executive Office Building five minutes later, drove through the Secret Service cordon, and parked on the west side of the building. The EOB was an impressive pile of marble and limestone in the French Second Empire style, which meant the outside was just a tad ornate. It had been commissioned by President Ulysses S. Grant, and for a while, it was the largest office building in the world. Both the president and the vice president had offices there, as well as the nascent National Security Council, whose staff had grown exponentially during the war. It was essentially across the street from the White House, where real office space was quite limited.

More Secret Service checkpoints and then we went up to the third floor and down a marble-tiled hallway to a conference room. The hallway had high-backed wooden chairs on both sides, along its full length, that looked like they'd come from a monastery choir. Our armed guard accompanied us, carrying two stuffed briefcases that I guessed contained Van Rensselaer's briefing materials. The conference room was richly appointed, with a stage at one end and a large movie screen above the stage. An overhead slide projector sat on a small table just below the stage, with a chair for the guy who flipped the slides every time the speaker nodded. I'd used a setup like that back in OpNav when we had to do a formal presentation for the CNO that required graphics.

Van Rensselaer nodded to me at the doorway, which I assumed was my signal to become scarce. I saw the entrance to another conference room farther down the hall, so I went down to that entrance and grabbed a chair. A Secret Service agent came up and asked for ID. We'd been given some visitor badges downstairs, but I dutifully presented my ID card. He nodded and walked away. In about thirty minutes the hallway filled with Secret Service agents. One came and stood by me, between me and the entrance to the fancy conference room. Perfect, I thought. I nodded at him but he ignored me completely. The Secret Service guys all dressed and looked the same: very fit, close-cropped hair, two-piece suits with loose jackets to accommodate shoulder holsters, narrow ties, laced shoes, and the sunglasses. Even inside, the sunglasses. I'd been told that the sunglasses were worn so that bad guys couldn't see where the agents were looking, which appeared to be everywhere. I'd also been told that they all dressed the same so that the covert agents, the ones who didn't look like that, could mingle with crowds.

A small commotion erupted down at the other end of the hallway and here came President Harry S. Truman. He was a fast walker, making some of his aides and escorts scramble just to keep up with him. His most prominent feature at a distance were large eyeglasses, which exaggerated the size of his eyes. Behind him came a portly Army major general. That must be Groves, I thought. The small crowd swept into the fancy conference room. The door closed and quiet resumed. Time to think, I told myself.

If the Japanese have an atomic weapon project, where is it?

How's about: Japan? The home islands. *Honshu*, probably, where the prestigious *Tokyo* Imperial University was located. Van Rensselaer had said it took battalions of scientists, chemists, physicists, math wizards, Nobel Prize winners, and also huge amounts of electricity, uranium, and other exotic elements to make an atomic bomb.

Except, ever since November 1944, B-29s had been bombing *Tokyo* and other major cities. Their targets had been aircraft plants, dockyards, shipyards, railroad junctions—the usual targets—in the hope of destroying the enemy's ability to wage war. So: if there'd been a large, secret weapons development program going on in *Tokyo*, would that have escaped the wrath of the B-29s? Especially after that firebombing raid in February of this year, which had incinerated most of central *Tokyo* and was rumored to have killed a hundred thousand people?

How about the rest of the home islands? *Hokkaido, Shikoku, Kyushu,* and maybe even *Okinawa*?

I had no data. I knew nothing. Who did? The OSS's Research and Analysis Branch, which used diplomatic-channel intelligence? The Office of Naval Intelligence, known as ONI? I'd been briefed on all of these organizations when I came back to Washington, but, given my minor role in OpNav, had never interacted with any of them.

Please don't call me in there, I prayed.

Van Rensselaer had to know that I wasn't the guy to brief the president on how the Navy could help find the Japanese weapons program, if one even existed. Besides, that old man could have been screwing with us. *Our* weapons program, idiot. And yet: he'd been aboard a German

U-boat filled with uranium. And a Nazi jet-powered fighter plane in a box, as a bonus.

"Captain Bowen?" I looked up. A civilian was standing in front of me. "Would you come in, please?"

"Oh, shit," I mumbled. I got a brief sympathetic look from the civilian, who was wearing a White House badge, and followed him back to the presidential briefing room. Inside there were far more people than I'd seen go in. The president was at one end of the table, close to the stage. General Groves was seated directly across from him. I didn't recognize any of the other individuals seated around the table, although some of them looked like academics. He led me to a chair at the back of the room and then left. Van Rensselaer was banging away up on the stage and pointing to an organization chart on the screen that seemed to include the entire government. The president had an occasional question but I couldn't hear him. Only Van Rensselaer had a microphone.

I scanned all those faces, and realized they were just a bit bored. Heard this all before. All except Groves, whose gleaming eyes were fastened on the president, and as I studied Truman's face, somewhat shielded by those thick eyeglass lenses, I realized that he was furious and getting madder by the second. Told you, my little voice sneered, triumphantly. I'd tuned Van Rensselaer's voice out while I was doing this but then heard him say something about the Bomb being capable of igniting the earth's atmosphere and extinguishing all life. That jerked me almost physically back to his briefing.

"Most of our physicists have dismissed that notion as ridiculous," he said. "But there is one factor in its favor: the temperatures created by this nuclear reaction will exceed the temperatures extant in the sun, however briefly. Until we test both devices, the uranium and the plutonium devices, and are able to measure those temperatures, we won't know."

The president said something.

"The tests are scheduled for late June, early July," Van Rensselaer said. "Out in the New Mexico desert. We're finishing site selection right now. As currently planned, the first test will involve the gun design. The second test, the implosion design. The gun design, as I said, would use highly concentrated uranium. The implosion device will involve plutonium, which, theoretically, should be even more powerful than the uranium device. But which one we test first will depend on which type we can assemble first. That equation contains a lot of unknowns."

The president asked another question, a short one.

"Sir, we have the best minds the country can muster working on this project. We have spent hundreds of millions assembling the materials, machines, factories, people, and installations getting this thing done on an incredible scale. There is one building at Oak Ridge that is one mile long. All of this multiyear effort is based upon the intellectual achievements of Nobel Prize–winning physicists, chemists, mathematicians, scientists, engineers, and far-seeing thinkers that goes back to the Curies in France during the late 1800s. We are confident, but, as I've heard about Missourians, the 'show me' day will tell the tale."

For the first time during the meeting, I saw Truman smile. It was a grim smile, to be sure. If the Manhattan Project failed to show him, there'd be hell to pay. Then the president stood up.

"I'm angry, as you can tell, but not at you," he said, loud enough that the entire room could hear. "I was never informed about this project, but that's not your fault. I'm behind you, and this project, one hundred percent. To think that you have managed to harness the basic building blocks of everything on earth is beyond amazing. Now: what was the intended destination of that uranium you found on that submarine? The stuff you sent to Oak Ridge?"

"Japan? Mr. President," Van Rensselaer quipped. It took a moment for the joke to register, and then the audience laughed appreciatively.

"And so it shall be, gentlemen," Truman said, moving his suddenly hard gaze around the table. "As soon as possible, please."

TEN
THE NAVY

The president and his entourage left the conference room. General Groves and Van Rensselaer conferred for a few minutes and then headed out. Suddenly Groves stopped, looking right at me.

"Who are you?" he asked.

I stood up. "I'm Captain Wolfe Bowen, US Navy, General."

Van Rensselaer quickly intervened. "Captain Bowen was with me when we opened up that German minelayer. The shipyard commander called him when the boat was first brought in, and he was present for the discovery of the uranium and the conversation with the Jap scientists."

"He has access?" Groves demanded, obviously getting angry. "I didn't approve that."

"I understand, sir, but—"

"No goddamned 'buts,' Van Rensselaer," Groves spat. "I am the only one who approves access. I did not approve this Navy captain's access. What the hell, over?"

I was suddenly tired of this guy's arrogance. "Did Captain Van Rensselaer tell you what the Japanese scientists said at the hospital in Portsmouth, General?"

Groves's face went red. Apparently a mere Navy captain did not dare to address a major general without permission. Van Rensselaer's face was a study in embarrassment. I decided to press on.

"They said that the uranium onboard that U-boat was destined for the Japanese weapons program. Did you know the Japanese had a weapons program, General?"

Groves's eyes went wide. I could see that he was about to start blustering, because obviously he had *not* been given this little tidbit of bad news. I cut him off.

"So the obvious questions are: where is it, how far along is it, does it even exist, and if it does, what are they planning to do if *they* get a bomb? Especially if they manage that before we get a bomb, right, General? Maybe wait for invasion day and all those fat and happy invasion ships gathered in one place, and then turn one loose?"

Groves's mouth fell open in astonishment. "What the *fuck* are you talking about, Captain?" he spluttered. The three colonels behind him were positively wide-eyed. One began to back away.

"Informed speculation, General," I said. "It may all be bullshit, but: there's no getting around that inconvenient submarine, loaded to the gills with uranium and two Japanese academics, fresh from Berlin, destined for Japan. Suppose it is true. Can the Manhattan Project find *their* project? You heard about a one-mile-long building at Oak Ridge. Have the Army Air Forces seen anything like that in *Tokyo*? So maybe it's not in *Tokyo*. China, perhaps? Korea? It sounds to me like you've got your hands full making our bomb. You're gonna need some help out there in the western Pacific *Ocean,* or in the *Sea* of Japan and the East China *Sea,* if you want to find out if this is true. You're going to need the Navy. Captain Van Rensselaer has had the foresight to reach out to the Navy. I work directly for Admiral King. I'm your way into your friends on the Navy staff."

Gotta give Groves credit. Once he heard me out, he deflated. A little bit, anyway. "Okay," he said. "I get it. Jesus, this is the last thing we need: the Japs with a gadget. Good *God*. We focused on the Germans. Turns out they didn't even get close. Hindsight. Never thought about the Japs. Okay. *Okay*. Van Rensselaer, you run this one. Tell me when you have anything of substance."

Groves and his retinue swept out of the room. I turned to Van Rensselaer. "What's a gadget?" I asked, innocently.

"That's the nickname the scientists have given the actual bomb. That way they don't have to say the word 'bomb' or 'weapon.' And thank you, by the way."

"You're welcome," I said. "I've met guys like him before. And 'gadget'? That makes it okay?"

"Something like that," he replied. "I think most of the scientists are pacifists at heart. Probably because they fully understand the thing they're creating."

"They have regrets?"

"I think the only regret they have is that they couldn't use it against Hitler. Many of them are German Jews. Probably why the German program got nowhere. They exterminated the best scientific minds they had. The ones who were forced to work on a German program probably led the Nazis down some pretty unlikely paths until they went to a camp."

On that cheery note we left the building and went back to the hotel for lunch.

Van Rensselaer was subdued during lunch. Thinking, I assumed. I'd saved his face when I told Groves about his so-called foresight. "What does Admiral King know about the Manhattan Project?" I asked.

"Theoretically, nothing," he said. "But . . ."

"Yeah, but," I replied. "Permit me to explain something. The CNO's top priority is to safeguard the Navy's role in national defense, which is to say to strive for naval budgetary preeminence. The chief of staff of the Army has the same mission. When both of them realize that hundreds of millions of budget money are going elsewhere, they're going to find out where and why. I'd be very surprised if Ernest 'Jesus' King didn't have a pretty good idea."

"You work this for him in any regard?"

"Negative. But my point is this: if you want, excuse me, *need* the Navy's help to find the Japanese weapons program, you're going to have to read him in. All the way in."

"Groves won't allow that. Not even Truman, when he was the vice president, was read in."

I sighed. "That was then. This is now. That was FDR. In my opinion, that was pretty dumb. Tell General Groves that he'll look like a perfect idiot if the Japs drop one before we do, especially if they hit our invasion fleet. I'll arrange the meeting for you to see the CNO."

"You'll go with me, then," he said.

"Oh. Goody," I said, knowing Admiral King all too well, but I knew I had convinced Van Rensselaer. The largest naval fleet in history would soon be assembling to invade and destroy Japan. But to do that, it would have to concentrate. The CNO would argue that he could spare no assets at this critical juncture to investigate a hypothetical Japanese atomic program. It would take everything we had to flatten Japan once and for all. Van Rensselaer and I would have to convince him that if the Japs were close to or had a bomb of their own, the only time it would be useful to them was when the entire American fleet concentrated within range of one of their bombers.

But first, Van Rensselaer had to get authorization to let Admiral King in on a whopper of a secret. As our car crawled through some traffic congestion toward Main Navy, I realized I was a long, long way from Johnson County, Kansas.

I entered the naval academy in 1922, having grown up in Olathe, Kansas, which at the time was a typical Midwestern town. My father worked for the telephone company that year; this was long before the large naval air station was built in Olathe. The country was recovering from the First World War and the economy seemed to be once again prospering. My father's older brother was a congressman, which is how I garnered an appointment to Annapolis. I'd been enthralled as a kid watching war films and news clips of the actions at sea, including grainy black-and-white scenes from the Battle of Jutland. I graduated from a small Catholic high school at a time when only the naval academy was again accepting applicants, following the huge military drawdowns after the Great War. West Point was still restricted to only two hundred new cadets per year.

Graduating in 1926 I'd gone off to sea on an Atlantic Fleet battleship, USS *Texas* (BB-35). I graduated as an Ensign, USN, and joined six other recent graduates aboard what was then a pretty big battleship. It was a two-year tour of duty, during which time we were not permitted to be married, because having a family was considered to be a handicap for a brand-new naval officer. The miserly pay may have had a bearing on that notion.

Following that "makee-learn" assignment, I went up the line through various ranks and assignments: division officer, department head, executive officer, graduate school, and then, eventually, a destroyer command that came on the heels of Pearl Harbor. My ship and I arrived off Guadalcanal right after the Savo Island disaster, where the Imperial Japanese Navy introduced the Americans to nighttime torpedo warfare. A Japanese cruiser formation sank four heavy cruisers, three American and one Australian, in the space of an hour without suffering a scratch. It was a real wake-up call within the US Navy, and it took the better part of two years before we began to sink consistently some of theirs. During the thirties there wasn't enough budget money to get out to sea often enough, and that cost us dearly when we went up against Japanese ships that had been training for years, especially in nighttime surface warfare. At the depth of the Depression, the fleet would get to sea once a year in the annual fleet battle problem, and then spend months sitting at the pier on mountains of coffee grounds. Real readiness was nonexistent. Officers' pay was cut in order to keep numbers sufficient to man the ships, and we were glad to still have a job. Even so, many fleet ships were laid up and their crews paid off.

I was glad at the time that I didn't have a wife and family. I barely had enough money to own a car and often lived aboard ship so as not to have to pay rent. I would meet attractive women from time to time, but the underlying consensus seemed to be don't marry a naval officer. They're always gone to sea and you'll be forever poor. Hard to argue with that, especially as the country began to prepare for another world war, brought to you by the same people who started the First World War. Realists in the Navy knew that we'd be drawn into it somehow once England was attacked, although no one in the fleet saw Pearl Harbor coming. Bachelorhood in the fleet was common prewar. It was overtaken by widowhood by late 1942. I'd never appreciated the crushing sadness suffered by so many wives whose husbands never came back from the vast Pacific. Every time I thought about it, I recalled that macabre poem by Shakespeare in *The Tempest*:

> *Full fathom five thy father lies;*
> *Of his bones are coral made;*
> *Those are pearls that were his eyes;*
> *Nothing of him that does fade,*
> *But doth suffer a sea-change*

ELEVEN
COMINCH

When we got to Constitution Avenue, we turned right to get down to the one-third-mile-long Main Navy and Munitions buildings, where reportedly fourteen thousand men and women worked. These "temporary" buildings had been erected in 1918 and showed some definite wear and tear. Supposedly they would all disappear when the armed forces headquarters staffs eventually moved to that concrete monstrosity going up across the Potomac called the Pentagon. The Army had already made the move. The Navy, as usual, was resisting the change.

I took Van Rensselaer to my former office, where now an aviator four-striper resided. I made introductions as his predecessor and told him we needed to set up a half-hour appointment with the CNO today.

He laughed outright. "Your name Harry Truman, did you say?" he snorted. "Get in line, Captain, and the end of that line's out the building. You worked here; you should know that."

Van Rensselaer spoke up. "My boss's name *is* Truman," he announced from way up there in the clouds. "I'm from the National Security Council.

I prefer to speak to Admiral King in his own offices. But if it's necessary, I can arrange a summons to the White House. An hour ago I was briefing the president on a topic of some importance. He told me to brief Admiral King. Today, if possible. Can you help me out?"

The captain's eyes went wide. "Sir, *I* can't, but I can call and check with the CNO's EA. It's just that—"

"I understand this is somewhat unusual," Van Rensselaer interrupted, as if the poor captain hadn't even spoken. "Don't call," he said. "*Go* to the CNO's office. Mention my name. It's Van Rensselaer." He spelled it out. "We'll wait here."

As in, discussion over. Do it. The captain blinked, got up, grabbed his uniform jacket, and went down the hall. He was back in three minutes. "The CNO will see you now, sir," he said, as if he was positively amazed at what he was saying. "If you'll come with me."

We went down the hall and entered the first of three anterooms. The first was the waiting room, where there was a rear admiral and his staff officers sitting. Then the secretarial office, where both Navy yeomen and civilian secretaries beavered away on shiny, black Royal typewriters, and then the EA's office, which led into the CNO's actual office suite. A captain wearing four gold *aiguillettes* on his dress khaki uniform shoulder stood up, and welcomed us to the CNO's office. The sign on the desk said he was H. R. Mayer, the executive assistant to the chief of naval operations. I knew the layout well and was, happily, recognized by several of the clerical staff, but they all stared at Van Rensselaer, who had to bend his head a little to get through the smallish Tempo-building doorways. This was definitely *not* the Old Executive Office Building. There were, however, Marine guards present in all the corridors outside.

Captain Mayer led us through the final doorway. The temperature dropped ten degrees as we went through that door. The EA backed out discreetly and closed the door. Admiral King was at his desk and he glowered at us both underneath that chrome-dome head of his as we came through. Then he recognized me.

"Wolfe Bowen, what's this all about, then?" he asked. "I thought you'd been shanghaied by the Army." Then he turned to Van Rensselaer. "Captain, my EA said I should see you forthwith. Do I know you?"

"No, Admiral," Van Rensselaer replied, as we sat down. "But you soon will. The president directed me to brief you on an extremely secret national weapons project just an hour ago. It's called the Manhattan Project. Before I begin, I need your personal assurances that you will not disclose *anything* I'm about to tell you to *anyone* on your staff or in your chain of command. Not the vice CNO, not the Secretary of the Navy, not to *any*one."

King's imperious face bridled. "Captains don't come barging into my office and say things like that to me, Van Rensselaer, even if they are White House staff. Admiral Leahy said I should see you, but *I'll* be the judge of what I tell my staff, as a function of what it is you want. I'm a fleet admiral, the CNO, and also the commander in chief of the entire US Navy, or need I remind you?"

Van Rensselaer closed his eyes for a full half minute, which, I think, made King even angrier. Then he looked over at me, ignoring King. "This was a mistake," he declared. "We need to seek an alternative modality to find out what we need to know. At a lower level. You know, at the operational level, perhaps. Someone at the sharp end of the spear, without all this gratuitous megalomania. Let's go."

King stood up and drew himself to his full height. "How *dare* you?" he thundered. "I forbid you to approach *any* of my operational commanders for whatever the *fuck* it is you're babbling on about. And, oh, by the way, now I'm going to make it a point to find out what it *is* you're all about, and then *I'll* decide what to do with that information. And with you, sir." He picked up the phone and told his secretary to get him the White House operator.

Semper Iratus, I thought. That was the unofficial and circumspect nickname just about the entire Navy staff had given Ernest J. King. Always angry. His own daughter had once rebuked a journalist who'd said that her father had an unstable temperament. "What?" she'd said. "He has the most stable temperament in the entire Navy. He is *always* furious."

Van Rensselaer stood up and fixed King with a stony glare. King was a tall man; Van Rensselaer was taller.

"*If* you so much as *pronounce* the words Manhattan Project out loud," he said softly, "you will be arrested by the US Secret Service and placed in solitary confinement at a location suitable to your lofty rank for the duration of the war. If you won't help, then we will make damn sure you can't hurt. Believe it or not, Your Highness, what I was going to brief you on supersedes anything you think you have power over. You. Idiot. You." A half-second pause. "Sir."

King's face went white with outrage. Van Rensselaer didn't give him a chance to say anything. He beckoned to me and we left King's inner office, got through two of the anterooms, passing the executive assistant, who was trotting anxiously back toward King's office. We got all the way to the corridor outside the waiting room before an alarmed-looking Marine guard caught up with us.

"Sirs?" he said. "Wait. Please?"

"What now?" Van Rensselaer spat.

"The CNO, sirs?" the frightened kid sputtered. "He wants you to come back. He *really* wants you to come back."

Van Rensselaer gave me a cold smile. "Fancy that," he said, softly. "I believe I detect the long, steely arm of Admiral Leahy."

We went back in, although Van Rensselaer made slow going of it. Boy, was I impressed. And, once again, fervently wishing I hadn't had to be there.

TWELVE
THE LADY FROM ONI

The briefing took one and a half hours, not thirty minutes, with Van Rensselaer taking his time to make sure that the CNO truly understood the ramifications of the Manhattan Project. I was a bit surprised at the scope of his technical knowledge. Even with my master's degree in chemistry from a highly regarded technical university, I learned stuff in that briefing that truly shocked me. At one point, Van Rensselaer again described the "gadget" as basically tapping into the power of the sun. Admiral King, who was no dummy by any means, immediately understood. He had one question. "Does Admiral Leahy know all about this?"

"Yes, sir, he does. He coordinates our interaction with the British program. General Marshall, however, has *not* been briefed in. Neither has General Eisenhower. Nor had the vice president, now president, until this morning."

Wow, King mouthed silently. "What do you need from the operational Navy?" he said, finally, with no trace of that unlimited hubris for which he was famous. I was wondering who he'd called at the White

House. He'd certainly changed his mind pretty quick. Had to have been Leahy.

"I think we'll need one submarine," Van Rensselaer said. "Just one submarine. And someone from ONI."

"To go where?"

"Korea," Van Rensselaer said. "We think. Or possibly to far northern Japan. But when we know, I'll need your immediate approval, no questions asked. And one other thing: I need a directive from you to ONI to cooperate with us, well, me, when I come calling. A blank check, actually. It won't be about money, but rather signals intelligence, and possibly, the use of any human assets they have in the eventual target area."

King smiled. "ONI will have a cow with that kind of tasking," he said. "They're such nannies. But you'll have it."

We got ready to leave. Van Rensselaer turned to King. "So, what do you think now, Admiral?" he asked. "And I apologize for my intemperate language."

King sat there for a moment. "Apology accepted, Captain Van Rensselaer," he said. "You've got a pair of brass ones, I'll give you that. But mostly I hope your Manhattan guys know what they're doing. Sounds to me like you people are about to tread on God's robes."

"Exactly so, Admiral," Van Rensselaer said. "Exactly so. We're going to test the prototype of this weapon in the not-too-distant future, somewhere out in the Western desert. Three of our most senior scientists still believe there's a chance the damned thing might ignite the entire earth's atmosphere. God's robes indeed."

King just shook his head, for once not knowing what to say. Who did?

We left Main Navy and got back into our waiting staff car. "The EOB," he told the driver. I raised my eyebrows. We'd just been there.

"I need to tell Admiral Leahy that we've read the CNO into the program. He'll be the one to see to it that Admiral King follows through. And *he* gets to tell Groves."

Admiral William D. Leahy was the essence of an *éminence grise* in Washington. In a forty-year naval career, beginning as a sailing ship cadet and now as the first five-star flag officer ever in the US Armed Forces, Leahy had been FDR's chief of staff and now served Truman in that capacity.

He'd been a most-trusted confidant, advisor, and close friend of Roosevelt for many years, on a par with his civilian counterpart, Harry Hopkins. He was discreet to the point of invisibility, and yet heads of governments and military chiefs of staff throughout the Western Alliance answered immediately if he called. He had an office in the White House itself, as well as a suite of offices in the EOB. He'd been the CNO five years before King.

Captain Van Rensselaer went in alone when we arrived. He told the driver to take me back to the hotel and then to return. I was a tiny bit disappointed at not getting to meet Leahy, but then again, the five-star admiral who was sometimes called the second most powerful man in the world probably did not need to meet yet another lowly captain. I also realized I probably wasn't going to get out to Chevy Chase to get my traveling clothes.

Evening was coming on and so I asked the desk clerk where the nearest gym was. He told me they had weights and exercise machines in a room next to the hotel's indoor pool. I put in a call to my neighbor, who said he could go in the house and bring me whatever I needed. I thanked him and told him what to gather up and where I was staying. I reminded myself to bring him a wartime souvenir of some kind the next time I went out there. That problem solved, I spent the next hour pumping iron, doing some laps in the pool, and then treating myself to the whirlpool bath next to the pool. I was wondering if one could get bar service in the pool enclosure when the door opened and a statuesque brunette came through from the ladies' changing room wearing a terry cloth bathrobe. She sat down on one of the pool benches, smiled at me, smoothed a bathing cap over her hair, and then slipped out of the bathrobe and into the pool, where she began a leisurely series of Australian-crawl laps. Very nice indeed, I thought, as I watched her slide through the water with a practiced, effortless ease, her head down, catching a breath every third stroke with a quick, minimal roll of her head. You've done this before, I thought, as I watched. The pool was shorter than a regular swimming pool, but she turned like a wet snake and never broke rhythm.

I closed my eyes and concentrated on soaking up the heat in the whirlpool bath and popping a couple of magnesium pills to urge all that lactic acid out of my sore muscles. Getting an occasional workout was no substitute for daily time with my beloved weights. I'd passed the stage where I needed coaching and instruction in a lifting gym. I did pretty much the same set of exercises each time, not pushing anything too hard, and my body rewarded me with some excellent sculpting and a complete release from whatever stupid stressors had come with any given day. I'd started lifting a long time ago, before the academy and then even aboard ship, to gain strength and a good-looking body, but eventually I'd learned that sustaining what I'd achieved was one of the best stress relievers out there. Charles Atlas, whose comic book ads had turned me on to weight lifting as a teenager, could relax. Plus, it was possible that I might, just might, be getting older. I'd watch the young bucks trying to impress each other with Herculean lifts that they'd later regret, and smile. You'll see, I'd think to myself. You'll see.

Fifteen minutes later she got out of the pool and went back over to where she'd parked the bathrobe. She took off the bathing cap and shook out her hair, giving me an opportunity to appraise at closer range. She was wearing an entirely modest one-piece bathing suit but there was no denying that she had an elegant and lovely body. She then turned and walked over to the whirlpool bath.

"May I join you, Captain?" she said.

Captain? My surprise must have shown. "By all means," I said. She stepped down the steps into the pool and submerged in the quietly bubbling waters right up to her chin.

"I'm Lieutenant Commander Janet Waring, from ONI," she said. "I was told to come to this hotel, get a room, and then meet you and a Captain Van Rensselaer for dinner at six thirty."

"How'd you recognize me?" I asked.

"They showed me facial pictures," she replied, with the barest hint of smile, as she rose out of the water to sit on the hot tub's bench. She had what I'd call a severe face, one that could have been conventionally pretty if not for that emanation of reserved authority with not a hint of coquettishness. "They told me that Van Rensselaer was exceptionally tall," she said. "And that you were a dedicated weight lifter." She pretended to briefly ogle my chest and shoulders. "So: all in all, not that difficult."

I laughed. Her voice was deeper than those of most of the women I'd met, and she radiated a degree of commissioned confidence. A lady lieutenant commander in ONI. Given her apparent age, mid-thirties, I guessed, she must have some important skills.

"Well," I said. "This is all news to me, but I suppose I look forward to it."

"Suppose?"

"I wasn't aware that I was in the ONI pictorial files," I said. "And I don't think you should tell Van Rensselaer that he is, either. I'm not anybody special in this man's Navy; he, on the other hand, appears to be exceptionally connected, so much so that he requested a meeting this afternoon with the CNO on a no-notice basis and was given an audience. Immediately."

"Yes, we heard about that," she said. "But not on the first try, correct? Captain Villem Van Rensselaer. Consorts with presidents, etcetera, etcetera. The Office of Naval Intelligence keeps tabs on people in Washington who either could be considered powerful or have powerful access. You have that access—now, and before, on the CNO's personal hit squad. That way if one of these people call, we know how to act. Makes us look good."

"Which is all-important," I acknowledged, and meant it.

"You betchum, Red Ryder," she said, and then we both laughed. Suddenly I liked her. I'd met one other ONI lady officer, and she would have fit right in with the flying monkey brigade serving that wicked witch in Oz.

"Okay," I said. "I'll check with the dining room to see if there's a reservation for us tonight. Van Rensselaer said nothing about dinner to me, but he did ask Admiral King for some ONI help."

"There is a reservation," she said. "I was told to wear civvies, and to arrive in the dining room at eighteen forty. My job in ONI is as the head of the division assigned to evaluate Japan's remaining capability to wage war in preparation for the invasion. I speak tolerably good Japanese and I can even read *kanji*. Other than that, I'm in the dark about this evening, too. I assume this must have something to do with Japanese weapons."

"Oh, yes," I said. "And ours, too."

"So," she urged. "Something new?"

I hesitated. "You have no idea," I replied unhelpfully and rose to get out of the hot tub. I think I was still a little disturbed at being in ONI's files. "But I suspect you soon will. See you at the dinner table."

THIRTEEN
THE GAME BEGINS

I went down to the main lobby at six. I'd picked up the suitcase my neighbor had generously delivered to the hotel. I was wearing a three-piece Gaskill-Chewning light gray woolen bespoke suit made in New York to fit my outsize frame. The hotel bar was just off the main lobby so I availed myself of a Scotch-rocks and then went back to the lobby and took one of the out-of-the-way chairs parked against the wall to watch the procession of new arrivals, hotel guests, and all the people waiting to meet other people that were filling up the lobby area. It was an eclectic crowd but typical of wartime Washington, more men than women, no children, everyone trying to watch everyone to see who was there this evening without being too obvious about it. There was an optimistic aura about it all, with Germany defeated, a new president, and Japan pretty obviously on the ropes. Tell that to the Marines, I thought idly.

And tell that to the Army, Navy, and Marines headed for *Okinawa* and beyond. On the ropes, perhaps, but in a corner, like a dangerous animal.

Dear God, I thought, as my imagination built a picture of Marines and Army grunts storming ashore—in homeland Japan.

And now this—*thing*. The gadget. The name all these wizards, magicians, alchemists, and scientific necromancers involved had chosen to call it, in order to avoid saying out loud what they were really doing. I could see the absolute utility of having a weapon like that. When you thought about it, what was the difference between flying 250 B-29s over *Tokyo* and setting the entire city on fire and this thing, this *gadget*? Well, 250 bombers, for one. If Van Rensselaer was to be believed this bomb, this *atomic* bomb, would flash the power and the heat of the sun itself, over its target in one-millionth of a second, reducing every living thing it touched to the purest form of interstellar carbon, and radioactive carbon at that. I finished my Scotch in one go.

"Captain Bowen?"

I looked up. Van Rensselaer and the lovely Janet Waring were standing in front of me. Van Rensselaer was wearing a suit that looked like a tux but wasn't. Waring had cleaned up very well indeed in a shin-length little black dress with a string of pearls around her neck. I had to stop myself from staring at her. "Sorry," I said. "I was miles away, thinking about—gadgets."

Van Rensselaer gave me a halfhearted warning look and then indicated it was time for dinner. Off we went, the impossibly tall Van Rensselaer easing Waring and myself ahead of him to our reserved corner table. People stared, and I had to wonder if it was Waring or Van Rensselaer they were staring at. Certainly not me, that was for sure. My bet was on Waring, but then I liked girls. I wasn't sure what Van Rensselaer liked, if anything or anyone.

He immediately assumed the duties of host. We ordered drinks— another Scotch for me, a vodka martini for Waring, and a glass of sparkling water with a lime wedge for himself. Having not had that much to eat that day, I took it slow with the second Scotch. The service and then the dinner were excellent. The conversation was innocuous, with Van Rensselaer treating the two of us to a colorful running commentary about who was who in the dining room. His knowledge was impressive. Clearly, we were seeing an exclusive clientele for wartime Washington. The prices on the menu were startling for someone like me, who rarely dined out, but I followed his lead. For some reason, visions of my commanding officer tour in a heavy cruiser kept flitting through my brain as I watched all these well-nourished swells. I'd seen my share of naval gunfights, and briefly wondered if official Washington, while Navy men were dying of burns, explosive shock, or fighting off sharks in oil-covered tropical waters after one of those deadly night engagements with the IJN, had been going to dinner in places just like this, talking knowingly about combat statistics and strategic advantage.

Waring had been gliding through the entire scene as if she had been to the manor born. I soon realized she was quietly playing up to Van Rensselaer, who was visibly enjoying her attention. Who wouldn't, I thought, but then I wondered: what was this dinner all about? Was he going to gather us both to the hotel bar after dinner and reveal the Manhattan Project to her? In a hotel bar? Not bloody likely. Then it hit me: she already knew. ONI already knew. She was playing up to Van Rensselaer because she knew he was a Washington kingpin in some important project. If that was true, I asked myself for the hundredth time, why the hell had Van Rensselaer pulled *me* onto this atomic web? And if that wasn't true, what was she doing here with the two of us? Suddenly I yearned for the happy simplicity of sitting in the captain's chair up on the bridge of my cruiser, sipping on serious coffee and waiting for the sun to set and the fun to begin.

Yes, I'd overheard the two Japanese prisoners talk about their own weapons program, but that could have been talk about anything at all. So what? Through a mildly Scotch-befuddled haze I began to wonder if I hadn't been drawn into something that went beyond finding out if Japan had a similar program. I thought about excusing myself for a head call and then keeping going, right the hell out of this hotel. It was the same feeling I'd sometimes gotten out there in the western Pacific, when everything went quiet, much *too* quiet, and the radars had no contacts, surface or air. I would order the bridge to sound general quarters, button up the ship, and begin to maneuver evasively in the dark. That back-of-the-neck crawling sensation had saved us from being torpedoed more than once. I was beginning to feel it now.

I was made no wiser through dinner. It was as if Van Rensselaer had been purposefully keeping the conversation innocuous. Over coffee, he asked Waring to describe the current organization of ONI headquarters. Not what they were doing, but how they were organized within the Navy department to deal with and cooperate with the rest of the Washington headquarters' intelligence departments, such as Army Intelligence, the State Department's INR bureau, or even the OSS.

"Poorly," she admitted. "In my limited experience, wartime intelligence is a parochial business. Each organization treats its collection of secrets, however obtained, as a treasure to be protected at all costs. That doesn't apply to the operational fleet commands, of course. They're our principal 'customers.' But other agencies? They're our bureaucratic competitors, not our allies. We're not an operational spy agency, like the OSS. Our information comes from naval attachés around the Allied world, the signals intelligence stations who work for the fleet commands, after-action reports from the fleet, and quite a bit from civilian industry. We also have connections in the various American laboratories and scientific research centers supporting the war effort. I think the other agencies and bureaus feel the same way. I think it cries out for centralization, but, with a war on, that's not likely."

"Captain Bowen," he asked, "what's been your experience with ONI, first as a cruiser skipper, and then recently, as part of the CNO's personal staff?"

"As a cruiser skipper, almost none," I said. "We'd get intelligence briefings from our operational commanders and the Pacific Fleet commander. ONI published some recognition guides—enemy ships and aircraft—but otherwise, ships had no contact with them. At the CNO staff level, ONI was, well, not highly regarded. Much too bureaucratic, unwilling to turn loose information, and usually hiding behind a 'you have no need to know' mantra when we mere mortals would ask inconvenient questions."

Van Rensselaer looked at Waring, who shrugged. "That's about right," she admitted. "We are in the *secret* intelligence business. We share with operational commanders, but most of our information is not time sensitive, as in, here they come, look out. We collect, we analyze, we sift out trends, we give estimates of the Japanese's war-making potential based on reports from the commanders of submarines regarding attrition of Japanese imports and after-action reports to estimate how many ships are left, or how many aircraft."

"You sound like military librarians," he said.

She bristled at that. "We like to think we contribute, if only because no one else in the Navy is doing anything like we do. Remember Midway."

"That wasn't ONI," Van Rensselaer pointed out. "That was a dedicated group of analysts working out of the basement of the Fourteenth Naval District headquarters building at Pearl. With opposition."

"But which ONI funded and staffed," she retorted.

"Fair point," he admitted. "But unwillingly. As I remember, Nimitz made ONI do it."

"Where we going with this discussion?" I asked, finally.

Van Rensselaer smiled. "Ah," he said. "Captain Heart-of-the-Matter speaks. Okay: I want to know if ONI headquarters could run an actual intelligence operation in the far western Pacific. Without any of the other Washington agencies' knowledge. Using strictly Navy communications systems. Based on Guam, probably. Driving Navy operational assets. In a highly dangerous place, well behind enemy lines. In the next month."

"What's the target?" Waring asked immediately.

"At this moment, you do not have the need to know," Van Rensselaer said, innocently.

Waring snorted. "Touché," she said. "But c'mon: we're not secret agents. That's not what we do. I mean, we'd need an op-con center, naval communications station access, area training, and—"

"Wouldn't you just," he observed. "Your 'we need' sounds to me like that's precisely what you do. You just don't talk about it."

She gave him an exasperated look. She was, like me, getting tired of these little verbal skirmishes. But then he changed the subject.

"Do you have direct access to Admiral Thebaud?" he asked.

"Well, yes, I do, but—"

"Ask him if you can manage an op like that on short notice," Van Rensselaer said. "And ask him tomorrow. First thing. Tell him who's asking, namely me. Then tell him I said for him to call Admiral Leahy at the White House and give him a yes or no answer. By noon tomorrow. I was told you can go in and ask him a question like that. Can you do that?"

She was clearly taken aback. "He'll demand to know what it is you're talking about, and I'll have to tell him I have no idea."

"Yup," Van Rensselaer said. His demeanor, however, had changed. No more the genial host of the dinner table. His expression revealed a personal sense of power, one I'd seen before in the Portsmouth shipyard and then in the CNO's office. You. Idiot. You. Command power and authority. Combined with his towering physical presence and those fire-bright eyes, he now had Waring's complete attention. Mine, too. And then he seemed to subside.

"Okay, forget that," he said. "I'll do it myself. Saves time."

I knew she wanted to ask more questions, but Van Rensselaer was clearly no longer in the mood. He got up, told us he had the check, thanked us both courteously for coming, and strode across the barroom toward the lobby. A Marine officer in uniform, whom neither of us had noticed, was waiting for him in the lobby and they headed for the front door.

We sat there for a long moment, both of us trying to absorb what had just happened. She tilted her head and asked me if I knew what the hell was going on here. In one sense, I did, but in another, this business with ONI had come as a complete surprise. Based on my experience, ONI was meant to be a support organization to commanders of operational forces: cryptography, indications and warning, intel on enemy ships and aircraft, classified maps and charts, and other matters. But individual ships' commanding officers rarely had any direct contact with ONI. For public consumption, anyway, it was just another Washington headquarters bureau, and definitely not a real cloak-and-dagger bunch. Time for some equivocation on my part.

"Yes and no," I answered. "All I can tell you right now is that it concerns something so important and so big that it could end the war with Japan in one day. And if it's any consolation, I have no idea why *I'm* involved, much less you and ONI."

She sighed and looked at her empty glass. "Nightcap?" she asked.

I'd had enough booze, but there was something in the way she asked that made me nod. "What's your poison?" I asked.

"Drambuie and Scotch on the rocks," she said. "With a twist."

I signaled the waiter, ordered her Rusty Nail and a Courvoisier for me, and then sat back in my chair, trying to sort things out. She turned her attention to the crowd in the dining room, looking around as if to see who was there. It gave me a chance to closely study her. Late thirties, not mid, maybe even forty, interesting, almost aristocratic face, some crow's feet at the corners of her eyes. Some gray strands in her dark hair. If she'd been a man, she'd have been at least a commander. But being just a lieutenant commander simply reflected the status of the WAVES in the Navy. WAVES: Women Accepted as Volunteers for Emergency Service. Until recently, the head of the WAVES Navy-wide had been a lieutenant commander. For someone like Van Rensselaer to ask for ONI support and get her in one day, she must be a player of some kind. A quick vision of her effortless swimming crossed my mind. If it looks effortless, then there's real strength in there. I admired strength.

"Interested, Captain?" she asked, giving me a sly sideways look. She'd caught me looking.

I shrugged. "I'm a sailor, Lieutenant Commander. I have a professional duty to ogle pretty women."

She smiled at that, and it softened her face. "Married, Captain?"

"No," I replied. "Got close, went to sea, and she—moved on to somebody more suitable. And present for duty, too, I suspect. Anyway, I plan to hang it up when the war's over. Maybe, then, possibly. But for companionship, I think. I'm well past the home-in-the-suburbs dream. You know, Momma Bear, Poppa Bear, two little baby bears underfoot. Mowing the lawn. Going to PTA meetings. I wouldn't know how to do any of that, I'm afraid. How about you?"

"Likewise," she said. "I'm from a Southern family. According to them I have failed utterly at Southern belle. I have good degrees, a mastery of Asiatic languages, and a keen interest in winning this war. Later, maybe, for domesticity. Right now, though, this war keeps me safe from all that."

"I completely understand," I said. "Plus, I've seen too much widow-making. It saddens me, and puts me off the whole proposition. But who knows. How do you know about me?"

"I read your file before coming in for this meeting."

"ONI keeps Navy personnel files in addition to pictures?"

She tried to give me a mysterious smile, but then simply grinned. "I lied. I called a friend on the OpNav staff, who told me you were a confirmed bachelor, a weight lifter, and one of the CNO's personal gunfighters. That you were a decorated destroyer and cruiser skipper, and that people who'd crossed the CNO never saw *you* coming until it was much too late. That you had a nickname in OpNav. Captain No-see-um." She paused. "Although, a no-see-um is just a tiny little bug," she pointed out.

"A biting bug, nevertheless," I replied. "Plus, you failed to mention that I'm also exceptionally brave, handsome, suave, rich, and debonair."

She rolled her eyes, but, fortunately, the waiter arrived with our drinks before she could retort. We tipped glasses and then she smiled again. I wondered if I'd overdone it just a wee bit. I liked her. In my business, especially in the CNO's office, I didn't meet many women officers, and none of them had been as appealing as she was. That little voice coughed up an ahem, and I realized I was getting way ahead of myself. Dutch courage, no doubt.

"I was married once," she said, in answer to my unasked question. "To a really slick Washington lawyer. Handsome, cruelly bright, rich and getting richer, an up-and-coming mover and a shaker, right here in downtown Washington. We had three glamorous years, with both of us career-driven and traveling a lot, until I accidentally discovered that he had a wife and two kids in another state. We'd done a civil ceremony, which meant there'd been no big-deal wedding and all that. My parents were furious, but not surprised. I only found out when she showed up at our Washington town house, kids and a bag of presents in tow. It was Christmastime. She wanted to surprise him. Mission accomplished."

"Wow," I said. "What happened?"

"I left them to it, the both of them facing each other with red faces, hers with tears and his with unreasonable anger. I got a hotel room for a week while I looked for a new home. Found something perfect, signed a conditional-on-financing, a cash purchase agreement, and then sent him a copy of the contract. He understood exactly what I meant by that and sent a check three days later. I now have a very nice river-view house, out near Glen Echo, mortgage free, and overlooking the Potomac River gorge, actually, at least in winter when the trees are bare. Navy friends who visit tend to say: wow, and then ask: how? I tell them I made an investment several years ago that handsomely paid off."

"Brilliant," I said. The lady indeed had some steel in her.

"This thing with Van what's his name," she said, changing the subject. "Is it dangerous?"

"Unauthorized knowledge of it can be," I said. "Some people have poked their noses in where they shouldn't have and are now languishing incommunicado somewhere for the duration of the war. Look: you were sent here today by your bosses at ONI. At Van Rensselaer's request, I'm guessing. Just like me. My advice? He'll tell us the what-for when it suits him. Don't talk about this to anyone, not your boyfriend, not your relatives, not your boss. Nobody. Go back to work and wait. Van Rensselaer does consort with people like Admiral Leahy and Admiral King, and gives personal briefings to Harry Truman. Who listens to every word—I was there for his briefing to the new president today, and everybody in the room was listening hard."

She looked down at the table for a moment. "Might this have anything to do with . . ." She hesitated. "Uranium?"

I about dropped my glass. I had to clamp my mouth back shut. She saw my consternation and leaned forward. "Listen," she began. "I'm the senior Japanese translator at ONI headquarters. I come from a privileged upbringing; my parents are descendants of the Warings of South Carolina. I went to Georgetown University to study East Asian cultures and the Japanese language for four years. Took some German in my spare time. German is easier. I then got a master's from Columbia in Japanese culture and history, which was taught *in* Japanese by a Japanese professor. I was an intern at State during the summers. And, most importantly, I spent nearly three years living and traveling in Japan right after graduation from Georgetown. When the war broke out for us in 1941, I signed on at State but discovered that they had older and better—just ask them—translators who didn't want mere ex-interns in their bailiwick. A friend from Columbia suggested I talk to ONI; they offered me a commission and some real work about real war. I snapped it up."

I nodded, not knowing what to say. Good for you, Princess? Rich Southern girl with a penchant for exotic languages, what else do you do with her but keep her in school until you can marry her off? I think she might have guessed what I was thinking, but pressed on.

"Here's the thing: the people are who involved in deciphering Japanese navy codes and such aren't at ONI headquarters. Van Rensselaer is right about that. Like he said, Station Hypo, for instance, *is* out in Pearl in the basement of the Fourteenth Naval District headquarters, and, yes, they're the people who brought us the Midway opportunity. ONI headquarters does ONI's budget and interacts with State, War, Navy headquarters. We get to see as many Japanese communications intercepts as we want to, but generally, our higher-ups aren't interested in that. Major policies, roles and missions, competing with Army Intelligence, INR, and the OSS for influence and money—sound familiar?"

"Absolutely," I said. "Just like OpNav."

"Okay, then," she said. "In the interests of keeping my Japanese current, I read the intercept stuff that does come through, looking for pearls. Early on, I found a mystery. They and the Germans were collaborating on technology. We called them the Axis powers, so no big surprise there. Then there was occasional traffic indicating they were exchanging 'stuff,' for want of a better word. Technology, research information, and eventually, actual 'things.' Evolving radar sets, tank machinery, specialized ammunition, synthetic rubber and synthetic fuels formulae, torpedo designs. Like that. I took this stuff to my boss, whose reaction was all too typical of ONI in 1942, 1943, even 1944. Of course they are, Commander Waring; that's why we call them the Axis, dear, isn't it? Right now, however, it's budget time, so unless there's something else?"

"That must have been frustrating," I said.

"Just a tiny bit." She sighed and finished her drink. "But then I discovered they were moving actual things via submarine. I thought that was important and worth possibly some interdiction operations. Talked to my Intel counterparts at the Atlantic command. Maybe hunt down these long-distance cargo subs? Nope. The Atlantic command has its hands full with wrapping up the Battle of the Atlantic. Attack subs, not *milch cows*. We hardly have the resources to seek out specialized submarines spending months underwater transiting from *Tokyo* to Germany and back, assuming they were even doing that. I told them their *Tokyo* government comms indicated they were. Swell. Pass it along to the Brits. Maybe they can do something with it, but we doubt it. One submarine? And besides, how long would a voyage like that take? You're talking thousands of miles."

"Good point," I said. "But that doesn't mean they weren't doing it."

"Yes, exactly," she said. "I kept watching, and I did pass some materials on to the British naval intelligence. They acknowledged, but then, silence. That's just their way; they're not famous for sharing."

"They did have other matters to attend to," I pointed out. "Especially in '42, '43. The U-boats were strangling them and then came V-1 and V-2 rockets."

She nodded. "Yeah, yeah, I know that," she said. "But then in '43 I began to see this word that I couldn't break. That hurt my pride. Went back to my university contacts. Drew a blank until a prof at Georgetown who knew a guy who knew a guy said that the word stood for the element uranium. I drew a blank. What's uranium?"

"And this was in traffic between—?"

"*Tokyo* Imperial University and some collection of consonants in Germany."

"Did you take *that* to your bosses at ONI?"

"I did; again, no interest."

I thought for a moment. The noise in the dining-bar area was getting loud enough to make that hard. "What happens to your decrypts once the higher-ups decide if they're important or not?"

"Filed," she replied.

I looked at my watch. Wait until Van Rensselaer hears this, I thought. "I'm gonna turn in," I said. "Van Rensselaer said we'd leave at 0830 for points unknown. Civvies. He didn't say where."

"And what if I don't want to play in whatever high-stakes game is going on here?" she asked.

I smiled as I gathered myself to leave. "That train has long since left the station, my dear Lieutenant Commander," I said in my best Peter Lorre impression. "Trust me on that."

"That was awful," she protested, making a face.

"I know," I admitted. "But it's the thought that counts. And it's also true. Breakfast at 0730?"

FOURTEEN
LOS ALAMOS

We met Van Rensselaer's driver in the lobby at 0830 and departed for the Executive Office Building, where he said he had a meeting with General Groves. Van Rensselaer was sitting in the right rear seat, as usual, so I had to go out into traffic to open my door. Waring hopped in front.

"Who's General Groves?" she piped up. Himself ignored her as we pushed through Washington traffic. He stared straight ahead, as if deep in thought. Waring sat in front with the driver so she couldn't see an annoyed expression flit across his overlarge face. I was next to him, nursing a small headache from all the booze the night before. *You're* gonna have to tell her, I thought. Or she isn't going to play. Once again, I was getting impatient with at all the hugger-mugger. If he wanted *me* to play, I'd need more information, too, secrecy or no secrecy. A fleet operation in a dangerous place? Come *on*.

When we got to the EOB, he told us that the car would take us to our respective homes. Prepare for a two-week trip, he said. Maybe even three. We'll leave by train at eighteen thirty this evening. Lieutenant Commander Waring, you are now under TAD orders to accompany me to Los Alamos, New Mexico. Call your office to confirm.

"You're meeting with General Groves?" I asked.

"Correct."

"Why don't you take Lieutenant Commander Waring with you?"

"Because—" he began, impatiently, but I cut him off.

"Right, she hasn't been read in. So, take her with you, explain why you need her, you know, in terms of this Japanese program development, and then ask his permission to read her in. As in, kiss the damned ring."

Van Rensselaer gave me a surprised look. "That's brilliant," he said. "I do believe you're better at Washington *kabuki* than I first imagined. Lieutenant Commander Waring, come with me, if you please."

That evening found all three of us on yet another military train bound for a place called Los Alamos. This time there were two of the new diesel locomotives, a fuel car, Van Rensselaer's "command" car, a dining car, and two Pullman sleepers, all followed by about thirty freight cars and a personnel caboose for the Army MP detachment. We left from Union Station at 1830 on the dot; the train had come from the Aberdeen proving grounds in Maryland. We had a twenty-six-hundred-mile trip on our hands. With military priority on the transcontinental routes, we still had a three-day trip facing us, barring mechanical delays. There were also a half dozen civilians on the train who purportedly were scientists, also bound for Los Alamos.

Waring and I met up in the dining car. As usual, we were in the dark about the purpose and even the duration of the trip. Two weeks, maybe three. The dining car had a tiny bar, but it was well stocked. Waring had a gin martini; I had my usual Scotch. We were both in civvies; Van Rensselaer had shown up in dress blues, stripes and all. He explained that he'd had to go to the White House; Admiral Leahy insisted that any naval officer coming to the White House had to be in dress uniform. He'd told Waring she'd been approved to be read in, and that he would give her a formal briefing about the program later.

"Any ideas?" Waring asked as we watched the darkening countryside slide by. Some of the civilians had come into the dining car, but nobody was mixing. The service staff looked to be military, and there were good smells coming from the galley at the back of the car.

"Nope," I said. "Along for the ride, at this stage. Los Alamos, from what I've heard, is the place where things get made, as opposed to Oak Ridge, where—" I stopped. I'd suddenly remembered that she hadn't technically been briefed in. "Sorry," I said. "I think you need to push on Van Rensselaer to do your in-briefing. Otherwise, he'll put it off. We're stuck on a train for three days and thus physically separated from Washington and all its prying ears and eyes. Now's a good time."

"If he says no?"

"Then tell him what you told me last night. That'll scare him into doing it. If a mere lieutenant commander knows what you know, that alone will do the trick."

"There's more, for what it's worth," she said. "Rumors. Senior intel people talking about big, *really* big, budget money being diverted to some kind of highly technical weapons project. You know how it is in DC: people pretend to know something amazingly secret while hinting at their insider status just to impress other people. And we've also heard rumors about people who try to find out about all that getting sudden, mysterious transfer orders. Unfortunately, all that kind of stuff does is give the original rumors more credibility."

"I understand that," I said. "Ask him, and make sure you tell him I won't give you one scintilla of information."

"What if he still says no?"

"We'll have fuel and food stops on a three-day journey. If he says no, get your stuff, get off at the first big-city stop, and go back to DC and ONI. But don't threaten to do that—just do it. In the meantime, I'll probably see him before you do, and I'll make the case. He's a strange duck, but a powerful one."

"Speak of the devil," she murmured, as Van Rensselaer came through the intercar door, spotted us, and headed over to our table. He said something to a waiter and then sat down with us.

"Lieutenant Commander Waring," he said. "Curious yet?"

"Oh, just a little bit, Captain," she said. "But present company won't tell me anything."

"Good for him," he said, as he looked around. Our table was three tables away from the nearest other people. The wheel noise made an acceptable sound cover. The waiter brought him his drink and said dinner service would begin in an hour. Once he left, Van Rensselaer surprised both of us.

"The project is code-named the Manhattan Project," he began. "In Allied circles, it's known as the Tube Alloys project. A deliberately vague name, meaning nothing. Its purpose is to create something called an atomic bomb. Currently, the biggest bomb in the Allied arsenal is the British Tall Boy, or Grand Slam, at twenty-two thousand pounds, or eleven tons. That's the one they finally used to put *Tirpitz* down. The atomic bomb will release, theoretically, at least, somewhere between sixteen and twenty *thousand* tons of high-explosive force, create temperatures hotter than the sun, generate deadly levels of man-killing radiation, and do so in one one-hundredth of a second. The Grand Slam is a bunker buster. The atomic bomb will be a city buster. The project has expended over two billion dollars so far, and done so in complete secrecy. The effort to create, build, and then test an atomic bomb has been going on since early 1942; the underlying research for twenty, thirty years before that. It's called an atomic bomb because the energy that is released comes from the energy contained in the basic building blocks of everything on earth—atoms. And *that,* in a nutshell, is what you are now involved in, Lieutenant Commander Waring. Comment?"

Waring was stunned. Hell, I was stunned. He'd told me earlier that it would be powerful, but those numbers were incredible. Twenty thousand *tons*? Both of us just sat there, speechless. Van Rensselaer smiled, but it was a cold smile. This apparently wasn't the first time he'd seen the expression of utter disbelief on someone's face.

"Don't feel unique," he continued. "The president had the same expression when he heard those numbers. He said what anyone who understands the magnitude of this device says: this changes *everything*. Indeed, it does. Whichever country gets one of these things first will theoretically rule the world. All the rigid secrecy, unending pressure, logistical priority, and twenty-four hours a day of superhuman effort on the part of about ten thousand people has been required for us to get one before Germany did. We knew they were working on one and a considerable intelligence effort has been expended to find out where they were with their project. We're pretty sure *now* that they didn't get far, but only because the two-front war caught up with them before they could. We, on the other hand, will test one very soon."

"So, why is all this pressure still on?" Waring interrupted.

Van Rensselaer looked over at me, as in: you tell her.

"Oh," I said. "Because we just discovered that the Japanese, who have definitely *not* surrendered, have been working on one, too, and if they've succeeded to the point where *they're* about to test one, the entire plan for the invasion of the home islands could suddenly be rendered impossible."

"*Jesus,*" she whispered. "But why is this news being 'just discovered'? You said we knew about the German program—why not the Japanese program?"

"Great question, Madame ONI," Van Rensselaer snapped, with a "gotcha" look gleaming in his eyes. "Why indeed?"

Waring actually blushed.

"Come on, that's not a fair question," I said. "ONI responds to tasking from the executive branch of the government and the fleet high command. If the whole idea of an atomic bomb's such a damn big secret, who would task them, if anybody, to find out?"

"Point taken," Van Rensselaer said, backing off a little. "But now we absolutely *have* to know if it's true. And, as best I can tell, along with every intelligence agency in our government, we have nobody *in* Japan who can confirm that there even is a Japanese atomic weapons program. But not too long ago we discovered that the Germans and the Japanese have been cooperating on a lot of technological matters by using submarines."

"Yes," she said. "I heard at headquarters that one had been surrendered to the shipyard up in Portsmouth. But—"

"What you may not have heard," Van Rensselaer interrupted, "is that it was a minelayer and not an attack boat. It had a cargo of partially refined uranium in the mine tubes and was bound for Japan when Germany surrendered. Uranium, or one of its isotopes, is what an atomic bomb is made out of. Why would the Nazis be sending uranium to Japan, unless they'd *both* been working on a bomb themselves? The Germans ran out of time, so they sent their uranium stock to Japan."

"Uranium," she muttered. "There it is again."

"What do you mean by that, Lieutenant?" Van Rensselaer asked, alarm clear on his face. She told him what she'd told me, and he swore again.

"Weeks ago," Van Rensselaer said, "we didn't even know Japan *had* an atomic bomb project going. Germany, yes. Japan? At the end of its tether? Being bombed continuously since *Iwo* was secured? Cities firebombed, with thousands of casualties? Most of its fleet sunk or languishing in port for lack of oil? Not enough naval air forces able to man up a single carrier? Bypassed garrisons in places like Truk starving to death because no supplies can get through to them? All the people *we* have working on this project are not being subjected to daily bombing raids and have all the resources this nation can offer up to make it happen. How could this be possible?"

"How indeed?" she asked.

"Good damn question," he snapped. "And yet, a German U-boat shows up in Portsmouth, loaded with uranium. Partially enriched uranium, even. Here's the plan, boys and girls. I'm taking you to Los Alamos, and then to Hanford, in Washington State, the other main production site, if there's time. And then to the test site. And then I'm going to use you two to find out if *any* of this, what's the word, *conjecture,* about a Japanese program is true. Preferably before the Joint Chiefs assemble the world's largest invasion fleet in a stationary formation off the shores of Japan."

I looked over at Waring, who had to be thinking the same thing I was: use *us* to find out?

Van Rensselaer smiled again. "I know," he said. "It's a lot to digest. That Army officer down there at the back of the dining room is telling me I have an important phone call. Tomorrow you two will come back to the command car for a fuller briefing on what you're going to see. In the meantime, have another drink. Maybe two. You're gonna need it."

Once again, I hadn't noticed the officer standing at the back of the car, but there he was. An Army major, with a piece of paper in his hands. Van Rensselaer finished his drink and took his leave. I looked at Waring. We mouthed the words together: What. The. Hell.

The waiter arrived with a second round. I think we were both more than ready.

FIFTEEN
HOT BRASS TACKS

Over dinner we kicked around our perceptions about our involvement in this massive project. There were few enough people on the train that we didn't think we'd be overheard as our iron horse rattled steadily into the western darkness. I did notice that we hadn't stopped even once as was usually the case with trains carrying passengers, but then I remembered all those freight cars. And the trip down from Portsmouth.

"I can see why *you* were folded into this project," Waring said. "A CNO's office executive who takes care of sensitive internal OpNav problems. But ONI? We'd love to be operating at your level, but we just don't. Our focus is on the fleet commanders' needs for operational intelligence. Our biggest claim to fame was Midway, which in fact was, as he reminded me, the result of some smart guys out in Pearl stretching their necks out, only reluctantly with our backing."

"I think I can see what he wants from you," I said. "Did you tell Groves about the word uranium appearing in high-level Japanese command traffic?"

She nodded.

"So that was a smoldering straw in the wind. Groves would have understood the significance of that immediately. You couldn't, because you didn't know about our project. So: how many other such straws in the wind have crossed other intelligence services' desks in the past three years? A word here, a word there. And strange words, too. Uranium. Cyclotron. Pitchblende. Centrifuge. Radiation. I think what he wants you to do is to canvass *all* the agencies back there in DC, and do so with a list of words in hand. Ask them if they've ever encountered these words. They may have seen stuff that means something to us but not to them. Like that."

"And you? What's he got in mind for you?"

"Beats me," I had to admit. "As you may have noticed, Van Rensselaer isn't given to explaining what the hell he has in mind on any given day. I do know he has communication channels back there in his so-called command car that probably rival Admiral Nimitz's. Seems to me that the burning question of the day is: if the Japanese have a program, where the hell is it? Van Rensselaer was taking me to see Oak Ridge when FDR died. He said that's where they make the bomb-grade version of uranium, and it's *huge*. There's one plant there that's over a mile long. I also learned that the entire output of all the Tennessee Valley Authority dams is going to Oak Ridge on any given day. Maybe ONI or one of its stations has imagery of something like that in Japan?"

"Our imagery of Japan these days comes from B-29s," she said. "It's mostly smoke. I can't imagine there's anything like what you're describing still standing."

"How about way up north? *Hokkaido*? The B-29s aren't going there."

"Because there's nothing up there," she said. "Not compared to *Honshu*, *Shikoku*, or *Kyushu*. Interesting wildlife, subarctic weather conditions. Coal mines, worked mostly by convicts and, sadly, POWs. One major city—*Sapporo*. Certainly not an industrial area like you're describing."

"Shit," I said. "So, once again, where the hell is it?"

"If it even exists," she said. "The Germans had the scientists, the labs, the universities and institutes, and a highly capable industrial capacity even before the damned war. According to you, the Japanese weren't sending uranium to Germany—it was the other way around, right?"

"How's about you asking the question?" I said. "*If* they had a program, where would it be? I'm thinking it can't be in Japan. So: There'd have to be almost unlimited electrical power. A source of uranium. Total secrecy. Vast quantities of labor—probably slave labor."

She thought about it for a full minute, if not longer. Then her eyes lit up. "Korea," she said. "It has to be in Korea. Or possibly even China, near Shanghai. But I'm betting it's in their vassal state of Korea."

"Seriously?"

"Yes, of course. Will Van Rensselaer let me use his comms suite?"

"Oh, I think so," I said. "Just tell him you think you know where their program lives. But Korea? They're still living in the tenth century."

"But they've been occupied by Japan since 1910. *Totally* occupied. Subjugated is a more accurate word. Korea. Whose borders touch Manchuria, which is a vast wilderness containing huge deposits of valuable minerals. Coal. Iron. Manganese. Copper. Gold. And just maybe? Uranium? Now the Communist Chinese are there. The Russian Army is there. The Japanese are certainly there. With all that treasure, it's probably the Asian version of the Wild West."

"Well, I'll bet *that's* why our dear Captain *Svengali* wanted an individual from ONI pulled into this, but he or she has to look like a free agent. Otherwise, none of those other intel agencies would give you the time of day."

She thought about that for a moment, then nodded in agreement. "Curiouser and curiouser," she muttered. Then she turned around and lifted her empty glass in the direction of the bartender. "Anyway, in the meantime, I'll see what I can find out about large Japanese industrial sites in Korea."

We were delayed during the night by a train-versus-automobile crash and the three-hour investigation that followed. These were becoming more frequent with the advent of these fast diesel engines on cross-country routes. The train, as usual, suffered no damage, but the car and its single occupant had been smashed into a cornfield in eastern Illinois. There was nowhere to disembark so we just stayed aboard and waited. Waring had gone to see Van Rensselaer with her theory and a request to use his secure comms link, which he quickly granted. She said he was fuming about the delay; no surprise there nor much sympathy for the poor driver of the car. Or the engineer, I thought, who was probably beside himself. Nobody ever thinks about the engineer, who knows exactly what's about to happen when his headlight first illuminates the hapless vehicle.

She reported at breakfast that ONI *did* have aerial reconnaissance photos of the northern parts of Korea because there'd been two Soviet army divisions perched on the Manchurian border since early 1944. They'd promised to get more details to her once we reached Los Alamos. We were summoned at ten that morning to listen to Van Rensselaer telling us more about the three main sites of our atomic weapons programs: Oak Ridge, Los Alamos, and Hanford. I knew a tiny bit about Oak Ridge, and we were headed for Los Alamos. Hanford was new to me. He explained that Oak Ridge and Hanford were pursuing two different designs and industrial processes. Oak Ridge was converting uranium in its natural state to uranium-235, a form of the element that would support a chain reaction, either controlled (a so-called atomic pile or atomic reactor) or an uncontrolled, runaway reaction, i.e., a bomb. Hanford was creating an entirely new, man-made uranium isotope called plutonium, using atomic piles to do it.

In simplest terms, U-235 was hard to make because it involved converting so-called natural uranium ore into a gas, then passing that gas through enormous centrifuges, where the heavier uranium isotope, the U-235, would precipitate out as a coating on the sides of the centrifuge. That would be scraped off at intervals and converted chemically back to a gas and then to a metal. The coating was more like a brownish smear, so it took either months, or many, many centrifuges operating simultaneously, to accumulate a useable amount. Hence that mile-long building at Oak Ridge.

Hanford, which was out in Washington State on the banks of the Columbia River, was using controlled reactors to separate out the brand-new element, plutonium. As opposed to physical separation, like in the centrifuges, they were using a chemical method to produce the plutonium, which was much faster. The downside was that the entire process required humans to be completely absent once the process began, because there was a huge amount of dangerous radiation produced when the reactors went into the production mode, or became breeders, as the scientists liked to call them. Plutonium would support fission just like U-235, but a lot more energetically. Plutonium was meant to make bombs, not atomic piles, although it could do that, too. The Hanford plant covered six hundred square miles and required fifty thousand people to run it. Oak Ridge wasn't that big, but given the fact that it had appeared suddenly in Appalachia and begun sucking up so much electric power, I was surprised that it was all that secret.

"We have a deal," Van Rensselaer said, "with the American news organizations, both in Tennessee and in Washington State. Absolute secrecy. So far, so good. The most important scientific and engineering effort of the war. Critical to winning the war. Once we can, we'll tell you what it's all about. If you blab, we'll make you disappear."

I still remember the case of that idiot congressman from Kentucky, who after a security briefing, blabbed to the Capitol Hill press corps about the fact that the Japanese were setting their depth charges too shallow to hit American subs, which subsequently cost us ten submarines and easily eight hundred deaths. If the entire American press was keeping its mouth shut about the Manhattan Project, that had to be a damned miracle. I asked, okay, so what's happening at Los Alamos?

"That's where they are going to assemble the first bombs," he said. "The fissionable material will be collected there, and then the bombs will be built. Two totally different designs, but each one aimed at creating a so-called critical mass of fissionable material in a blink of an eye, so that the resulting neutron flux will initiate an uncontrolled fission event."

I looked at Waring. Van Rensselaer was speaking in tongues, as far as I was concerned. She seemed equally baffled.

"Look," he said. "The trick is to use high explosives to create a critical mass of uranium or plutonium suddenly enough that the neutrons have time to make the thing go bang before the high explosive blows the assembly apart, creating a dud. That takes some serious electrical engineering. The first bomb will be a design that just about has to work. Two subcritical chunks of enriched U-235 will be encased, one at each end, in the barrel of an artillery tube, with explosive packed behind them. The space between them will be a vacuum. The two chunks will be fired at each other. When they hit each other, a critical mass will be created, and the uncontrolled reaction will be initiated at the speed of light. Timing, as all the wags say, is everything. One ten-thousandth of a second."

"What's a critical mass?" Waring asked.

"A typical atomic reactor, or pile, is a big twelve-foot-on-a-side cube made up of blocks of pencil lead—graphite, a pure form of carbon. The pile is salted with pieces of U-235, and a matrix of cadmium rods is drilled through the pile. The point of both the carbon and the cadmium is to absorb neutrons being emitted naturally from the uranium. As you withdraw the cadmium rods, the neutrons are freed to produce more neutrons and the so-called nuclear reaction starts up. It creates heat. This is the promise of atomic energy, by the way: that heat can boil water, making steam, which can make electricity through the use of steam turbines. But: if you take too much of the cadmium out of the pile, the reaction will run away. Now you're talking about a radioactive bomb, or a huge explosion. You control the reaction going on in the reactor by watching the neutron flux and keeping it below that critical stage where it can run away.

"We, on the other hand, are specifically after that runaway, or uncontrolled, reaction, meaning an atomic bomb. But we can't fly a pile out over the target and then start to remove cadmium rods—nobody would be coming back from that mission, would they?"

"And a critical mass?" I prompted.

"A critical mass of uranium is an amount of enriched uranium that can initiate a runaway chain reaction. That's why, in a bomb, in design one, there are *two* subcritical chunks of the stuff, one at each end of the tube. Separated, they can't do anything. There's not enough uranium to start and sustain the reaction. Smash them together by firing one chunk into the other, there *is* enough, and off it goes. Same thing in design two: a ball of plutonium is placed in the center of a hollow sphere made of graphite or some other moderator. That ball is loosely made so that, just sitting there, the atoms of the radioactive material are not close enough together to go critical. Then the sphere is coated on the outside with what are called high-explosive lenses. Get all those lenses to fire simultaneously, and we're talking about creating a perfectly spherical pressure wave, focused on the ball at the heart of that hollow sphere. A basketball-size piece of material gets squeezed down into a Ping-Pong–size ball of fissionable material. Off it goes. In both weapon designs, you drop the bomb, but you don't fire the explosives until it's had time to fall right over the target. By then the plane will have made its escape."

"*God!*" Waring said. "How do they do that? Make every one of those lenses go off at the same time without blowing the entire sphere apart?"

"That, Commander," he said, with a rare grin, "is a really big goddamned secret. Even I don't know how they can do that. Nor does one want to ask. We're going to Los Alamos to get a briefing on how close the program is to testing one. We might even get to watch the first test, if it's close enough. Then maybe we'll go to Hanford and see how close they are to making enough plutonium to make even more bombs. Faster. Or it might go the other way: if there's enough plutonium available, they'll build the test bomb for an implosion test, using plutonium. The gun design pretty much has to work, so that one might become the first bomb used against Japan. Lots of variables here."

I finally decided to ask the question that had been bugging me since I'd been swept into this horrifying secret program. "Why are we accompanying you now, this late in the program?" I asked. "All of this, all the things you've revealed to Lieutenant Commander Waring and me, are so far above our pay grade that—"

He put up his hand to shut me off. "Given what I'm going to ask you both to do, you, a senior OpNav operative and an expert on Japan who can speak their language, have to be believers. The consequences of success in this program will be to change the very nature of warfare—forever. Everything about it is incredible—meaning literally unbelievable. Once you see it, you won't be able to unsee it. And then, I'm confident you'll be eager to do what I ask you to do. That's all I'm going to tell you right now. Enjoy this trip out to Los Alamos. And, perhaps, beyond."

His eyes burned with a passion that surprised both of us. I studied that lean, aristocratic face and wondered if we weren't dealing with a fanatic after all, someone who had been entrusted with a burden so big that he was running on nervous energy alone. I'd met some ship captains like that back in early 1943, determined, totally sleep-deprived and driven men who were fighting the Japanese twenty-four hours a day, their faces studies in fatigue and facial bone structure because they weren't eating, living instead on coffee and cigarettes. Back in the fall of 1942 the Japanese had clearly demonstrated to us that the US Navy was punching way above its weight class. It had taken a year and a half and thousands of dead Navy men before we became confident enough and sufficiently proficient at surface ship warfare for us, the survivors, to take the war to them. A lot of the Navy's peacetime bright lights had had to be extinguished before we reached that point.

To me, Van Rensselaer was beginning to look like one of them. The fact that he and Major General Groves were operating at such a high level—briefing the president, keeping the awful secrets, driving other men, mostly civilians, to work to capacity and beyond on an end-of-the-world weapon, created an overwhelming pressure all of its own. I wondered if combat at sea wasn't a simpler proposition than what these guys faced in Washington. We seagoing commanders knew who our enemy was and whether or not we'd prevailed; the bureaucrats were never quite sure, especially when the fights were about budget dollars, power, and influence. Either way, I wasn't going to get in his way if I could help it, and I sensed that Waring felt the same way. That didn't mean that we weren't feeling an element of apprehension of our own. What did he have in mind for us, that we had to be "true believers"? Believers in what, exactly?

"Okay," I said, after he'd left. "I need to hit the rack. All this hugger-mugger is making me tired."

She smiled and then finished off her drink. I'd had more to drink than I was used to. In a different place and under different circumstances I might have asked the sporting question, but the time wasn't right. I liked her a lot and we seemed to be simpatico. But thoughts of atomic bombs, cataclysmic invasions, and the deadly urgency of the whole situation made the possibility of our entering the seduction dance seem wrong. Still, the look on her face was unmistakable.

"Hey?" I said. "Rain check?"

She gave me a direct look. "Why not right now?"

"Have you seen the beds in our compartments?" I asked, looking for a diversion. "I can barely fit. We'd end up on the floor in a heap of shins and elbows, and then the night porter would be knocking at the door asking if there was anything we needed. And then we'd end up laughing hysterically."

"That doesn't sound all bad," she said, trying to keep it light.

"I'm afraid," I said, surprising myself. "Not of you, not of us, but this *thing*. Something tells me we're getting entangled in something that's gonna look like the end of the world. I have the sense that we're getting swept into something so awful that . . ."

She reached across the table and took my hand. "You're a good guy, Wolfe," she said softly. "I'm a woman. I seek refuge from scary monsters in the arms of a strong man, but I can wait. All this talk about the power of the sun being unleashed against the Japanese scares the shit out of me, too. I have been a part of the Japanese people and their ancient culture. Not the ones who brought us Pearl Harbor, the *samurai,* but the real Japanese. I have this terrible feeling that they—the ones I knew and loved, the mystics, the *bonsai* artists, the real *geishas,* not the whores, the calligraphers, the temple gardeners, the coastal fishermen, the rice farmers—are going to be immolated in order to convince the nutcases to give it up. They are the enemy, but I don't want this to happen, not to them. The generals, the admirals, the fanatics, they deserve it. But not the people of the land. And yet . . . listening to Van Rensselaer, I don't want to be alone tonight."

"Will you settle for a hug in the dark, then?" I asked.

"Oh, hell yes," she said.

SIXTEEN
TRINITY

We arrived at the test site at 0330. It was dark and surprisingly chilly for July in the high deserts of New Mexico. It had been raining for the past three days, so the ground was uncharacteristically muddy. There were already several people out there, milling around in the chilly darkness. We couldn't see the test tower that was ten miles out there in the desert, but there were several soldiers huddling up in small knots behind sand dunes, trying to keep warm. There were endless tests of the announcing system going on, with *test, test, test* blaring from speakers mounted on telephone poles. Neither of us had thought to bring a coat. Janet was shivering in slacks and a long-sleeved blouse. We'd been wearing civvies our whole time in Los Alamos at Van Rensselaer's direction. Most people at Los Alamos had been in civvies; if you were in uniform, you were part of the guard forces, and there'd been plenty enough of those. More people kept arriving over the next hour in those incongruous, brown-painted school buses appropriated by the Army.

Van Rensselaer appeared out of the darkness and handed us our black-lensed goggles.

"The scientists tell me that the initial explosion will produce a blinding, literally blinding, white flash accompanied by a pulse of intensely strong radiation," he said. "So, we're going to head over to the trenches now. The countdown will come over those speakers. At the ten second count, you'll need to get down below ground level in the trenches, face away from the test stand, cover your eyes with those goggles, and then close your eyes. Once the white flash subsides you can stand up and look at what's happening. But not before."

"If our eyes are closed," Janet asked, "how will we know the flash has subsided?"

"According to Dr. Oppenheimer, you'll see the flash, even with goggles and your eyes closed. When you can no longer see it, and we're talking a few seconds here, you can take a look. But remember, there's going to be a shock wave coming out from ground zero. Stay low until that passes, too. Peer over the edge of the trench, but expect it. And then there's going to be a return shock wave, as the atmosphere roars back in to fill the vacuum created by the explosion."

"I think I'm just gonna sit down in the trench and wait for everything to stop moving," I said.

"No," he said. "I need you two to see what happens. White flash, flash goes dark, stand up and take a look over the edge of the trench. Your ears will sense the shock wave coming, duck down, let it pass, and then look again. And put your fingers in your ears. The sound will come right after the first outbound shock wave. And it will be impressively loud. But you need to see it. Witness it."

And then he was gone. We tripped our way down into one of the trenches and walked to the other end, followed by lots of other people, splashing through the mud at the bottom. The speakers had finally gone silent, for which we all were grateful. Janet moved closer to me and I put my arm around her shoulders to quiet her shivering. She then moved in front of me so I could shield her from the piercing desert cold. I wasn't sure if she was frightened or just cold, but it felt natural to hold her. You're imagining things, I told myself. And yet, the close-hold night on the train had been a surprisingly delightful interlude amid all this urgent madness.

"Wanna fool around?" I whispered in her ear, and she laughed quietly, but even so, I still sensed she was a bit frightened. So was I, truth be told. What in the name of God Almighty was about to happen? An *atomic* bomb. Okay, we'd both been digesting the notion for a couple of weeks now, listening to endless academics, seeing close-up the enormous industrial efforts going on with this Manhattan Project, meeting with Nobel Prize–winning scientists who were both proud and discreetly nervous about what they were fooling with. I think I'd understood about one-tenth of what individual scientists had told us, but they'd all been politely patient.

We'd come from Los Alamos by car to Alamogordo, a tiny town in New Mexico attached to an Army Air Forces base bombing range. This was the place where the first test bomb, made of plutonium, as it had turned out, had been assembled. The original plan to test a uranium bomb first had been discarded. Van Rensselaer had shared some truly inside information with us. The president was being lobbied hard by some of the project's own senior scientists to conduct a demonstration of the Bomb off the coast of Japan, rather than hitting a population center. The problem was that we had only one of each type ready; if we used the gun-type bomb, which we pretty much knew would work, for such a demonstration without *knowing* that the plutonium implosion weapon would work, the whole thing could backfire on us. There was no point to demonstrating what we now had in our arsenal if we only had one bomb that we *knew* worked. The good news was that Hanford had assured the president that more implosion devices were on the way, and soon.

The afternoon trip to Alamogordo took us through scenery both beautiful and utterly desolate. Everyone on that bus sensed we were on the verge of something life-changing, even world history–changing. The final hours of the trip were in darkness, as if the world itself recognized that something awful was imminent and didn't want to see it.

Assuming it worked. Every conversation about this thing was always prefaced with that condition. The basic problem remained as a single great unknown: would the firing of all those explosive lenses blow the sphere apart before enough atomic energy was released to do the job. The spherical blast wave would be going in, toward the center of the sphere. But that still meant that the pressure *in* the sphere would rise from nothing to something huge in the space of a millisecond (one-thousandth of a second) or two. In theory, the chain reaction would go out of control in a microsecond (one-millionth of a second) so it should work, the operative word being "should."

The only people out there who didn't seem to be worried were the soldiers, who were doing what soldiers do when they're not being shot at: bitching about the cold, the lack of coffee, and those seemingly unending tests of the announcing system. Then the speakers blared again.

"Take positions for the final countdown."

It was a few minutes before 5:00 a.m. We anxiously made our preparations. Hunker down into the muddy trench, turn around, away from the test stand, put on the black goggles, keep your head down and below the top edge of the trench. When the countdown gets to ten seconds, clasp your hands over your ears, close your eyes. When it gets down to five, close your eyes hard. On no account look over the parapet of the trenches until "the flash" subsides. Then do look. Be alert for the shock wave. You *will* feel, and maybe even see, it coming. Duck back down until it passes. But then stand back up and look. I need you to see this.

I need you to see this. That's what he'd said. But that's not what happened. I'm convinced it was the other way around, that *it* saw *me,* crouching in my little trench, and made its presence known. The white flash hurt my eyes—eyes that were squeezed shut, facing the other way, down below the top edge of the trench, wearing glasses covered in black paint, and ten *miles* away from where it went off. I felt Waring jump next to me. The flash was over in a few seconds, but it seemed longer, much longer, and left a bright red image on my retinas. I turned around, raised my head over the parapet, and looked. Only then did I remember to take the damned glasses off.

Rising off the desert floor was this monstrous sphere of fire. It looked to be as wide as my entire field of view. The colors were fantastic, shades of red, yellow, cobalt, orange, and others I couldn't name. Off to one side there were six tiny, white, vertical vapor trails rising into the sky as if somebody had fired off rockets at the time of ignition. They were quickly absorbed into the main fireball, which was now forming into a pulsing, horizon-wide dome of hideous light. And then I did see the shock wave coming, a two-hundred-foot-high wall of dirt, sand, and lightning flashes coming toward us at incredible speed. I grabbed Waring by the shoulders and pulled her down into the trench as this titanic wave of sound, pressure, and heat boomed over our heads and on out into the desert behind us. It was so loud that our ears couldn't comprehend it; we could only feel it, like a battleship muzzle blast.

We raised our heads and looked again as the fireball, still expanding, its colors fainter now but no less appalling, pushed its way up into the cold desert air, every part of its surface boiling and curling into fantastic bulges and shapes, as if it couldn't dispel the energy it contained fast enough. The ground shook continuously, and I remembered the warning about the return shock wave, where the earth's atmosphere tried to fill in the spherical volume of space *consumed* by the fireball. I remembered the scientists saying it might set the earth's atmosphere on fire, and that's exactly what it had done. I tapped Waring's shoulder this time, and we ducked in time to endure hurricane-force winds arriving from behind us, howling like mortally injured banshees desperate to get back into that unearthly vortex of roiling incandescence that was still rising, forming a mushroom-shaped cloud and getting bigger and bigger, up into the stratosphere now, where the jet stream winds finally began to misshape the top of it.

Nobody spoke. There were no "My Gods" or "Jesus H. Christs" or any other exclamations of horror from anyone down there at what we were seeing. Ten miles away. There were barely any words that could do it justice, only a sense of absolute terror—contain your bladder, blink through the tears that were forming in your eyes, hold your breath, terror. I'd never felt so helpless in my entire life as in the face of this epic explosion.

I want you to see it, Van Rensselaer had said. No—I *need* you to see it. I looked over at Waring, who had to be thinking the same thing I was thinking: are you true believers now? God, yes.

SEVENTEEN

THE MISSION

On the late afternoon of the test, we were once again on a train. I was pretty sure it was the same train we'd taken from the East Coast to Los Alamos, minus one diesel engine and the freight cars. It obviously wasn't just an Army train—it was Van Rensselaer's Army train. Same crew, same cabin attendants, same dining room staff. Up front was the command car, and we saw familiar faces in the guard detail. Waring and I even had the same sleeper accommodations. The big difference was that everybody who'd seen the test was pretty subdued after witnessing what I was now mentally characterizing as the face of an extremely annoyed God. One insignificant detail stuck in my humbled brain. There'd been some tumbleweed out in front of the observer trenches. As the light from the initial blast dimmed, I could see the tiny branches of the plants glowing red in the shattered darkness like dying light bulb filaments. The passenger cars' crews could tell something was up with us, but of course they had no way of knowing what we were upset about. Van Rensselaer had told me he needed to communicate with the White House, who would then have to communicate with the president, who was currently overseas meeting with Stalin and Churchill.

We were bound for the Davis-Monthan Army Air Field in Arizona, not too far from Tucson. We hadn't been told why, as yet, but Van Rensselaer would send for us when he was ready. Fortunately, the dining car's bar was open, so we'd both ordered drinks the moment we sat down. Even before we sat down, in fact. The bartender, a genial Black man named Charles, saw our distressed faces and asked if he should hammer things just a little bit. Waring nodded emphatically before I could get a word out. I still couldn't erase the picture of that immense explosion from my mind. Describing it almost defied words. At one point I thought we should have been jubilant—the damned thing worked. The round-the-clock effort of ten thousand of the brightest people in the country for years had produced . . . well, I couldn't conjure up the word. Armageddon? Still, I sensed that neither one of us could avoid the elephantine question in the room: what are we going to do with such a thing? As if we didn't, deep down, know exactly what we were going to do with it. For the first time since Pearl Harbor, I began to feel a little sorry for the enemy. God Almighty!

"There you are," Van Rensselaer said, appearing out of nowhere as usual and sitting down at our table. He parked a briefcase under the table. "Why the glum faces?"

We both just stared at him, lost for words.

"Okay, okay, I understand," he said. "You saw something today—we all did—that shook the foundations of absolutely everything you know. I felt that way, too, if it's any consolation. I was, perhaps, more knowledgeable about what to expect than you were. When the heavy-duty scientists, the ones with Nobel Prizes, would describe what *might* happen, they had the same expressions on their faces that you do now. One of them, Oppenheimer—you remember him, the chief scientist?—said we wouldn't understand it until we used it, or something like that."

He lowered his voice, even though the train noises gave us complete privacy in the empty dining car. "At *Iwo Jima* we had twenty-six thousand casualties," he began. "At *Okinawa* we had twice that. The closer we get to Japan, the worse it's been. The JCS has been working on the plan for invading the major home islands; as you know it's Operation Olympic. Part of that planning involves figuring out how many men we'll need for that, and how many of those will survive the effort."

He looked around the empty dining car.

"I think I may have told you this. The current estimate is that we'll lose up to a half million—*million*! That's because the Japanese will enlist every human being in their homeland—men, women, children, the sick, the lame, the old—to fight off our invasion. We put one hundred thousand Marines on *Iwo Jima* and lost twenty-six thousand. We put a hundred ten thousand on *Okinawa* and lost more than fifty thousand. We're talking Antietam- and Shiloh-scale numbers here. But the big difference is that the Rebs fought to win. The Japanese fight for the opportunity to die honorably in battle."

He closed his eyes and took a deep breath. "What you saw today is the only way any of us know to prevent a galactic-scale bloodletting. As you know, we've been bombing Japan's cities and industrial centers relentlessly for months now. One firebombing raid over *Tokyo* killed ninety thousand people. They took it. They just—*took* it."

"We're going to use this thing to bomb a city?" Waring asked.

"Yes, we are," Van Rensselaer said. "We're going to tell them to surrender or face the end of their world, the end of their civilization. And when they tell us to fuck off, yes, we're going to use this *thing* to obliterate an entire city in a single flash of unnatural light. The one you saw today, facing away, in a trench, with black glasses, and your eyes squeezed shut. But, still—you saw it, didn't you?"

We both nodded. How could we forget it?

Waring finally asked *the* question. "How does this change our role in this, this—shit, I can't name it."

"The JCS think there's a problem," Van Rensselaer said. "The president has been informed that the Trinity test was a success. When he gets back, he'll get to see films of what we all saw today. Not the same as being there, but still—"

"So what's the problem?" I asked.

"Apparently he's having doubts," Van Rensselaer said. "About using it on a city full of civilians. And once he sees the films, these doubts will harden. I told you there are civilians around him who are telling him that it would be immoral to use such a weapon over an occupied city. That we should first demonstrate it to the Japanese by firing one off the coast so they can see, firsthand, what's coming unless they surrender. Or that he should go ahead and order the invasion and then see what happens, and only use it if things get so bad that we have no choice."

Waring slapped her hand down on the table. "Out with it, Captain Van Rensselaer. Why did you need us to see that thing go off?"

I could see that he took momentary offense at her tone, but then he relented.

"You personally saw what happened today," he began. "Harry Truman did not. I told you that I needed the both of you to become believers. Especially you, Lieutenant Commander Waring. So when someone asks you what's so important, what's the hurry, and so on, you turn into a wild-eyed, fanatic apostle to convince all those spooks that they need to look hard and right fucking now for evidence of a Jap program, however small, so that if you get the least bit of corroboration, you can stand tall in front of Mr. Truman and say: yes, Mr. President, we're pretty sure the Japs have a program."

"And that will convince him to go ahead and use the thing?" I said.

"If he finds out that the Japanese have been working on a similar weapon to use against *our* final invasion fleet, and you must admit that an invasion force of a million men and the thousand ships to support them is the perfect target for such a weapon, *and* if he knew that they were close to perfecting it, or even that they were only a few weeks behind where we are right now—one test, two or three more being assembled in a building or a laboratory somewhere, then yes."

We nodded. But then why'd he need me?

"Okay," he said. "Now, Captain: we have some new intelligence. From the Army Intelligence command, of all people."

"Army Intelligence," Waring sniffed contemptuously. "Oxymoron."

Van Rensselaer grinned, breaking the tension a little bit. "Thought you might say that," he said. "But they have direct ties into Generalissimo Chiang Kai-shek's intelligence network, through the good graces of our SACO command in China. I asked them to explore Japanese efforts, if any, to obtain uranium in the past year. At first, we got nothing, but then, one week ago, they came back by naval message with a disturbing picture of Japanese efforts to acquire uranium, mainly in the Shanghai area."

"In China?"

"You are aware that they've been occupying most of China since the early thirties. You've heard the term the Rape of Nanking?"

I said yes, although I had to admit that my knowledge of the Japanese war against China was pretty superficial, especially since December 7th, 1941.

"There is uranium to be found in Shanghai?" Waring asked.

"There is pitchblende to be found *near* Shanghai. That's actual uranium ore. But this is the interesting part: several hundred pounds of it were sent to a Japanese industrial center in northern Korea, to a place called Hungnam, on Korea's eastern seaboard. We've been baffled as to where their atomic project might be, since most of Japan's industrial infrastructure has been repeatedly bombed since October of last year. You've seen our atomic infrastructure, and there's nothing like that in Japan. But *you* then said it might be in Korea.

"The Japanese have been interested in Korea for decades for its natural resources—all the war materials that are in critical short supply in Japan itself, plus the entire population to use as slave labor to dig it out of the ground. The Russians are also interested in Korea, for the same reasons, probably. The OSS has confirmed that there are two Russian armies assembling on the Korean border with Manchuria."

"Have we attacked any of that?" Waring asked.

"Our submarines have made the Sea of Japan prohibitively dangerous for any Japanese shipping trying to get back home from Korea to Japan or from China to Japan, but for Washington, the civil war between the communist Chinese and Chiang Kai-shek's nationalist Chinese is a sideshow. We're focused on defeating Japan; their colonies will wither on the vine once we accomplish that. Just like all their big bases in the South Pacific that we chose not to invade. That said, I talked JCS into sending some recon flights over eastern Korea. One of the planes disappeared, but another one brought back these pictures. We now think you were right."

He fished a roll of black-and-white aerial photographs out of his briefcase and spread them over the table. They showed a single large industrial strip, some five to ten miles in length, along the eastern shore of northern Korea, and even more factories north of that. There were small, dark islands scattered about five miles offshore. Everything looked grainy, even sooty, but every chimney and stack in the pictures, including locomotives, was pouring out smoke.

"That's a bombardier's dream," I said. "All concentrated like that with three mountain ranges behind and everything vulnerable to an attack by sea. No place to run and hide."

"One of the Army's photointerpreters said there's evidence of even more 'stuff' in tunnels behind the factories you can see. Plus, air defenses, lots of barbed wire compounds, searchlight gun towers, and military barracks throughout the complex. It's well guarded. There's one big pier complex, and what looks like three naval gunboats at the pier."

I looked again but couldn't make out any of that. Waring told me the PIs had these large magnifying light stations they put the actual aerial films under, where you could blow up the image and see in much greater detail.

"And this is where you think their atomic bomb project is?" I asked.

"That's where the pitchblende ore went," he replied. "That's the Hungnam complex. And now, in answer to your unasked question, Captain, while Lieutenant Commander Waring beats the intelligence bushes in Washington, I want you to go there. To Hungnam, for the final piece of the puzzle."

EIGHTEEN

HUNGNAM

*H*ungnam? He could have bowled me over with a feather. Go there? To *Korea*? Waring and I looked at each other in disbelief. I was sure Van Rensselaer was enjoying the moment. I couldn't think of what to say, so I declared that I needed a drink. Van Rensselaer nodded in approval. Waring remained silent, probably waiting for me to work it all out. If we could tell Truman that the Japs had a program, and I could somehow confirm to the president that it appeared to be a mature program, i.e., something they could bring to bear on our invasion, there'd be no more hesitation at the top about using the Bomb on a city in Japan. Or, hell, maybe even in Korea.

With a drink in my now trembling hand, Van Rensselaer gave me more details about what he had in mind for me. "This train is bound for Davis-Monthan Army Air Field, where you will be transferred to a modified B-29 bomber for a trip to Manila, in the Philippines. From Manila you will board a Navy P-5A flying boat, which will take you to a rendezvous with one of our submarines somewhere in the Sea of Japan.

That submarine will then proceed up toward Korea and get as close to Hungnam as the minefields permit."

"Minefields permit?" I squawked. "What the hell, Van Rensselaer?"

"I know, I know," he said. "But the Sea of Japan is well known for its Japanese minefields. Happily, most of them are wrapped around ports, channels, and straits. The mean depth of the Sea of Japan is around five thousand feet, which is where submarines can go without fear of mines. It's not like we're going to put you ashore."

I started to respond but he raised his hand. "Listen to me. We have one further piece of intelligence that makes this . . . expedition necessary. I call it an expedition because it's a ten-thousand-mile trip from Davis-Monthan to the Korean coast. Admiral 'Mary' Miles, in China, has an asset in Hungnam who is part of the chemical plant research division that is supporting a 'very secret' Japanese project there. He has reported that the entire industrial area in and around Hungnam is preparing for a major event, one that will require movement of many assets in and around the port, and then a lockdown of everybody, in every plant, rail operation, harbor, barracks, guard post, and factory in their facilities for twenty-four hours on a date to be announced. But soon. Within days. Now, we're making a big assumption here, that this will be their test of whatever they've achieved in the way of atomic weapons in this heretofore secret location. One we never looked for.

"And that's your mission. A submarine will get you close to Hungnam, as close as the minefields permit, as I said before. And then you will wait, offshore. If we get a date certain, you will be informed. If not, you will just wait."

"Wait for *what*?" Waring asked, but I already knew. Van Rensselaer *had* taken us to the Trinity test for a reason. Waring could now confront a possibly indifferent intelligence community in Washington with the fervor of a "true believer" and direct White House backing. And I was probably the only officer in the entire Navy that knew what an atomic bomb looked like. An impartial Navy captain not from the Manhattan Project, but rather from the CNO's personal staff. If the Japs tested an A-bomb, I would recognize it in an instant. And then transmit that news to Washington, allowing Harry S. Truman to justify the use of our weapon on the Japanese homeland. Before they used *their* weapon on our invasion fleet.

Van Rensselaer raised his eyebrows. "Understand?" he asked me quietly.

"I do," I said. *Two* witnesses. One for the intel indications that something was coming. One for the really bright light. Truman was nothing if not a professional skeptic.

"I don't," Waring complained.

Van Rensselaer stood up. "That's okay, because you're not going, remember?" he said. "You will accompany me back to Washington. You're going to be the captain here's point of entry into the Washington intel community. He and that submarine are going to need help as to where to look and what to look for that might narrow down an impending test site. I'll also need you to help me convince the intelligence community, as well as the president."

He smiled when he saw the look on Waring's face. I think he liked to surprise her. "Have another drink," he said. "Enjoy your dinner. And Captain? Try not to think about the fact that what you see and what you do off the coasts of Korea might end up determining the outcome of this whole goddamned Pacific war. Lieutenant Commander Waring, be packed and ready to board a plane back to Washington by 0600 tomorrow, please."

Our train arrived at 0500 at the airfield. We had to wait for a car to take me to the base ops building near the runway and Waring back to wherever "his" train was waiting, giving us time for a quick coffee and a fat pill in the dining car. I apologized for Van Rensselaer's endless course changes, but she just smiled. "As if you had anything to do with it," she said, nicely. "I don't envy you your trip. Ten thousand miles? How the hell will they do that?"

"Big airplanes, I guess," I said. "But I swiped a pillow from my Pullman berth. I anticipate a lot of nap time. He did tell me I'd be going through Pearl, where I could get some fresh uniforms. I don't want to be on a sub in civvies."

"I toured a submarine in Norfolk once," she said. "I found out I'm a bit claustrophobic. And the 'boat,' as they called it, smelled, to tell the truth. I don't know how those guys stand it. They all seemed so bright."

"Usually they're too busy keeping both the enemy and the ocean from killing them to notice," I said. "But the submarine force has done as much or more than all the surface ships combined to bring Japan to its knees. They're a special breed."

"Well, good luck," she sighed. "I'm still shook up about that test. I shiver every time I see it in my mind. And now he wants me to go convince the president? I'm not exactly a silver-tongued headquarters briefer."

"Truman doesn't strike me as a man who likes silver-tongued devils all that much," I said. "Your job will be to convince him Japan has a program, and that there have been indications of that available for some time, except no one was looking. It's evidence he'll want, not rumors. As for me, I think the chances of my being there when they conduct a test are pretty slim. But Van Rensselaer's right—if I *do* witness a test that looks anything like what we saw out there in Alamogordo, that and whatever you unearth will be the final straw for Truman."

"But I'm just a lieutenant commander," she said.

"I think that'll be an advantage. You'll be able to penetrate the lower echelons of the Washington agencies. Talk to the backroom boys who actually listen to or read the hundreds of intercepts coming in from all over the world. The 'bigs' are all worried about budget money and their status in Washington, just like your bosses at ONI. Like that old saying goes—you want to know where the general's gonna be today, go have a cigarette with his driver."

She gave me a discreet hug and a wan smile. "With any luck, to be continued," she whispered. Then she headed for the waiting staff car. One of Van Rensselaer's guards came and motioned for me to follow him. The base ops building was a combination air control tower and operations center. We'd been in the waiting room on the ground floor. The guard took me through the building to a jeep waiting outside. We drove a mile or so to a hangar that had its own control tower on one side. He pointed me into that control tower building, where I found Van Rensselaer waiting. Outside, two aircraft were parked on the nearby tarmac. One was a standard, twin-engine military DC-3, the transport workhorse for all the services. There was a fueling truck under one of its wings, while some men in flight gear were walking around, inspecting the aircraft. The surprise was the other plane, which positively dwarfed the DC-3.

"Big, isn't it," Van Rensselaer said, indicating the second plane. Big it was—four-engined, a massively tall tail, bright, silvery fuselage, with stubby antennae and one long-wire HF antenna running from behind the top of the nose all the way back to the tail. A B-29. I'd never seen one. "That what I think it is?" I asked him.

"Yup," he said. "Only this one was factory modified as a VIP transport aircraft. Nimitz took one of these when he moved his headquarters from Pearl to Guam. MacArthur has one, and there are two more in Washington. It has extended range because they took all the air combat and bombing equipment off and replaced it with a pressurized passenger compartment and extra fuel tanks. The inside has been configured for extralong flights, with a couple sleeping compartments, passenger seating, a galley, and berthing spaces for an extra set of pilots and navigators."

"But no windows," I said. "And no doors that I can see."

"Correct; windows in the midsection would have compromised the airframe. You still board by climbing up through a ladder well up front. You'll leave here, fly to Travis air base in California, near San Francisco, refuel, then on to Hickam Field at Pearl Harbor, Wake Island, Guam, and finally Manila. You'll pick up a PBY in Manila harbor and then fly across the South China Sea and into the Sea of Japan for a rendezvous with the sub, at sea. When you get to Pearl, buy some books."

"And some more khakis," I said. "I didn't exactly bring a full sea bag to Los Alamos."

He nodded, but I could see he was distracted. "Look," he said. "I wasn't kidding about how important this mission is, but I'm also aware there are a whole lot of big assumptions hanging in the air. Nor do we have much time: ships from the States are already in motion for Olympic. We don't *know* when they might test their weapon, or, to be totally honest, if they even have a weapon. Our most recent intelligence comes from halfway around the world and from OSS people, living in the primitive Chinese countryside, hunted by counterspies, who are pulsing sources from both sides of the Chinese civil war to hunt down Admiral Miles's Americans. The key thing is that you've seen what this new bomb looks like. If that sub can get you close enough to Hungnam and they *do* hold a test, you'll be the only guy onboard who will know what the real thing looks like. Everyone else will be crapping their pants."

"I know that feeling," I said, remembering having a similar reaction when I saw the test.

"Good luck, then," he said. "We'll be going back to Washington as soon as they fuel that DC-3 out there."

"Not the train?"

"No time." He hesitated for a moment. "She's an attractive woman," he continued. "Do you think she has the moxie to convince all those intel prima donnas in DC that her quest is all about a weapon that's the biggest thing to happen in America since electricity?"

I told him yes. "She has graduate degrees, comes from an old-line Southern family, and thus she's independently wealthy. So I'd expect her to be quite comfortable mixing with all those Foggy Bottom aristocrats and the Georgetown set. And, being a lieutenant commander, she'll be able to get to the ground-truth guys, too."

"I wasn't aware of all that," he said.

"She does not like surprises," I pointed out, deciding to take a small chance. "You've been surprising her a lot, lately. Me, too. I would advise you to *fully* brief her on what you want her to do, and then just get out of her way."

I think he was taken aback for a moment; my lord Van Rensselaer wasn't accustomed to criticism, actual or implied. "And how about you?" he asked. "Do you 'dislike' surprises?"

I laughed. "Up until my assignment in the CNO's office, I'd been a seagoing naval officer, in both peace and war. Two wartime commands, a destroyer and a cruiser, so surprises at sea were my daily fare. I've never had the luxury of liking or disliking them. I was too busy looking for my GQ gear. You needn't worry about me, shipmate."

"I'm not in the least worried about you," he said. "Nor is the CNO. Admiral King told me you were exactly the right guy to do what I had in mind."

Aw, shit, I thought, as I saw that familiar gotcha grin spreading across his face. He'd planned this caper all along. I should have known.

NINETEEN
WAIT AND WATCH

The B-29's navigator, an impossibly young-looking Army captain, came to the field to get me. We stopped just outside the terminal door while the DC-3 taxied away toward the runway in clouds of blue smoke. I wondered if Waring had been told that Van Rensselaer was flying back. Probably not. We crossed the concrete tarmac to the B-29, which got bigger and bigger as we got closer. The navigator kept looking at his watch, as if escorting some Washington wienie wasn't exactly part of his job.

"We'll get aboard by climbing a ladder under the nose into the flight engineer's compartment," he said. "Then we'll go aft to the passenger section. Leave your suitcase at the bottom of the ladder; one of the crew will bring it aboard."

"Okay," I said. I was dressed in slacks and a short-sleeved white shirt with a tie. I don't think he even knew I was a Navy captain. We climbed the ladder up into the front section of the aircraft and turned right. I later found out that a real-deal B-29 had two pressurized compartments, one forward, one aft, with the middle third of the airframe dedicated to two massive bomb bays. The two pressurized compartments were connected by a long tube that ran over top of the bomb bays, which were not pressurized. Boeing had created an entirely new midsection passenger compartment and pressurized the entire aircraft. The navigator showed me to what had to be a senior officer's seat, complete with a small desk. He then brought me a flight jacket and a pamphlet containing emergency procedures in case of an in-flight problem.

"We'll be cruising at twenty-two thousand feet to Travis," he said. "This compartment is heated and air-conditioned, but it can still get a bit cold at altitude. From Travis to Pearl we'll be closer to thirty thousand. You'll want the jacket then. If you have no further questions, I need to get back up front."

I had a million questions, but none worth taking up any more of his time. "I'm fine," I said. "And thank you."

He nodded and made his way back up front. It appeared that I was the only passenger, at least for this leg of my ten-thousand-mile journey. I wondered how Waring was faring, and then smiled at the unintended rhyme. It struck me then that I kept calling her Waring, not Janet, her first name. I was sure that that was somehow important, as if, despite our recent intimacy, I was mentally keeping her at arm's length. But then the first of the bomber's four engines lit off. They might have pressurized the new passenger compartment, but they had surely *not* soundproofed it. Wow. Those were enormous engines. Once we had taken off and hit cruising altitude, and with all four of those monsters humming, I was asleep in thirty minutes. Clickety-clack had clearly been rendered insignificant.

And that's how the entire trip went, all three days of it. Travis base in California was somewhat primitive looking, with a single runway that had recently been extended to cope with the B-29's thirst for takeoff concrete. We pulled into the refueling area, where a small team of fuel mechanics began crawling the wings. Three more passengers boarded for the flight to Hawaii, each carrying a white in-flight lunch box along with their briefcases. There was also a crew change, with two new flight crews coming aboard for the upcoming long legs of the flight. One of them brought me a boxed lunch, and then we launched for Hickam. It was twenty-five hundred miles, so about nine hours' flying time. At Hickam we rolled down to one of the bigger hangars for some engine work. I was told the plane would be there for three, maybe even four hours for a "cylinder pull," so I took that opportunity to get an Army car over to the Pearl Harbor base Navy Exchange for a uniform run. I also bought an enlisted canvas sea bag, into which I packed my new khaki uniforms and insignia, a khaki raincoat, a fore and aft cap, toiletries, shoes, skivvies and socks, and some towels, in the middle of which I buried a bottle of Scotch from the package store next door.

With two hours to go, I had the car take me to the officers' club. I was still in my Los Alamos civvies, somewhat wrinkled by now, but my ID card got me a table and lunch. The club was expanded now and totally recovered from December 7th, when it had been used as a medical aid station right after the attack. During my at-sea time in the PacFleet I'd been through Pearl several times. The Pacific Ocean was vast, and Pearl was one of the first of the many fuel stops any transiting battle group would have to hit. I was finishing up lunch and looking at my watch when a stir began in the crowded dining room. I looked up to see a two-star admiral in khakis making his way across the room to my table, followed by an aide. I started to get up but he waved me back down and took a chair.

"Captain Bowen," he said. "I'm Admiral Matthews, from Admiral Nimitz's Pearl Harbor staff. I understand you're bound for Manila and then a rendezvous with one of our subs. And then you're going to Korea."

I was a bit taken by surprise. It had never occurred to me that Van Rensselaer would have alerted the top brass at Pearl, although I guessed that I should have expected it. Instead of answering, I nodded. I wasn't being coy—I simply didn't know what to say.

"We got a call from Admiral King's office," he said. "As you know, the Boss is in Guam now, preparing for Olympic. The CNO told us to make sure that nothing, absolutely nothing, got in the way of your mission.

We've been advised that you will go from here to Wake, then Guam, then to Manila, and that time is of the essence. Is there anything we can do for you right now? Any problems? Logistics? Communications?"

"My plane is doing an engine change over at Hickam," I replied. "I'm told that B-29s do that a lot. But, no, sir, the Army Air Forces are doing whatever it takes to get me to Manila and then a PBY to the submarine. I must admit that I'm a little taken aback by—"

"Don't be," he said. "I don't know what this is all about, only that the message from King was put in terms we haven't seen out here in a long while, even from Admiral King, who doesn't ordinarily mince words."

"Yes, I know," I said. "I was on his executive staff recently. He doesn't mince words, only people."

The admiral grinned. "Yes, indeedy," he said. "Of course, I'm dying to know what this is all about, but I know better than to ask. Just this—if you run into any bullshit delays or obstacles, from anyone, anywhere, get a message to me and I will take immediate action."

"Thank you, sir," I said. "You will in time realize what my trip was all about, although I'm a pretty small cog in a gigantic undertaking. All I can tell you is that if I succeed, there won't be an invasion and the astronomic loss of life that an invasion of Japan entails. And that's not knowledge you can share with anyone. Not until this war is over. Please respect that."

He stared at me for a long moment, and then nodded. "Any problems at all, Navy, Army, or anyone else—I'm the guy who will solve them for you, okay?"

"Yes, sir, and thank you again. And, um, can you get me a ride back to Hickam?"

TWENTY
THE REALLY LONG HAUL

Manila was in ruins. I'd been there many times during my career as an Asiatic fleet sailor, and it was heartbreaking what the Japanese had done to the city as they withdrew in front of MacArthur's determined assault. It must have been even worse for him, because he'd been governor general of the islands, as had his father. The Filipinos I saw were making the best of it and it was clear that the overthrow of their occupiers was probably worth the destruction of their capital city to them.

I was taken to a relatively undamaged building that had been commandeered as the headquarters of the American Army in the Philippines. A colonel from General MacArthur's office met me and told me they'd been expecting me. He was, of course, curious but professional enough not to ask what this was all about. They'd been told that I was from the White House, on a secret mission, and to be given anything I needed to facilitate my trip to Manila and beyond.

What I needed most was sleep, real sleep. The colonel told me that my PBY flight would leave at noon on the next day from Manila harbor.

He summoned an Army doctor, who pointed out that I'd been through several time zones during my flight from California, and recommended that I take a pill and then retire to a room in the next-door hotel. I was happy to agree with him. He had a medical aide escort me next door and administer the magic pill, and then I gratefully turned in to cool, clean sheets while the aide pulled the wooden shutters over the windows, adjusted the overhead fan to low, and then turned on a small radio and tuned it to the white noise frequency spectrum. Nice touch, that.

I woke up thirteen hours later, when a hotel waiter brought in breakfast and hot coffee. I showered, shaved, and felt a thousand percent better. I changed into khakis with a fore and aft hat and my captain's insignia. A car and driver called and then off we went through the shambles of the Intramuros area to the Manila Yacht Club, where a US Navy PT boat lay alongside one of the piers. A somewhat emaciated lieutenant (junior grade) welcomed me onboard, nodded to the Filipino line handlers, and then we were off into Manila Bay. All the crewmen were combat thin, with drawn faces and circles under their eyes, nineteen-year-olds looking like thirty. I could remember being that thin after a month of operations in The Slot above Guadalcanal. The PT boats had been fully involved during the final fierce months of the campaign to take the Philippines back. Once the ship cleared the actual marina harbor, its three engines began to howl and we headed for Corregidor at great speed. The skipper asked if I wanted to go below, but the fresh and as yet cool morning air felt wonderful after an eternity in an aluminum tube. The wind and the engine noise made conversation impossible, for which I was grateful. I only hoped my sea bag had made it onboard.

The historic island of Corregidor is forty-seven miles down the bay from the actual city, almost all the way to the open South China Sea. I recalled the Bataan Death March that followed the surrender of that fortress in 1942. I wondered if they'd caught up with the monstrous Japanese general who'd been in charge of that atrocity, *Yamashita*. It was on a PT boat just like this one that MacArthur had escaped, promising that he would be back. I'd read that Filipinos had interpreted that to mean "in a few months," not the three years that it actually took, during which time the occupying Japanese had lived up to their reputation for extreme barbarity. And then some.

An hour after leaving the marina, the boat slowed down as we approached Corregidor Island. We rumbled past the shattered remains of *El Fraile* Island, where years ago two now-wrecked battleship turrets had been mounted onto a concrete fort to protect the approaches to Manila Bay. There, to my great relief, floated a PBY flying boat, bobbing calmly at anchor just off the main island. The PT boat was too big to go alongside the PBY, so they sent a small rubber raft out to get me and my sea bag. I climbed aboard the plane and the engines started immediately. They strapped me unceremoniously into a canvas bench seat behind the cockpit and then we were taxiing, bumping over the waves until the flying boat became "unstuck" and lurched into the air. Once we'd hit cruising altitude and the engine noise subsided somewhat, a lieutenant naval aviator in a flight suit came back to welcome me onboard.

"We've got a six-hour flight to a point fifty miles southeast of *Jeju-do* island, northeast of Shanghai, where we'll rendezvous with USS *Cragfish* right after sunset. We've got some box lunches and a coffee mess back aft. Until then, feel free to stretch your legs. Once we link up with the boat, we'll land and transfer you over to them."

"Sounds fine, Lieutenant, thank you."

"Are you really from the White House, sir?"

"Yup," I said. "And you know what? Once I've done what I came to do, I'll need a hop back there. Might even be you guys."

His eyes widened. "How far is that, Captain?"

"Ten thousand miles, give or take, Lieutenant. Assuming no delays, of course."

He shook his head in wonder. "Jeez. Well, good luck, Captain. I guess this must be truly important."

I nodded back at him. "You have no idea, Lieutenant. Now just get me up there."

It was dark when we made the rendezvous. I'd been alerted by a crewman that we were an hour out, which had given me a chance to repack my trusty sea bag and test fit a kapok life jacket in case the water landing went off the rails. I'd asked one of the pilots how an airplane meets up with a sub out on the dark ocean. He explained that the position and time was prearranged, but since the sub, which necessarily spent her daytime hours submerged, might not have the best position information way out in the middle of the South China Sea, it was the PBY's responsibility to find *Cragfish,* not the other way around. The plane had a good surface search radar; the sub was supposed to surface after dark and establish UHF comms, after first checking that she didn't have unfriendly company. The PBY had homing equipment that could give a bearing of on the sub's radio signal. We would fly down that bearing with our nav lights turned on, something no Japanese plane would ever do. Once the boat was acquired on radar, the pilot would ask for local winds and sea state, land near the sub, and then taxi over to make the transfer. The sub would put her rubber raft in the water and make the PBY's water hatch to pick me up. The way the pilot described it, this was all pretty much routine, since PBYs had been picking up rescued naval aviators ever since Midway, back in 1942.

The landing was uneventful and within minutes a small rubber raft with an outboard engine came out of the darkness. There was no moon, but, with no competing lights in the area, I could just make out the sub's conning tower a hundred yards away. I also heard the deep rumble of her diesels as she recharged her batteries. The PBY had completely shut down and had deployed a sea anchor, as the crew intended to get some rest before their predawn launch back to Corregidor. Somebody would keep a radar watch in the plotting compartment to make sure nothing snuck up on them in the night, but this was one of the beauties of a flying boat—they could land out at sea, float around as long as the weather allowed, expending hardly any fuel, and thus stay out for days if they had to. Earlier in the war, traffic coming out of Shanghai, including Japanese naval units, would have posed a problem. But now, in the summer of 1945, most of the Japanese shipping going between China and Japan was on the bottom, courtesy of the Silent Service.

As a heavy cruiser skipper, I'd always envisaged our submarines to be small vessels, but from the perspective of a bobbing rubber raft, this boat looked pretty substantial as we got alongside. I was helped aboard by two strong sailors, followed by my sea bag and then the rubber raft. I could feel the muscular vibrations of her engines as soon as I stepped onto her steel weather deck. A five-inch deck gun, wrapped in waxed canvas, stood silently as we headed for the forward hatchway. Behind us the conning tower, fully darkened, loomed in the darkness, enveloped in a cloud of diesel exhaust that was blowing forward from her stern. A young officer led me to the hatch and then down into the forward torpedo room, which was under red-lighting conditions. Once down from the hatch and ladder, I was surprised by the somewhat surreal smell of fried chicken. The raft came down along with the deck handlers and then the hatches were secured. Regular lighting was restored as the hatch going aft was opened, and I was greeted by the captain, who introduced himself as Commander Russ Remington.

Russ looked too young to be a submarine skipper or even a commander, for that matter, which probably said more about my advancing years than his. I got the impression that this mission to get me to the east coast of Korea was something of an imposition. He was polite and outwardly respectful while at the same time radiating impatience, as if my being here was denying him and his crew the opportunity to gain glory by sinking Japanese ships. Which it probably was, although everything I'd heard in OpNav about the current submarine campaign indicated that the biggest problem SubPac faced these days was the lack of respectable targets. They'd done their job too well, with so-called fleet boats like *Cragfish* reduced to sinking Japanese fishing boats, junks, and small patrol craft with their deck guns instead of the usual spread of torpedoes.

"Welcome aboard, Captain," he said. "I understand we're bound for— Korea?"

The way he said it confirmed my suspicions that he was less than pleased with his new assignment. I suddenly got an attack of the yawns. My brief stop in Manila hadn't quite cured me of the sleep deprivation created by traveling ten thousand miles in only a few days. I think I was also distracted by the smell of fried chicken that permeated the boat. Box lunches only go so far.

"What I need right now, Commander," I said, "is perhaps a meal and then some sleep. It's a long way from Washington."

"Of course, sir," he said, with a friendly grin that took some of the sting out of his previous demeanor. "Forgive my bad manners. Let's go to the wardroom. As you can tell it's fried chicken night. Hopefully there's some still left. We can only do that when we know we'll have a night on the surface. Follow me, please."

I did, trying not to bang my shins on the series of elevated hatch coamings between compartments. We diverted into a tiny room that I assumed was the boat's wardroom. As I plopped down into a chair, I realized that I was pretty exhausted. It must have shown because a steward appeared immediately with some coffee. The commander sat at the head of the table and asked about my trip. The XO came in as we were talking, and soon there was real food on the table, which was when I remembered that the best food in the Navy was to be had aboard submarines. I tucked in rather impolitely, hoping they'd already eaten. Then I remembered why I was there.

"Are we headed north?" I asked.

The commander seemed surprised. "Is it urgent?" he asked.

I had to take a deep breath before replying. "Look," I said. "We need to be in position off the port of Hungnam. Tomorrow morning would be nice, although I realize that might be a stretch. At the moment, I'm not firing on all eight cylinders, if by some chance that's not already obvious. I've been in the air for hours and hours, mostly on a specially configured B-29, which got me to Manila. From California. I need to be as close to Hungnam as the minefields and Japanese patrols will permit, and I need to be there as soon as humanly possible."

They just stared at me as if I was crazy. I soldiered on.

"Once I've gotten some sleep and my brain clears," I said, "I'll brief the both of you fully. But not just now. And, by the way, once I've accomplished my mission, I'll need to get back to Washington as quickly as possible. That will mean you'll be running night *and* day on the surface at full speed to get me back to the Philippines and my ride home on Chester Nimitz's personal B-29. It's ten thousand miles from Manila back to the States, and then another three thousand back to Washington. Where I'll be taken to the White House to brief the president within the hour of my landing at Andrews. So: make for the east coast of northern Korea immediately. Full speed. Now, I need a rack and eight hours of sleep."

The captain and the exec, somewhat wide-eyed, said yessir, simultaneously. The exec took me to his cabin, where my friendly sea bag stood in one corner. I apologized for taking his room, and was asleep in three minutes. Fried chicken. By God, that was, so far, the highlight of my trip. I tried to compute what day it was, counting from the day of the Trinity test. I wondered what Waring was up to back in the semicrazed politico-military cauldron that was Washington, DC. For about ten seconds. Then I succumbed to the sudden enhanced throbbing of the boat's engines. My last conscious thought was of Van Rensselaer's gotcha smile, and wondering if any of this was going to work.

TWENTY-ONE
THE HUNGNAM APPROACHES

I was awakened by the diving alarm and a sudden squeeze of air pressure on my eardrums. It must be daylight. The lullaby motion of the boat ploughing at twenty-two knots through the long swells in the East China Sea and on into the Sea of Japan died away as the boat sought the dark safety of a couple hundred feet underwater. I sat up in the narrow rack, nearly hitting my head on the overhead shelf. I could hear men moving out in the main passageway and commands being given by the diving officer nearby. I got up and put on clean khakis. I had only one set of collar insignia so I had to switch them over to the clean shirt. My eyes felt sandy and I needed the head. I grabbed a manila folder out of my sea bag and then asked a passing crewman where the head was. He was obviously startled by the sudden appearance of a full captain in the passageway, but he dutifully took me to the head and gave me instructions on how to align all the valves and in what sequence, depending on what business I had there. Using and then flushing the toilet in a submerged submarine can be an explosive event if done incorrectly. There even was a card of illustrated instructions taped to the bulkhead.

He took me back to the cabin where I could wash up and then to the wardroom, where officers were moving in and out, grabbing rolls and coffee before turning to. The XO spied me and offered his seat. I deferred and got in line for coffee and a fat pill with the rest of them. In a moment the wardroom magically cleared out and then the skipper showed up. He drew the curtain across the entrance, then bade me to sit down at the table while he got some breakfast.

"Okay," I began once we were all seated. "My name is Captain Wolfe Bowen. I'm a member of the CNO's executive staff where I and three other captains solve problems for Admiral King that he doesn't want the Navy's headquarters staff involved in for whatever reason. I'm a ship-driver, and my last command was a heavy cruiser. I've been mainly a PacFleet sailor, starting the war with a destroyer command at Guadalcanal before going on to my cruiser command."

"Not too long ago I was sent TAD to the National Security Council to work a top-secret program called the Manhattan Project. It has nothing to do with Manhattan and I must tell you right now that if you even mention that name outside of this little séance and anyone in the Navy's security organizations hears about your saying it, the consequences will be dire. You'd be in less trouble if you told the Japanese we'd been reading their naval code ever since 1942. Got it?"

Two sincere nods. The skipper reached for his pack of cigarettes and then so did the XO. I didn't smoke but I didn't care if they did, even if we were submerged. The boat might even smell better.

"What's our ETA off Hungnam?" I asked.

"We'll be thirty miles southeast by 1800 this evening," the XO said. "We're making six knots now, not twenty-two, and we'll definitely need a charge this evening."

"Good, because I need to be on the surface, or at least at periscope depth, as soon as it's dark. Do you have a mine-hunting sonar?"

They nodded. I'd assumed they had one because *Cragfish,* a *Balao* class boat, was only one year old. She'd been built back in Portsmouth, where this whole caper had begun.

"Okay," I said. "I need to be somewhere between ten and twelve miles off Hungnam, in a position where I can see everything between Hungnam and a group of small islands directly east of the port. ONI says the seacoast directly off Hungnam is heavily mined, especially the area nearest the port's approaches. Where I need to be should be too deep for sea mines, but you'll need to take great care as you approach the Korean coast."

They both nodded again. In this part of the world, most of the subs we'd lost over the past two years had most likely been killed by sea mines. I reached for the folder and withdrew three color pictures, taken during the Trinity test. I stood them on end, their backs to my little audience. I took and exhaled a deep breath while I considered how to put this. The first picture showed a glowing, rising fire dome as it turned ten square miles of desert sand into radioactive glass. The second was even scarier, as the dome expanded to full shape, with that gelatinous-looking, quivering surface of intersecting sunbursts, and the third showed the gigantic mushroom-shaped cloud take shape as it lifted into the stratosphere, still boiling with otherworldly fire.

"The Manhattan Project is an extremely secret effort on the part of the national government to create an atomic bomb," I began. I watched their faces. Atomic bomb? What was that?

"An atomic bomb harnesses the latent energy of atoms, the basic building blocks of all matter on the earth. Everything is made up of atoms, infinitely small particles, invisible to even powerful microscopes, and held together by intense fields of pure energy. Everything from the earth itself, to the atmosphere, to the oceans, to human beings, the mountains, and every element on the periodic table of the elements, and even some that aren't, is made up of atoms. An atomic bomb taps that energy for a single instant and releases it into the atmosphere. This is what that looks like."

I handed over the three-pack of pictures to the skipper, who swore silently when he saw them. He passed them to his exec, who literally gasped.

"In the second picture," I started. "The one with the big glowing dome, can you see the tiny black dot at the bottom right?"

They nodded. "If that bomb had been dropped over New York City," I said, "that black dot would be the Empire State Building. It's that big."

I let them look at those three pictures for as long as they wanted. The muted sounds from outside the wardroom, the sounds of the boat settling in to normal, submerged operations, were in stark contrast to what they were looking at. They were shocked. As they should be, I thought. I got up, refilled my coffee mug, and passed the pot around. Then I retrieved the pictures.

"Those pictures are of the first test of the weapon, conducted in the western deserts of the United States. When that damned thing went off everybody out there in the desert who saw it understood that this atomic device changes *everything* about war and warfare. And when that black dot is pointed out, showing the sheer scale of this weapon, disturbing questions arise. I mentioned New York City. I could have mentioned *Tokyo*. The Army Air Forces have been bombing the cities of Japan on almost a daily basis. Hundreds of thousands of civilians are being killed, especially by the firebombing raids. Japan has moved its war industries out into city suburbs to disperse legitimate wartime targets—airplane factories, munitions factories, and the like—into the civilian population, with what we would consider unintended consequences. They don't think that way. Death as a consequence of military action is an honor to the Japanese, even if it means trying to figure out how to give a dead two-year-old a medal."

I let them think about that. The skipper got it first. "They're never going to surrender, are they?" he asked. "They'll fight to the last man, woman, and child, won't they?"

"Which is why the United States is going to introduce them to the atomic bomb," I said. "To prove to them, in the most outrageous manner possible, that they *must* surrender."

The skipper nodded. "So," he said. "Why are you here? Why are *we* here? Assuming I can ask that question."

"There's a problem in Washington," I said. "There are some trusted senior voices, who've seen these pictures, that are advising the president *not* to use it on a city. It's too much. It's over the top. Thousands will die. *Hundreds* of thousands will die. On the other hand, JCS points out that if we have to invade Japan, as we invaded *Iwo Jima* and *Okinawa*, hundreds of thousands of *American* GIs will die. Right now, as best we understand, Mr. Truman remains undecided. He has seen these pictures, and others. It always comes back to that little black dot."

"Fuck me," the exec mumbled.

"Yeah," I said. "That's the human reaction. But there's an unexpected wrinkle."

"Jesus *God,*" the skipper said. "There's more?"

"The Manhattan Project has been ongoing for years now, with everybody involved—we're talking about ten thousand people all told—Nobel Prize–winning scientists, electrical, electronic, and chemical engineers, metallurgists, medical doctors—going as hard and as fast as they could in order to beat Germany to the punch, because we had intel that Nazi Germany had been pursuing an atomic bomb as hard as we were. When Germany surrendered, we found out that, yes, they had a project like ours, but the war caught up with them before they could muster the materials, the scientists, the universities, the labs, the enormous industrial infrastructure, and the hundreds of millions of dollars required to bring the thing home. What we, the United States, didn't know, what *nobody* in all our many intel organizations knew, what our main allies in this effort, the Brits, didn't know, was that the goddamned Japanese also had a program. To build an atomic bomb."

"How could that be possible?" the exec exclaimed. "We've been technically ahead of them throughout the course of this war—radar, sonar, aircraft, shipyards, oil, munitions—and ever since Midway and Guadalcanal, they've been on defense, beaten back to where we are now. Shit, we can't even find any ships to sink. Japan is wrecked. Japan is *starving,* for oil, food, steel, coal, ships. The B-29s have set the whole fucking country on fire, if you can believe the Army."

"Right," I said. "Except: they've been building *their* bomb in Korea."

I gave them a moment to think about that. I realized there was much more that I could tell them, but I didn't have the time. It would have taken hours. There was only one more thing I needed to mention.

"We have intel from China that they might be far along in the development of a bomb," I said. "Maybe even close to a test. If they are, it will be done at night to avoid our long-range recon flights. And if, in fact, they have managed to duplicate *our* program in secret facilities in Korea, then any thoughts of a million-man Allied invasion of Japan are moot. Just think about one of these things"—I rattled the three pictures in my hand—"being dropped above the biggest amphibious invasion fleet ever assembled, bigger even than D-Day, in one place."

"Why are we finding this out just now?" the skipper asked.

"*Good* question," I said. "But I have people back in Washington beating the intel bushes to see what else we've missed—and where. That's why I've been flown ten thousand miles to this little patch of the Sea of Japan. If they *do* test, I can tell Washington two things: that they tested one, and that it worked. I can tell them that because I'm probably the only naval officer in the whole damn Navy that's actually seen one go off. I was at the test of our first one. And then we think Mr. Truman will say, well, goddamn! Use it. Tomorrow. And then tell the bastards we'll keep using them until they surrender, unconditionally. Simple as that."

I sat back in my chair. "That's why we're here. I'm going to spend tonight and every night hereafter looking through the periscope, because I know what to look for. It might happen tonight. It might happen a week from now. It might never happen, but if it does, the United States will probably drop one in Japan, and if *that* works, there'll be no invasion or thousands of dead GIs, either."

"Captain," the XO said. "Don't you think this—you being here, waiting—is a really, really long shot? This intel you've mentioned—that's pretty thin gruel."

"Yes, of course it is," I admitted. "Probably *the* long shot of the war. But: the war's entering its endgame. The shameful thing is that there's been no intel on a Japanese program because no one has ever looked. Everybody just assumed they couldn't do it, and, besides, we were fixated on the Germans. Now we've got the entire national intel community looking hard—for fresh stuff and for stuff that might have been there all along, had anyone been looking. But you're right about this being a long shot: this could all be BS or even deception on Japan's part. Washington thinks we need to try. Remember, nobody thought about looking in Korea, China, and nearby Manchuria. Which Japan has been occupying ever since the nineteen thirties. Which are rich in minerals, hydroelectric power, coal, iron, absolute secrecy, and an infinite supply of slave labor."

I let them absorb all this in the suddenly quiet wardroom for a long moment. Then I gathered up my pictures.

"Be alert for messages from ONI," I told them. "We need to be close enough to see it, but not so close that we get caught up in whatever underwater shock wave might come our way. If it does happen, we will then need to head south at best speed while transmitting a short, uncoded message on three long-haul HF frequencies, four times an hour for two hours. Every NavComSta in the Pacific and on the West Coast is already guarding these specific freqs, looking for this message. I then have to get back to Washington to be personally able to stand tall in front of the president and tell him what I saw and what it means."

"I assume this message will say, yes, they tested one," the XO said. "Why do you need to go all the way back there to confirm it?"

"Because the president is from Missouri. The Show-Me state, remember? He's always making a big deal about that. Before he makes this decision, he's going to want to hear it from someone who saw it, who had also seen one before. That would be me."

The XO exhaled loudly. "Then they'll . . . what? Drop this fucking thing on a city?"

"That's way above my pay grade, XO," I said. "But, yeah, I think they will. In a way, it'll be a continuation of the current bombing campaign. The thinking in Washington is that until the Japanese people or their emperor are so shocked by what's happening to them, they'll never just surrender and end it. That said, there's a lot of resistance to hitting a city with one of these things. On the other hand, if we can prove they have one, too, that takes a lot of the guilt out of it, doesn't it. I assume you guys have heard how bad *Iwo* and *Okinawa* were in terms of casualties, yes?"

They both nodded.

"Well, there you go. It all comes down to: their guys, or our guys? And as I recall, those bastards started this shit."

I handed the XO a card with the three HF frequencies they'd need if we saw something. The message to be transmitted was simple: affirmative, affirmative, affirmative. If we saw nothing, we'd say nothing. I told them there might be messages from ONI to me. Then I asked to be taken to the attack center, where the periscopes lived. Once we got there the XO wanted to say something.

"We can probably be on the surface at night," the XO said. "Unless there are heavy patrols, or aircraft. You won't need a periscope to see— that."

"'That' begins with an incredibly bright white flash, which also sends out a pulse of nuclear radiation that will kill everybody aboard if we're close enough *and* on the surface. I won't have to be looking through a periscope: if they set one off, the periscope optics will light up like there's a welder on the conning tower and then you're gonna need new optics. And another thing: somebody has to keep watch for the bearing of any explosion we see, and then you need to turn the boat's head to that bearing immediately to minimize shock damage. Even at ten miles."

They nodded simultaneously. Clearly, they hadn't been thinking that the boat itself might possibly be in danger. Or themselves. Now they were. The other officers and the crew had seen their faces since coming out of our little meeting. I didn't envy the skipper's dilemma in figuring out what to tell them.

TWENTY-TWO
WAITING

By explaining my presence way out here in the Sea of Japan to the skipper and his XO, I now absorbed Van Rensselaer's need to have someone physically out here who could tell the difference between an ammo ship blowing up in a harbor and an A-bomb. As the XO had pointed out, this entire mission was a titanic long shot. I just had to assume that there was some kind of intel back in Washington that pointed to the near term. The Japanese had to know Olympic was coming. Daily photo-recon flights, the gathering of logistical forces throughout the Pacific at large, the lack of any more island targets like *Iwo* or *Okinawa*, the mobilizing of Russian armies on the mainland to their west, the ever-tightening blockade of our submarine forces, who had been reduced to killing seagoing fishing boats, small trawlers, interisland cargo luggers, even small coastal boats, because there were no more ships coming toward Japan. The big problem with *bushido* was that you couldn't eat it.

The skipper took me up to the attack center and explained some of the periscope machinery, navigation instruments, and torpedo firing computers. I was surprised to find three periscopes, not just one. The center was cramped because of all the equipment. I found it hard to believe that up to six men would be up here during a submerged attack. He let me look through all three periscopes; none of the images looked much like anything I'd seen in propaganda movies. I settled on the one with the widest field of view. The problem was that my eyes were still leaden. I didn't think I could stay awake to keep watch all through the night.

"Can I sleep here?" I asked. "Let's look at the charts and determine a bearing to the waters between Hungnam and some small islands offshore. You'll know it if they torch one off. I believe this whole attack center's gonna light up through those 'scope lenses."

The captain nodded and sent for some kapok life jackets and a blanket. I lay down in a corner and was gone in sixty seconds.

Sometime during the night we surfaced, but I was so tired I missed it. The rumbling of the boat's diesel engines as they recharged the batteries probably put me into an even deeper sleep. I remembered one of the docs in Manila talking about the physical effects of crossing multiple time zones. I qualified.

I was awakened by the diving alarm as the boat submerged in dawn's early light. The skipper took her down to 250 feet and put her into a five-mile circle at just enough speed to maintain stability underwater. The water depth beneath the keel was 5,500 feet, so mines were not a concern. I grabbed some breakfast in the wardroom and apologized for crapping out in the attack center. Not a problem unless a nice fat tanker comes by, the XO said. Bomb or no bomb, we'll go after it.

"No, you will *not*," I said. "My mission supersedes any other opportunities you might encounter."

They stared at me as if I'd committed blasphemy, which, to a submarine command team, I had. "Sometime after the war, assuming this bomb will end it," I told them, "you'll understand, but right now I need to make it clear to you that *nothing* is more important than *my* seeing with *my* own eyes if they've succeeded in making a bomb. Nothing, got it? I hate to be a hard-ass, but if you want, I can get ComSubPac on the horn to clarify that for you . . . You want that?"

There was an embarrassed silence, until I asked if there was some coffee available. Then the skipper said there'd been some fishing boat contacts during the night so he'd had to settle down to what they called the decks-awash position, where only the conning tower showed. Otherwise, nothing had been moving off the Korean coast. He did say there was the loom of many lights along the coast, indicating a major industrial center was there.

A radioman came into the wardroom and said he had a TS message for Captain Bowen from ONI. The tape was available in radio central. If I'd thought the attack center was cramped, radio central was this tiny little cupboard on one side of the control room. The radioman drew a curtain and handed me the top-secret message. The text ran down the length of the ribbon:

"Gun gadget ready to go to Guam/Tinian XX Second PU gadget ten days away. XX SACO says second source reporting project at Hungnam is Jap version of ME-262 XX. But: source at Shanghai Jiao Tong University reports a shipment of thorium to *Tokyo* University in late 1943, plus Korean source claims deuterium being produced in Hamhung, below Chosin Reservoir. XX ALSO project confirms Jap/Nazi tech cooperation. Keep watching. Endit JW."

I handed the paper back to the radioman, told him to shred it, and went to the wardroom looking for fat pills. The XO was there, surrounded by three piles of paperwork.

"I recognize those," I said, sitting down at the tiny table.

"The eternal constant," he said. "Even out here. I heard you got a love note."

"I did," I said. "Indications remain nebulous, squared."

The XO had the bulky physical features of an ex-athlete. "You lift, sir?" he asked.

"Whenever I can," I said. "Charles Atlas devotee as a teenager, now for stress relief, mostly."

"Guys back in after-torpedo have some steel; rest of the crew calls them the goon squad. If you'd like . . ."

"Yes, please," I said. "I'm just another run-of-the-mill CruDes guy," I said. "Pumping iron is what I do to keep sane in Washington. That's a crazy place."

He laughed. "I doubt that run-of-the-mill stuff," he said. "But lemme introduce you to Chief Gomez."

"Thought so," the chief said when we got together in the last compartment in the sub. He and I had similar shapes. He was even bigger than I was. "Heard our special guest was a big boy up top. Sir."

"Nowadays I use it to substitute pain for stress," I said. "On account of I may possibly be getting old."

He snorted. "Welcome to the goon squad," he said. "We've got some metal back here; help yourself. If you're gonna need a helper, the crew's usually back here after evening meal. All this good chow and nowhere to run, this is the only way we don't get too fat."

"Got it, Chief," I said. Gomez was a big boy, but he was definitely not a fat big boy. "Unfortunately, nighttime is why I'm here."

"Word is, we're looking for a big boom."

So much for top-secret security, I thought. Well, of course. Ninety guys, locked into a steel tube. Secrets? Gimme a break.

We shot the shit for a while about the war, the lack of respectable targets, the invasion, whether or not the enemy would ever give this shit up. Despite the difference in rank, senior chiefs and O-6s had a natural affinity because we were about the same age and possessed many of the same professional experiences. I was surprised he wasn't Chief of the Boat, but there was another chief senior to him by about three years. A young-looking sailor interrupted us and said I had another message up in radio. Back to business.

This message was again from ONI. OSS had sources in the Russian army, one of whom had revealed that the two Soviet armies stationed on the Chinese-Korean border had been told to get ready to invade Korea along its eastern shore and to seize the entirety of the Hungnam industrial complex. That was it—no estimate of when or why.

So, Janet's beating of the bushes in Washington was paying off. I'd been to intelligence briefings in DC earlier that postulated the Russians would declare war on Japan at the first sign that she was even thinking about surrender, with the object of seizing some of the northern Japanese island territories below Sakhalin Island. Two full divisions already positioned on the border would give credence to that. With Germany prostrate, the Russians had armies to spare. A second message an hour later said that gadgets were staging for the trip to the Marianas. Maybe Harry Truman had made his decision, in which case I might just be wasting time out here in the Sea of Japan.

We spent another night of waiting and watching the Hungnam industrial area in a flat, calm sea. By now I was able to stay awake between catnaps in the attack center. There was some kind of welding going on in one of the distant waterfront buildings, manifested by lightning flashes in upper-story windows. I had to use the high-power setting in the periscope to see that well; otherwise, all I could see was a line of dimmed lights running north up the coast until they disappeared behind a promontory. The mountains behind the industrial area remained dark. We'd moved a little closer this night, but the skipper drew the line when the water depth got any shallower than one thousand feet. He was afraid of mines and nobody was arguing, least of all me. If these guys popped an atomic bomb, even underwater, we would not have to be any closer to see it. As it was, I thought we'd feel it as well and I'd warned the skipper to secure the boat. An underwater blast would produce a monster tidal wave.

At dawn the next morning one of our lookouts thought he heard an approaching aircraft, which resulted in a crash dive down to three hundred feet and no little excitement in the boat. The skipper ran south, back out into greater depths, for an hour before slowing back down to a battery-saving creep. We heard no bombs or depth charges, but that didn't mean somebody wasn't out there looking for snoopers. In fact, when we crept submerged back toward our "surveillance station" we detected the sounds of patrol boats in the distance. Boats, plural, as if a barrier patrol had been set up. The skipper waited until full dark to surface, after plotting the boat sounds for an hour to determine their distance. Then came a surprise.

The sonar detected a growing sector of boat-engine sounds to the north of us. Everything from putt-putts to larger marine diesels, typical of the bigger fishing vessels. There were no lights in evidence out on the water, and the industrial area looked unchanged in the dark. Given what the sonar, operating in just the passive or listen mode, was telling us, however, he submerged again, but this time to periscope depth. He took over the periscope as we glided at three knots on an east-west course until he suddenly shouted: *shit!* Flood negative to the mark! Make your depth two hundred feet.

I could feel the boat sag underneath me as we settled down to two hundred feet instead of the sixty feet that was periscope depth.

"It's a mob," he said. "Coming straight at us. Junks. Sailboats. Bigger fishing boats. Hopefully no sonar-equipped patrol boats."

Even as he said it, I could hear the sudden swarm of boat engines passing overhead, as if all the occupants of the Hungnam harbor were fleeing for their lives.

Which is what they might well be doing, I thought.

"As soon as you think that gaggle has passed, get back up to periscope depth," I ordered.

The skipper clearly wanted no part of that, based on the expression on his face.

"They may have told everybody to leave the Hungnam harbor area," I said. "I can think of only one reason for that. I must have a periscope look."

There followed lots of discussion between the attack center and the sonar shack—are they gone? Down Doppler on everything? Anything else out there, just drifting and waiting for us to fuck up? Make *damn* sure, Sonar. Even a wooden fifty-foot patrol boat can carry two five-hundred-pound depth charges. That's what happened to Sam Dealey, remember? So be *goddamned* sure.

We waited for what seemed like an eternity to me, and then the skipper finally relented. Up we went. Deliberately and very slowly.

Okay, I thought. Do it right. This isn't the Chesapeake Bay. I realized then why I had never even thought about becoming a submariner. On a cruiser, you could see—and shoot. Or run away at thirty knots. Or both. A submerged submarine could run away at—eight knots, tops, maybe? For five minutes until the batteries coughed and said: all gone. I started mumbling my mantra when I felt cornered like this: "This was a good idea; this was a good idea . . ."

The skipper heard me and then grinned. He didn't say anything; he didn't have to.

Finally, we reached periscope depth and put the stick up. The skipper did a walk-around, and then another one.

"Darker than a well digger's ass up there," he said. He backed away from the periscope and invited me to take a look, but before I could, the two optics at the base of the scope blasted a searing white light against the bulkhead of the attack center. So bright that the crewmen up there covered their eyes and exclaimed out loud. The intensity of the light was beyond normal human experience. Except mine.

"Mark that bearing," I yelled. "Come around to that heading, *Bendix*! For the love of God!"

I scared the entire control room with that order, but it had the effect of a thrust of power from the screws as the boat leaned into a sudden, hard turn and came about to the heading of the initial flash. And that was a good thing, we all discovered, as moments later the bow lifted twenty degrees up angle and we began accelerating *backward*. I grabbed the nearest metal and hung on desperately. The entire boat then hogged, making every steel beam of her hull groan and crack so loudly that some of the younger sailors in the attack center cried out, their terror echoed by other sounds of total panic from the control room down below. Then she rolled to starboard an incredible fifty or even sixty degrees, throwing any loose objects everywhere and eliciting more terrified screams throughout the boat. Part of my brain knew what was happening, and yet it took everything I had not to scream in fear like the rest. I held on to the base of the periscope well as the second and the third shock waves hit. The burst at Alamogordo had only two, but the sea expressed its displeasure in a *series* of shock waves as water was compressed outward and then flooded back into the fiery vacuum, and then back out again in a series of hydraulic convulsions that hurled poor *Cragfish* around like a chip of wood at the base of Niagara.

I dimly became aware of the skipper's frantic orders as he tried to regain depth and attitude control of his floundering submarine. I felt my lower lip stinging; I'd been kicked in the face by the periscope well coaming.

Jesus, I thought. And we were at least ten miles from the Bomb.

And a bomb it had to be. An atomic bomb. A *Japanese* atomic bomb. I wanted to cry.

I picked myself up from the deckplates and started giving orders to the skipper.

"Surface, immediately," I said. "Proceed south at maximum speed on the diesels. Begin the radio transmissions."

He looked at me in consternation, having just barely rescued the boat from a multiple shock-wave convulsion and a trip to the bottom of the South China Sea.

"*Do* it, goddamnit," I shouted. "Surface, come about, head south and get that HF radio going. Maximum speed. Two hours. Send it again and again."

"But," he began.

I wanted to throttle him. "You wanna be the guy who's responsible for half a million GIs dead?" I yelled. The other people in the attack center were looking at me as if I were a madman.

"*Surface!*" I shouted again, and then hit the alarm switch I'd seen them use to bring the boat back up on the surface.

Training kicked in. He took over, surfaced the boat, gave the conning orders to point us in the away direction, and, when the diesels roared, ordered up a course and speed to get us the hell out of there. When he hit the bitch box and ordered radio central to start sending the critical message, I subsided down onto the deckplates in the attack center and concentrated on my breathing.

I'm too old for this shit, I thought again. Except, suddenly, I felt good. That surge of combat adrenaline, followed by that hand-quivering "I'm still alive" elation, flooded through my body as the boat settled down.

Plus: we'd been *right*! The goddamned Japanese *had* been working on an A-bomb the whole time with the help of Adolf fucking Hitler. And now? Here comes the end of the world, you sonsabitches. You'll never get the chance to "die with honor" on *this* battlefield. You will be burned to cinders in a man-made version of Hell itself.

We ran for two hours on the surface toward the Philippines. The skipper then wanted to submerge but I ordered him to keep going at twenty-two knots throughout the night and into the next day. He balked at running on the surface in daylight.

"Friendly aircraft," he said. "That's what I'm afraid of. They see a sub on the surface they attack. I'm not that worried about Japanese subs. It's *our* guys, trigger-happy aviators."

"Proceed on the surface," I said. "Use your radar and your electronic listening gear. Dive if you have to, but I have an appointment with the commander in chief and it concerns the go-ahead for what I showed you in those pictures. And, most likely, the end of this war. Do as I say, Commander. That's a fucking order, in case you have any doubts."

He protested. He was a submarine skipper. Too many times "friendly" American aircraft had attacked and even sunk American submarines. I fully understood, but I also understood that, if Truman did want to see and hear from a live human being that he had witnessed a Japanese atomic bomb test, time was, as they say, of the fucking essence. I knew the skipper was right, but this time, I was righter.

We didn't have to wait until daylight for trouble to appear. We were running full out in the South China Sea, pointed at Lingayen Gulf. The problem was that we were leaving a trail of phosphorescence in the warm sea fifty yards wide. Subs didn't carry an air-search radar, but they could slant the beam up a few degrees on their surface-search radar to catch low-fliers making a bombing run. More importantly, they could also detect enemy radar signals and even American radar signals on a basic signal-intercept screen down in the control room. That's what happened at 0430. The radar operator shouted excitedly that he had a friendly radar signal target angle 030. Range was unknown—the system was a passive listening device.

We did an emergency dive down to 250 feet and initiated a ninety degree right turn as we hurried down. One minute later we heard "things" hitting the water behind us and then four thunderous explosions, far enough back that we were safe, but close enough to make unsecured items in the boat dance around. I was in the control room. The skipper gave me a hard look. "As I was saying," he began, but I waved him off.

"Remain submerged until daylight," I ordered. "Then surface and continue the high-speed transit." He just glared at me, but surface we did at 0730, but not before having a good listen for that radar signal.

As if to reinforce those orders, we received a high-precedence message just before dawn giving us the rendezvous instructions for meeting a seaplane at noon that very day. They'd sent the plane out farther this time. On the plane I could travel at two hundred miles per hour instead of twenty-two. I lay down on my borrowed rack for some shut-eye. Wouldn't it be ironic if the plane that picked me up was the same plane that attacked us a few hours before? Ironic probably would *not* be the word the skipper would use, I thought with a small grin. That grin faded when I realized I was in for another halfway-around-the-world airplane ride. I groaned out loud.

TWENTY-THREE
STANDING TALL

Van Rensselaer was waiting for me in the Travis operations tower when I finally landed at dawn two days later. I was a bit groggy and I stumbled a little bit after dropping down from the forward hole to the tarmac. My fancy B-29 had crapped out at Hickam in Hawaii, so I'd been transferred to a real warbird for the final leg to the West Coast. I'd spent the flight sleeping on a pile of inflatable life jackets in the radio compartment. By then, I didn't care—I was that tired. One of the flight crew walked beside me to the tower just in case. California was warm and I could tell it was going to be another spectacular day; I wondered idly if it ever changed out here.

"Welcome home, Captain," Van Rensselaer said as we met in the waiting room. "I think you've set a record for passenger hours in one trip."

"I believe it," I said, my voice dry from the pressurization on the bomber. "I need a coffee."

"Coming right up," he said with a welcoming smile. "Right over there, in the met room."

We walked over to the weather office, where I was pleased to see coffee and donuts on one of the desks. The weather-guessers must have been asked to make themselves scarce until we were done.

I sat down heavily in a chair and tasted fresh coffee and the fat pill.

"Absolutely no doubts?" he asked.

"Absolutely no doubts," I replied. "The blast wave damn near rolled the boat completely over—and in theory we were ten miles away, if not more. That flash came down from the top of the periscope, through the observation lenses, and projected two round spots on the attack center bulkhead. Even then, it hurt everyone's eyes and stained the paint. One guy was looking at a gauge right next to those two spots, and he couldn't see for an hour. No doubts."

"Fireball?"

"No, a water column with a fireball inside. Even scarier."

He thought for a moment while I worked on the coffee. My eyes had that by now familiar sticky feeling. I needed sleep, with real rest. The thought of getting back on another airplane to get back to the East Coast made my heart sink.

"Did they drop it, you think?" he asked.

"Couldn't tell," I replied. "There was nothing to see out there except the loom of the lights along the Korean coast. I'm guessing they put it on a barge or a boat, moved it ten miles offshore near those little islands, and triggered it. They probably swamped half the factories along the shore. I'm assuming the messages got through?"

"Oh, God, yes," he said, pouring himself some coffee and refilling my mug. "They moved two gadgets from Guam out to Tinian the next day. The Army Air Forces have been training a special squadron of B-29s for the mission for six weeks. They're out there on Tinian right now. Hanford has sent enough plutonium to Los Alamos to make two more implosion bombs."

"What's the president's thinking?"

"That," he said, "is something you're going to find out in about twenty minutes. We decided on a phone call from here rather than waiting for you to get to Washington."

"Praise God," I said. "Can I walk back, then? I never want to even *see* the inside of another airplane, much less ride in one."

"After you talk to the president," he said, "you'll take my train back to Washington. Given what you know and what you've seen, you'll be escorted all the way. I'm going west, to Tinian, with General Groves."

"Happy trails," I said, irreverently. He grinned.

"Two gadgets in the forward theater," he said. "He's much happier now. It all comes down to how convincing you'll be talking to the president."

"That's no problem," I said. "I saw what I saw, and I knew what to look for. I only wonder, how did we miss it?"

"We weren't looking," he said, his face suddenly somber. "When Lieutenant Commander Waring started beating up the intelligence establishment, all sorts of stuff came bubbling up, like debris from a sunken sub. From an amazingly disparate set of sources. The OSS in China and Korea. Our ALSOS project in Germany. Norway. Even Italy, for God's sake. No one, from the JCS on down, ever asked the question: does Japan have one? Not until that old man in the Portsmouth hospital ran his mouth did we even *suspect* they were working on one. I'll tell you one thing: the postwar analysis of this intelligence failure is going to be truly interesting."

"Postwar—you think this will do it?"

He nodded. "It has to," he said. "Assuming the damned things work. It *has* to."

A Marine lieutenant came into the meteorological office. "The link is up, Captain," he announced.

Van Rensselaer nodded. "Showtime."

We walked to a stairway and went to the second floor of the tower, where there were offices. The actual control room for the airfield was on the next floor up.

The secure phone station was different from the ones I was used to, although I shouldn't have been surprised. Every piece of technology I'd encountered during this war had been improved again and again. Van Rensselaer picked up the handset and spoke to someone in Washington. He waited a minute for a reply and then handed the phone to me.

"The president," he announced.

"Captain Bowen," came Harry Truman's distinctive voice. "They tell me you've been on a rather long plane ride."

"Indeed I have, Mr. President," I replied. "And I don't even like flying."

"Me, neither," he said. "I'm a much better walker. Tell me, Captain: what did you see?"

"The light at the end of the world, Mr. President," I said. "Through a periscope on a submarine that was about ten, maybe twelve miles away from some small islands off Hungnam, Korea. It was nighttime and the periscope was pointed in the general direction of the Hungnam harbor area. Nobody was looking through it when it happened, but the attack center on the submarine was lit up like an electric welding arc for about five seconds, which is the same thing I experienced at the Trinity test. Unbelievably bright white flash. One of the officers in the attack center was pretty close to the periscope's eyepieces, and he was blind for an hour after it happened. From the *reflection*. I did look immediately afterward and saw the fireball, then the illuminated mushroom cloud. Then the shock wave hit and damned near rolled the boat all the way over on her beam ends. We were partially submerged, decks awash, or I think we'd have been completely capsized."

I stopped then to see if he had anything to say.

"And you were present for the Trinity test, correct?"

"Yes, sir. They had us down in a deep trench for the initiation, wearing black glasses, with our faces turned away from the test tower. Even so, that white flash was painful. As was this one. I could still see it whenever I closed my eyes on the way back. This was not some ammo ship blowing up. This was an atomic bomb."

"As big as the one you saw at Trinity?"

I had to think about that for a moment. "No, sir, I don't think it was as big, but it was identical in profile. The white flash, the bright yellow, then red, fireball that began rising and then becoming an even bigger sphere of fiery colors and weird layer boundaries within the fireball. I barely had time to shout: brace for impact! before that shock wave hit and knocked everybody and every loose thing onboard galley-west."

I heard the president sigh. "Okay, Captain," he said. "You've convinced me. And if it's any comfort to you, your amazing odyssey all the way out to Korea and back was very helpful to me and my Joint Chiefs. I've got a big decision to make. You understand me?"

"Yes, sir, I absolutely understand."

"All right then, thank you again, sir."

The connection was terminated and I handed the phone handset back to the secure station operator. Then I realized the people standing around me were desperate to hear what he had said.

"He thanked me for telling him what I saw," I announced. "And then said he has a big decision to make."

"That's it?" Van Rensselaer said.

"If you mean, did I get any impression on which way he's gonna decide?" I said. "No, I did not. But I think that now he knows and believes that Japan has one. I think there's only one possible outcome."

"Okay," Van Rensselaer announced. "Great job. I know you're bone-tired. My people will get you to the train. When you get back to DC, pay a call on Admiral King. Tell him where you've been and what you saw. Then go home and take the rest of the week off. You've absolutely earned it."

The rest of the week off, I thought. Hell's bells, I didn't even know what day it was, much less the date. But I thought it would be fun to sit down with *Semper Iratus*. Just once more.

TWENTY-FOUR
AFTERMATH

They got me to the train station an hour later. It was almost comforting to see the familiar lineup of cars and guards waiting on the tracks. My train, Van Rensselaer had called it. He was a Captain, USN, just like me. How come I didn't have a train?

Hah!

One of the staff showed me to a berth in the Pullman car. This one was a little bit bigger than my previous accommodations, complete with a shower and a real bed. I stripped off my well-used travel clothes and told them to stand at parade rest outside the bathroom. No problem, Boss. Then I took a long, hot shower and climbed into the bed. I was hungry, but not that hungry. It was just past ten o'clock in the morning. Maybe dinner. Maybe breakfast. My bet was on breakfast, tomorrow.

We were rolling comfortably through the countryside when there was a knock on the door. I roused myself and opened my sticky eyes. Sundown was playing reddish colors on the compartment's walls. I made a noise. One of the dining room staff, whom I recognized, poked his head in and told me dinner would be going down in about a half hour. He then pointed to a clean uniform on a hanger and a pile of necessities on the chair. Obviously, someone had come in and taken charge of my laundry. I thanked him and he grinned. He came back in five minutes and held a second reveille on me and helped me get up and get dressed, and then steered me down the passageway to the dining car. He sat me down in that corner table, our table, I thought, and brought a Scotch.

Bernard, that was his name.

"Thank you, Bernard," I said. "I've been up for a while."

"Yessir," he said. "We heard tell you went around the whole damn world since we saw you the last time. That must have been something, all that flyin'."

"It certainly was," I said. "A B-29, set up for passengers. I can still hear those big-ass engines."

His eyes grew big. "B-29?" he said. "Man, that must have been something else. Sir. Ain't nobody here ever even seen one of those things."

"If I never see one again, it's gonna be just fine with me, Bernard. Thanks for the Scotch."

The dining car was starting to fill up. I closed my eyes and sipped the whiskey, trying not to let that clickety-clack put me back to sleep. Then someone sat down at my table. The last thing I needed just then was company, so I kept my eyes closed and willed them to go away.

"You sure know how to make a girl feel welcome, there, Captain," Janet Waring said.

I opened my left eye; the right one was still resisting. There she was. I kicked my right eye in the ass and tried to smile. She laughed out loud. "Oh look, a zombie," she said with that infectious grin. "I'll have you know that I am your official escort, charged by many higher powers with keeping you from running your mouth about Japanese surprises, and you—what? Bare your teeth at me?"

Van Rensselaer, I thought. You sly old dog. "Sorry," I said. "I'm a wee bit tired."

"Oh, you poor thing," she went on with visibly fake sympathy.

"That's poor thing, sir, to you," I grumped.

"Well, getting closer," she said, tapping her shirt collar.

I looked. *Silver* oakleaf now. Full *Commander* Janet Waring, now. I tipped my Scotch in her direction. "Many congrats," I said, finally waking up. I caught Bernard's eye, raised my glass, and nodded in Janet's direction. He brought a partially consumed martini over to the table and took my empty glass. Then I realized she'd probably been sitting at the bar the whole time I'd been in the dining car.

Zombie. Yup. She was still grinning.

"What did Mr. Truman have to say this morning?" she asked.

"He thanked me for my interest in national defense," I said. "But I think he's gonna do it."

Her face sobered. "They've taken two weapons to Tinian. I found out the Army Air Forces have been training an entire squadron of B-29s to drop one. Training for some time, actually, back in the States. They had to strip the bombers down in order to make weight. Reduced the crew. Took off all the guns. Added some fuel tanks. Developed a special maneuver so that they can get away from the explosion and make it back to base."

"I believe it," I said. "Let me tell you what I saw off Korea."

We had dinner and then I asked her what she'd been doing during her vacation in Washington. She snorted.

"My boss had a good idea," she began. "He got Van Rensselaer to get me a White House building pass. I put that on top of my ONI, Navy Department, and State Department credentials, so when I went to see somebody, it was prominently visible. Made asking questions go a whole lot faster."

"I'd have thought that asking if there were indications of a Japanese weapons program would have shocked some people."

"Well, I got one of two responses: oh, shit, is that even possible? to what's an atomic weapons program? So, I changed tack: any reports of uranium ore on the move in Asia? Heavy water? Large centrifuges? Cyclotrons? New, unusual concentrations of electrical power, especially hydropower?

"Then I started chasing down the names of prewar Japanese physicists and chemists, from the early 1930s forward, at the major universities in Japan. I interviewed a bunch of the Nobels working out there in Los Alamos, the project people at Stanford, University of Chicago, and others, and came up with a list of names. And locations, where their labs had been, how far along they were. Three names kept coming up, and one lab complex at *Tokyo* Imperial University. This was, according to the older scientists, all about basic research—structure of the atom, isolation of particles, the possibility of a chain reaction. Not weapons work."

"It wasn't weapons work when the good guys were doing the same thing, either," I said. "But I think they all knew, especially once Fermi proved a chain reaction was feasible, that a controlled one could provide limitless electrical power, and an uncontrolled one could produce an explosive amount of energy. And that became the elephant in the room no one would talk about."

She nodded. "I actually talked to Dr. Oppenheimer. I told him I'd been at the Trinity test, and then what I was after. He said something interesting about the Japanese. He said their contributions were nil, but their research was tracking right along with ours and the Europeans'. Their biggest problem was that their government wasn't interested, so they had no money, which meant little equipment, or even radioactive substances to work with. Their research program was operating on a shoestring. Their military was urgently interested, but also had no money.

"I asked if their scientists were good enough to initiate a weapons program if they were funded. He said their scientists were certainly as good as ours, if the scientific literature being exchanged worldwide was any indication, especially in chemistry. Then he woke up. Why are you asking? he said suddenly. I filled him in. He got excited, especially when I told him about the facilities we'd discovered in Korea. He cut off the conversation, saying he needed to talk to General Groves right away. That kinda confirmed my suspicions."

"I'll bet," I said. "Although I'm sure Groves was aware of my mission by then."

"Maybe, maybe not," she said. "I asked Van Rensselaer if anyone knew about your vacation out to Korean waters. He told me to keep digging and to focus on recent intelligence by asking the OSS and SACO to poll their agents in China, Korea, and Manchuria."

"In other words, he didn't answer your question. Typical—Svengali to the last."

She nodded, then raised her empty glass. We took a break. I stayed with Scotch; she switched to a liqueur involving Scotch. The dining car was thinning out and it was full dark outside as we rumbled east through the Rockies toward Kansas.

"I have this vague memory," I said, "that Oppenheimer once said something rather opaque. Kinda like that no one in government or the military would understand what 'the project' had accomplished until they used it. The way he said it made him sound like *he* was having some regrets, in the humanitarian sense."

"We're at war with the original implacable enemy," she said quickly. "Humanitarian issues are of no consequence. Look at what we found about what the Germans had been doing to European Jews. And what we already know that the Japanese have been doing to captive nations and prisoners of war. I told Van Rensselaer that the fruits of my labors convinced me the Japanese were trying hard to get an atomic bomb and that the president should flatten the bastards at the first opportunity."

I smiled at her fierce aggression. "What did he say?"

"He said, with a very straight face, that he'd inform the president, forthwith."

We both laughed, but then the amusement drained away. From what I was hearing, in the not-too-distant future a Japanese city would be subjected to total annihilation by atomic fire. Maybe even two or even three of them. For all our efforts, hers and mine, that didn't bear thinking about. A wave of fatigue rolled back over me. Bernard brought drinks and we both subsided into our own thoughts and enjoyed the clickety-clack as the darkness rushed by. I couldn't shake the feeling that we were rushing toward something unspeakable.

TWENTY-FIVE
THE SUN BOMB

Things happened quickly after the *Hiroshima* bombing. Russia declared war on Japan and sent those Manchurian divisions south into northern Korea, aiming at that vast industrial complex farther south. Truman told the country and the Japanese that he would immolate every city in Japan until they came to terms—our terms—on unconditional surrender. People in the Manhattan Project knew that this threat could eventually be carried out. Americans everywhere were still trying to digest the significance of an atomic bomb when the second one was dropped on *Nagasaki*. Janet told me she nearly cried when she heard about *Hiroshima*—she'd been there during her sabbatical years in Japan. The best news for all those in uniform was that the invasion probably wasn't going to happen, and certainly not in the month of August. Truman might be bluffing, but I was willing to bet that any survivors in those two cities were more than ready to fold.

In the event, after *Nagasaki* the emperor ordered his people and his armies to surrender. The Second World War was officially over. We learned later that the surrender had been a close-run thing. The militarists in charge of the Japanese government and armed forces had been ready to assassinate the emperor in order to force the entire nation to fight to the death to uphold *bushido*. The emperor, having finally been told in gory detail what had happened to the two cities, got the jump on them and sent out the surrender message to the Allies and then made a public radio broadcast in Japan. After that broadcast, the Japanese people, having been drilled since infancy into utter subservience to their god-emperor, whatever they thought about *bushido*, fell into respectful line. Many of the prospective assassins had committed suicide, or had been shot.

On September 2nd, the Japanese signed the surrender documents aboard the USS *Missouri* in *Tokyo* Bay. General Douglas MacArthur became the military governor of Japan. And then began the extremely difficult process of standing down from the largest and most brutal war in the history of the entire world. MacArthur himself acknowledged the role of the atomic bomb in his final statement about the war to the entire world at the end of the signing ceremony. We have had our last chance, he said. If we do not devise some greater and more equitable system to resolve international conflict, Armageddon will be at our door. And that was before any Americans got a good look on the ground at what had happened to *Hiroshima* and *Nagasaki*.

Van Rensselaer contacted me by phone a week after the signing of the surrender. I had been staying with Janet at her home on the Potomac, catching up on sleep and renewing our acquaintance in ways that were mutually satisfying. I had just finished my first cup of coffee for the morning, and it hadn't had any effect whatsoever. Janet had left around six thirty to get to work. He politely asked after my health, mental and physical. I told him I was a bit numb, probably like most Americans. We'd been at war for so long that nobody knew quite what to do when it finally stopped. From everything I'd read, the Brits were in a similar state of emotional confusion. They'd been at it for two years longer than we had, but their country was wrecked. Upbeat, defiant, jubilant that it was over, but economically wrecked nonetheless. I did not envy the victorious statesmen in all the Allied governments. Educated people understood the lessons of the punitive Versailles treaty after the First World War. Something different had to be done this time. And then, of course, loomed the increasingly dreaded fact of the atomic bomb. Van Rensselaer was going to go to Japan to see for himself, and he wanted me to come along. I told him that I had zero interest in that.

"Take Oppenheimer and the Nobels," I told him. "They might find the experience informative."

"Don't be a smart-ass," he said. "I'll need Waring, too—she is fluent in Japanese and also knows the culture. The president concurs. You're right: there's an entire herd of people who want to go, want to see what happened. He wants a couple observers whose career future does not depend on what they see or what they say. He learned a thing or two from FDR, who always had his own people who could go and see, whatever it was about, and then come back to tell him the God's honest truth. He doesn't want politicians and he doesn't want professional voyeurs. Remember that it was your report, person-to-person, and the stuff that Waring dug up that convinced him to use the Bomb."

I took a moment to consider, mostly, how to get out of this. I'd had well enough of going halfway around the world to do a job of work. And yet, I was an American naval officer, whose commission as a captain was signed by the president of the United States, in my case by FDR.

"I'd go on one condition," I said.

Van Rensselaer snorted. "Navy captains don't—"

"Wait," I said, interrupting him. "I want the president himself to tell me what he expects from me—us—if we go. Like you said, there will be lots and lots of scientists, doctors, high-ranking officials, generals, admirals, who are eventually going to go out there and see for themselves. If we're going as *his* eyes, I want to hear it from him. Use the term: 'show me.' He'll go along."

"Your impudence passeth all understanding," he growled. "No deal."

"Then I won't go. You go. I understand why you'd want me to after the past three, four years, but at this point, I'm ready to hang it up and subside into the ooze somewhere. I've done my goddamned duty. As for Waring, she might agree to it, but you're gonna have to ask her. I can't speak for her."

"One wonders," he snapped. "You're living at her home, aren't you?"

That pissed me off. "Screw you," I said, surprising myself. "And the white horse you rode in on. The emergency is over, remember? The Navy, hell, *all* the services, are gonna have to shed hundreds of senior guys like me. And you. Captains and colonels, especially. I *volunteer* to retire from active duty. One less guy for the next hump board to send a Dear John letter to. I do not want to see what your precious gadget did to a Japanese city."

Then I hung up. The phone rang back immediately. I ignored it. It wasn't my number, after all, and Janet was, conveniently, at work. There'd been no Navy hump board organized yet, but I knew there would be. A hump board was just what it sounded like. If you graphed the numbers of captains, commanders, lieutenant commanders on a straight line, you'd see a big hump at the senior end. As long as all those senior guys were still on active duty, the junior officers coming up could never get promoted, since the total number of senior ranks was limited by law, and that number depended on the total number of enlisted men in the force. Soon, several hundred *thousand* enlisted people would be coming home for discharge. Draftees, volunteers, even career sailors. The war was over; we no longer needed a million men under arms. Each service would then have to convene a commissioned officer hump board, which would decide who stayed on and who got to retire, as in, within ninety days, if you please, sir.

I realized I was more than ready. Something about this atomic bomb had gotten to me. It had changed *everything* having to do with war, as even MacArthur had alluded to. Armageddon next time. After twenty years of being a professional warrior, I guess I'd lost my taste for it in the face of that dreadful rising fireball. It had ended the war. Good for you, atomic bomb. Now let go of me.

Janet got home—her home, just as Van Rensselaer had nastily called it in his cheap shot—at six that evening. I told her what had happened between Van Rensselaer and me, and about the new mission to Japan.

"I know," she said. "He called me at ONI. Actually, he called my boss, who congratulated me on the opportunity to represent ONI on the first 'strategic survey' of defeated Japan. I told him I was afraid of the residual radiation that just *had* to be there, just like the guys at the Trinity site told us in terms of going out to the tower to see what was left. The admiral drew a blank, so I explained it to him, and told him I did not want to go. He was shocked—the career opportunity of a lifetime, and more like that. Obviously, I knew a lot more about what might be lurking out there in the cinder field that *Hiroshima* is now, so he said he'd inform Van Rensselaer. That's how we left it. And by the way, my dear captain, you look like you got shot at and missed, shit at and hit."

"That good, huh?" I said, gamely, although the description fit. "I slept almost the whole day; I wonder when this wears off."

"I need a long, hot shower," she said. "Maybe you could do my back."

"Only if you carry me up the stairs," I whimpered.

"You can do it," she said brightly. "There's a future in it, if that helps?"

"I'd probably fall asleep the moment the hot water hit me."

She sighed and then began to take her uniform off, piece by piece, as if I wasn't even there. She left her underwear—which was not, I discovered, exactly regulation—on. Then she walked slowly up the stairs. I groaned and followed, hoping the fancy balustrade would stand up to my pulling my way upstairs. Things got much better after that.

The house was interesting. Three levels and built like one of those Frank Lloyd Wright things I'd seen in *Life* magazine. The ground floor was built into a hillside and contained a spacious entrance-cum-lobby, a two-car garage, and a storage area. The entrance was accessed from the front by a circular driveway that came up from the main road running along and above the river. The second floor was the main entertainment area, with a large living room overlooking the river gorge across the full width of the house, which protruded six feet over the front walls. The windows were floor-to-ceiling on the front and sides. Toward the back was a dining room, kitchen, and a pantry big enough for a caterer. There was a see-through fireplace situated between the living room and the dining room. The third floor had the master bedroom and bath, and two guest bedrooms with their own baths. This floor also extended beyond the walls, so that each floor above the entrance was cantilevered above the one below. The master bedroom windows gave one a view of the entire river gorge below and the Virginia side of the Potomac Palisades. Part of the overhang deck was screened off as a balcony off the master bedroom. There was a streetcar line that ran parallel to the old C&O Canal and the main road, which went out to an amusement park called Glen Echo.

That night we sat on the third-story balcony, pretending we could see the Potomac through the thick stand of trees along the C&O canal. The traffic out on Canal Road had thinned considerably by seven thirty. She'd lit an anti-mosquito coil on the coffee table to attract any mosquitos getting through the screening. Some locusts were buzzing away out there somewhere in the dark, although it was nothing like a full-fledged outbreak. It was hot and uncomfortably humid—late summer in Washington, when anyone with any sense at all and enough money left town until mid-September. People tend to forget that our capital was built upon a swamp. Summers here would remind you of that fact, especially along the remains of the old Chesapeake and Ohio Canal.

Down in the living room a radio station was playing a Brahms symphony quietly, which I thought was something of an offense to the composer. I loved so-called classical music. Benny Goodman and other contemporary music left me cold. I wasn't sure what Janet liked, but the Brahms was a good sign. Suddenly a pair of white headlights turned into her circular driveway. Shit, I muttered. Had to be Van Rensselaer. But then two more cars, big ones—Cadillac limousines, I guessed—followed the first one up the driveway and stopped by her front door. Janet was in a summer bathrobe and nothing else; I had on slacks and a sport shirt. She fled for the bedroom while I went downstairs. Opening the door, I discovered a small crowd of what had to be Secret Service men, complete with dark glasses, even at nightfall, wearing three-button suits and identical ties. Behind them came a spry man who zipped up the steps, making his oversize glasses bounce on his nose.

I smothered a holy shit! and stepped briskly back away from the door so that the president and some of his Praetorian Guard could come in.

"Mr. President," I began, louder than necessary, so that Janet might hear me say it upstairs. "Welcome, sir."

He smiled, put out a strong handshake, and looked around for a second at the spacious main entrance hall. I took him upstairs to the living room, where he headed for the nearest armchair.

"Captain," he said, sitting down. One of the agents trotted up the stairs to the second floor. He better knock, I thought.

"I'm told you don't want to go to Japan on another special mission for me," he said, raising his eyebrows.

"Not quite, Mr. President," I replied. "I'm still trying to get over my last one. A Navy doc told me it had something to do with traveling through so many time zones. I've been mostly sleeping since I got back, and I am well and truly 'whupped.'"

"I know that feeling," he said. "I had to go meet Uncle Joe Stalin in Persia and it took me a couple of days to get back on my horse. I understand you traveled to the Philippines by B-29?"

"Yes, sir," I said. "Although it was a pretty spiffy B-29."

"Nothing like the one I've got, I'll betcha," he said. "Where's Commander Waring?"

Janet came down the stairs as if on cue. She'd changed into a summer dress and applied some minimal warpaint. A red-faced Secret Service guy followed her down the stairs. Must not have knocked. Truman stood up and greeted her.

"Mr. President," she said with a smile. "Welcome to my home. I'm guessing we're going to take a little trip, then?"

Truman grinned. "Smart and beautiful," he said. "I certainly hope so. And let me tell you two why. You know who General Marshall is, undoubtedly."

We both nodded. Who didn't?

"He has come to me with a plan for what to do with the so-called postwar world. Both Europe and East Asia are wrecked. Germany is flattened.

Angry, but flattened. Japan is, well, I'm not sure yet. China is engulfed in civil war. Russia has been bled dry but is frothing at the mouth with communism. South America is infested with escaping Nazis. India? Not even the Brits know what's happening there, although Churchill knows they're going to have to hand it over to the natives. America alone stands free and mostly undamaged. It's a brand-new world, and only America has the resources to reshape it. And the biggest stick Teddy Roosevelt could have ever wished for.

"General Marshall, genius that he is, proposes that we set the world back up on its feet. That we rebuild Germany, that we recognize all those former colonies who want to stand up their own nation-states, that we re-form the Japanese state into something that looks more like a parliamentary democracy than an imperial dictatorship, and that we pay very close attention to the rise of communism in Eastern Europe, China, and Russia."

"We rebuild Germany and Japan?" I said. "With American tax dollars? After we've spent—"

"Yes, yes, yes," he said. "It's a pretty heady proposal, I know. But I assume you're familiar with the terms of the armistice with Germany in 1919? And the unfortunate consequences of that?"

"Yes, sir," I said. "I am. I'm also familiar with that theory. But selling such an idea to the American people? While the bodies are still coming home? And every major newspaper predicting a massive recession once all those GIs come home when the wartime factories are shutting down nationwide?"

"That's why they pay me the big bucks, Captain. This is what presidents of the United States wake up to every morning. Understand?"

I apologized. "I'm sorry, sir. I didn't mean to challenge—"

"Yes, you did, but no offense taken. But the challenges, as you term them, are enormous. Worldshaking. We have to get it this right, this time. And surely you know why."

I remembered MacArthur's words. Next time, Armageddon. I nodded.

"If my soothsayers are right," he continued, "Russia, and possibly a communist China, with its millions and millions of people, will be the boogeymen of the future. Especially Russia. We're learning they've had spies in the Manhattan Project the entire time it existed. They stole every one of our atomic bomb secrets. If that's true, our A-bomb monopoly will soon be over. And that means that we will need allies in East Asia. Not the rice-paddy, mud-jungle countries of Southeast Asia, but the only real industrial society out there—the Japanese. The guys who introduced us to the aircraft carrier age of warfare. The guys who were right behind us with an atomic bomb, until you two played a big role in making me finally decide to use ours before they got a chance to use theirs. Thank you, both, and I mean that. Your role in that decision will probably never be publicly acknowledged, but take it from me, a grateful nation ought to thank you."

Janet said it before I could. "How can we help you, Mr. President?"

Truman looked over at me pointedly. I sighed and nodded my acquiescence.

"Okay, good," he said. "Here's what I need, and you two are perfectly suited to get it for me without my having to depend on bureaucrats who will be wondering if they'll have jobs in the near future. I need to know how bad it was in *Hiroshima* and *Nagasaki*, from someone who is familiar with military damage. And, more importantly, I need to know if the Japanese people might ever be willing, even after all that's happened to them, to become our ally in East Asia. Not necessarily to become like us and our form of democracy, but to see the world as we see it, and to join in our efforts to prevent anything like the war we just 'won' from ever happening again, precisely because of the existence of the atomic bomb. I'm not talking about you having discussions with what's left of the Japanese bureaucracy. Do the people of Japan realize what happened to them, and would they be willing to move into a new age where war is no longer possible?"

Wahoo, I thought. I needed time to absorb what he was asking, and

Harry Truman knew enough to wait patiently. I wished my brain had fully recovered from the last mission.

"I think I can give you an unvarnished report," I said, "on what happened to those cities and the people who lived there. But Commander Waring is the one who speaks the language and who lived there for long enough to absorb their culture. She's the one who will have to appraise your second question."

"Right," he said. "That's what I thought all along. That's why I came here tonight." He paused. "And to get out of my gilded cage in the White House, truth be told."

We all smiled.

"I know it's a lot to ask, but I—we—have this terrible feeling that we've evolved, without knowing it, from a war of ships and planes and armies to a different kind of war, overshadowed by a weapon whose widespread use can end mankind. We'll have squadrons of experts going to Japan. All kinds of experts, especially ambitious ones. But the two of you can bring me a perspective that no one else can, so, saying please here. Will you go?"

I looked at Janet and then we both nodded. As if we'd had any choice, I thought, irreverently. Truman's eyes gleamed. As if he'd had any doubts, I realized. I remembered Janet kept a bottle of Wild Turkey in the liquor-locker, so I offered Truman a drink. That got a big smile and so we spent the next half hour listening to him explain the impact of over a million young men coming home from the war. His grasp of the domestic economy and the banking system surprised me, but then I realized he'd been a US senator before becoming vice president under FDR, who himself had been no slouch when it came to those two topics. An aide came in finally from the front porch and gave the president the high sign. Janet thanked him for gracing her house with his presence. He thanked us both for agreeing to go on the mission and told us Admiral Leahy would be in touch shortly.

We sat there in the living room once he'd gone.

"So, how's about them apples?" I asked the air.

"It's funny," she said. "You see his pictures in the papers or on a news-reel, and he's not all that impressive. But in person he's definitely a pres-ence. Not like FDR, of course, but *I* wouldn't fool with him."

"Power does that," I observed. "And remember, FDR had many years to perfect that presence, even from a wheelchair. I still kinda wonder what the hell he *really* wants from us."

"I don't," she said, promptly. "Like he said, he'll have a hundred dif-ferent experts reporting back to him. But all of them will be dealing with the Japanese through interpreters or English-speaking Japanese bu-reaucrats. I, on the other hand, arrived there several years ago speaking Japanese at the *Tokyo* Imperial University level. Kinda analogous to peo-ple who 'come down' from Oxford and Cambridge with an accent that proclaims their special status. Then I had almost three years to absorb their culture, their manners, their oblique approach to difficult problems, especially social problems. The importance of 'saving face.' The etiquette of bowing. The iron-clad rules of deference. The rules for drinking. Their delight in playing subtle mind games, and a general agreement that men are all-important and women are lesser beings, unless you're talking about the bedroom. Then, women rule."

"Um—" I began, but she shook her head.

"*I* know all this stuff, but I have to tell you now that, if we're going to be dealing with Japanese men, we'll have to make it look like I'm your official lackey, and *you're* going to have to listen to my instructions while acting like you're some kind of visiting *daimyo,* or lord. And the higher the lord, the less he ever shows emotion of any kind. You're a big guy and that's going to help. You will have to be remote, aloof, impatient, and speak to me in short sentences while not looking at them—or me. They will take their cues from how *I* act around you; if I display total respect, maybe even a little fear, while practicing low-bowing deference, then that's how they'll act."

"Wow," I said. "I've heard the term *kabuki* when bureaucrats are talking about blowing smoke up someone's behind."

"Not a bad analogy," she said. "Here in America, we strive to make friends with people, even those on the opposite side of any issue, so we can get to direct, frank discussion as soon as possible—and solve the problem. Not so in Japan. Even if you and your opposite Japanese number understand the problem, whatever it is, you would both pretend that's not why you're sitting across the table from each other. The indirect approach, always. The last thing you want to do is cause the other guy to lose face. You make sure he always has a way out.

"The president wants to find out if their reaction to the atomic bombs precludes them from *ever* indulging in a cooperative effort. I think the smart ones, who are legion, will understand immediately that that is what we want to know—no, what *you,* the important guy in the room, want to know. But you can't allow yourself to get frustrated by their indirect approach, their seeming focus on tangential issues, maybe even their feigned indifference to what we're talking about. I think, from an intellectual point of view, you might even enjoy this."

I let out a deep breath. "I think I'm not qualified for all this subtlety and chess-playing," I said. "I almost wish we could reverse the roles. You be the important guy, me the lackey."

She smiled. "I will be the important guy," she said. "We'll both be role-playing. That's a reversal game the Japanese would truly appreciate. But: the problem is that we will be playing these cultural games amidst the carbonized ruins of a flattened city, where the dead will be considered the lucky ones, and where the survivors are just beginning to realize that there's some invisible death sentence coursing through their veins. Combine that with the numbing shock of having experienced, not just watched from afar, the Bomb. There's been enough time for them to absorb their losses of family, friends, and children, and experience the overwhelming sadness every time they look around, all framed by their national embarrassment for surrendering. They might talk to us, or they might erupt into fury and seek revenge."

I was still not convinced that we were the ones to make such an important appraisal. "He'll have his science experts," I pointed out. "His diplomats will eventually talk to their diplomats, our bankers to theirs—what do *we* bring to the table?"

"Our insignificance. In America the people matter. We have the vote. Piss off enough people, you'll get voted out of office. In Japan, the people have never mattered. But I think this damned A-bomb experience is going to change that. I think they're gonna look around at the incinerated remains of their cities and then ask the question: who brought all this on our heads? The emperor? Never! All those nobles, Prince this and Baron that? Those nasty generals and admirals pretending to be *samurai*? Because *we* ordinary people sure as hell didn't. I think one of the things Truman wants us to find out is whether or not they might be seeking, however politely or deferentially, a change in the way Japan works. I'll be talking to ordinary civilians, not government functionaries. I'm going to ask that question and maybe even plant some seeds."

I hadn't thought about the possibility that the survivors might see Americans and start whipping out swords. "We'll need some security, then, right?"

She thought about that for a long moment. "We'll need to work that out," she said, finally. "I have an idea of how to prevent that, but it's gonna be a reach. We'll definitely need MacArthur's help."

I was so impressed with her. I will be the important guy, she'd said. Why not? She was the one with all the answers. She was the one who understood the Japanese. And then I had an idea.

"You know," I said. "They really ought to send Van Rensselaer, not me. He looks the part, he'll tower over any Japanese, he's beyond smooth, he's—"

"A professional courtier is how they'd see him," she said. "He's too goddamned arrogant. No, I'll need a large man who scowls a lot and hardly ever speaks. I only wish I could put you in costume—headdress, robes, three swords, warpaint, and six brutes standing behind you, itching to kill someone. Trust me, they'll recognize you in an instant."

"I think I like your attitude," I said. "Let's get to bed. Although all this Oriental play-acting sounds a lot like too-hard."

She rose from her chair. "Remember what I said about the respective positions of men and women in Japan."

"Hunh?"

"Where's the one place I told you about where the roles reverse?"

I pretended to not remember, but the sexy grin spreading across her lovely face entirely blew my cover. Damn the woman.

TWENTY-SIX
BACK

For some reason I woke up at 0500 the next morning. Janet had called the ONI operations duty officer last night and told him that she would not be in today as she had to prepare for a trip to Japan. I myself had to tend to some logistics of my own, including trip preparations and going to at least see my house in the city. I also knew I needed to go make a call on Admiral King so that he knew about our new "mission" to Japan—and, of course, where those "orders" were coming from. I went downstairs and made coffee, feeling rested for the first time in the week since my return from the Far East, despite the Scotch from the night before. I was also thinking about a quick pre-work trip over to my gym, except I didn't have a car here. That brought up thoughts about having moved in, temporarily, of course, with Janet Waring. These were most definitely new waters I was sailing in, having been a "confirmed bachelor" for my entire Navy career. *Terra incognita,* as the old navigation charts used to put it. Or was it: dangerous ground?

The phone rang at 0630 and I let Janet answer it on the extension upstairs. I didn't want a repeat of the Van Rensselaer conversation yesterday. She came downstairs a few minutes later dressed in a bathrobe and poured herself a coffee.

"Tell me that wasn't Van Rensselaer," I said.

"Okay, I won't," she said. "But if it had been him, we'd be due for a meeting with Admiral Leahy at the EOB at ten this morning. He sounded—distant."

"Remember, he and I had a frank exchange of views yesterday, as the diplomats put it," I said. "He made a snide comment about me shacking up here, in your house. I told him to go fuck himself, or words to that effect, and hung up on him. That was after I told him I wasn't interested in another vacation trip to goddamned Japan."

"Ah," she said, remembering. "And for what it's worth, that would have been my response as well, Big Man. I'm delighted you chose my digs to go to ground in. For a variety of reasons."

She gave me a comical leer, slipped out of the bathrobe, and headed back upstairs, naked as a jaybird. A variety of reasons, the lady had said. I needed to think about this. All done, I announced to myself, and followed her upstairs at a great rate of knots, any trip to the gym long forgotten. There's stress relief and then there's stress relief.

We arrived at the EOB at 0930, courtesy of a Navy staff car that had shown up in her driveway. I'd half expected to see Van Rensselaer in the back seat, but no such luck. We were both in summer khakis, which is what I'd been wearing when I first crashed at Janet's house. Mine were a bit wrinkled, but nobody was looking at me when we went into Fleet Admiral Leahy's outer office. Janet, on the other hand, fairly radiated some definite "It" factor in that tight khaki skirt and those gleaming, brand-new silver oak leaves on her shirt.

Admiral William D. Leahy was an imposing figure with heavy black eyebrows and a stone face. Known throughout Washington as FDR's chief of staff, he was often touted discreetly as the second most powerful man in Washington, if not the world. He could speak for FDR, presumably after prior consultation with the president. But he'd been doing it for so long that it became obvious that he often didn't need to consult the president. When the five-star rank was created in 1944, FDR appointed Leahy as the first fleet admiral. One day later he appointed the others, Marshall, King, Nimitz, Eisenhower, and MacArthur, which had the effect of making Leahy senior to all the others.

With FDR gone, official Washington might wonder if Leahy would stay on. So far, he had, mostly because Truman recognized the value of having FDR's "flywheel" chief of staff working for him. Leahy had known all about the Manhattan Project from its inception, for instance; Harry Truman, even as vice president, had been kept in the dark. That had to have made an impression.

We got to the EOB and went upstairs. The fleet admiral did not have a personal staff, per se. No aides, executive assistants, or the usual gauntlet. Instead, the entire National Security Staff worked directly for him. He had a secretary, who showed us into the inner office. She'd told us before that the admiral did not invite visitors to sit down or have coffee. The protocol was that you stood before his desk, introduced yourself, spoke your piece if you had something to tell him—or answered his questions if that's why you'd been summoned—and then he'd nod and you'd leave. It's nothing personal or bad manners, she'd told us. It just keeps things moving smartly along. You are not the only visitors today, okay?

I looked at Janet, shrugged, and said yes. In we went. I suppressed an urge to click my heels like the Germans did once we'd approached his desk. He was working on something at that moment, so we stood there for about fifteen seconds before he looked up. I made the introductions, which elicited a brief nod. His most prominent feature was an outsize, chrome-dome head.

"The president wants the two of you to go to Japan," he began. "You'll go first to *Tokyo* and make your manners with Douglas MacArthur. Captain Van Rensselaer will be your point of contact at MacArthur's headquarters.

"Now then: the General will have been told that you are on a discreet, personal mission for the president and that it involves you going to the two A-bomb cities. He will want to know more, but you will courteously demur. He will then say something along the lines of: sorry, but I can't just let two American naval officers go gallivanting around Japan, especially in its current state of disrepair and, even more importantly, all the unknowns about the current physical conditions in *Hiroshima* and *Nagasaki*. Your answer to that will be, yes, sir, and that you will return to Washington and so inform the president. A few hours later you will have his authorization to go wherever you want to, along with a promise to provide whatever logistical support you might need.

"As to what the president wants from you, Captain Bowen: he wants private eyes and ears to appraise both the damage caused by the Bomb and what the Japanese people who were there when it went off feel about what's happened to them. Secondly, you, Commander Waring, are being asked to appraise how the Japanese might react to gaining a voice in their own government and also becoming an ally of the United States in the face of rising Soviet power and hostility and a vengeful China, based on your knowledge of Japan.

"There will be several issue-specific, formal, and publicly conducted government investigations, made up of experts, but those delegations will take time to investigate and then draft up reports via their bureaucratic chains of command. The president wants you back here in twenty days to report directly to him, to the best of your capabilities. You may talk to anybody, but try to avoid the remnants of the wartime Japanese government and military personnel. Initial reports indicate that military personnel are so ashamed at surrendering they won't come out of their houses."

He paused for a moment. I was hoping he wouldn't ask for questions. I had a million, but sensed that he had just told us all he knew about the president's wishes.

"Very well; thank you both and good luck." Then the nod and we got out of there. As I closed the door behind Janet, I saw that he was already on the phone. Then she had an idea.

"If Van Whatssit is already there, why don't we sit down with one of the Japan experts here, or maybe at State, and draft up a realistic itinerary, and from that what we'll need in the way of logistical support from the occupying forces office. Then get Leahy to transmit that to his lordship in *Tokyo*, as opposed to us starting from scratch upon arrival."

"Brilliant," I said. "Who do we talk to?"

Janet queried the secretary, who said she knew just the guy and he was right down the hall. I started laughing when I saw who it was: one Colonel Billy Peterson, US Army. He grinned sheepishly when we came into his office.

"I thought maybe Leavenworth," I said after we shook hands.

He said, no, not exactly. Are you familiar with the term *kabuki*? I told him I was a recent student of the political version.

"That's what the gym scene was all about," he said, as we got some coffee and sat down at a small conference table. "And the subsequent warnings at HQ. Don't snoop, or you might disappear like Colonel Peterson. No one said it, but the message was pretty clear."

"Your better half was pretty convincing," I said.

He nodded. "She knew," he said. "But the kids and neighbors didn't. I came over here to the EOB to work originally for Van Rensselaer, then the National Security Council at large. Japan country expert, with a specialty in their industrial production capabilities."

"Can you speak Japanese?" Janet asked.

He shook his head. "I've taken some lessons at the language school over in Roslyn, but I'm just no damn good at foreign languages and accents. I can read it fairly well if it's in Roman, but every time I tried to speak, the language tutor would start to cry."

Janet laughed.

"How can I help you guys?" Peterson asked, glancing at his watch. We spent the next twenty minutes describing our recent taskings since being pulled into Van Rensselaer's orbit. We could speak about the project now that the Bombs had become sensational news around the world. Then the specific question about how we'd accomplish our new mission and what support to ask for from MacArthur's staff.

He thought about that for a long moment. "You'll probably enter Japan at *Haneda* air base, just outside *Tokyo*. MacArthur and his staff are billeted in an undamaged insurance company's downtown headquarters building near the palace and the diplomatic quarter. The imperial palace district was off limits for the B-29s, which is not to say some stray bombs didn't find their way there. The rest of the city is a wreck, especially after the firestorm in October of last year. Your problem will be that all the normal in-country travel modalities are also wrecked. Trains. Interdistrict bus lines. Highways. Interisland shipping. Bridges.

"One of MacArthur's first requests was for a thousand Army trucks. Repair and rail-laying trains from Union Pacific. We now have a continuing stream of passenger-cargo ships coming from West Coast ports to *Tokyo* and points south. They unload food, medical supplies and personnel, bulldozers, tents—stuff like that. Then they go to Guam or the Philippines to pick up troops for repatriation, precedence being given to ex-POWs. It's a massive effort."

"Well, it's not for an invasion, though," Janet said. "That has to be a good thing."

"Pretty good imitation of one," Peterson said. "The Japanese are astounded at how fast we brought in what we—and they—needed. We don't tell them it was all pre-staged on the West Coast for Operation Olympic—the invasion. Now there's a central logistical office at MacArthur's headquarters, trying to coordinate the world's biggest food fair. They're the guys who will provide you a means of traveling within Japan, and within the two forbidden zones."

"Forbidden?" Janet asked. "Radiation?"

"Fundamentally, yes," Billy replied. "Lot of confusion on that subject right now. One bunch of scientists say that since the Bombs went off high up, there should be very little residual radiation on the ground. Another camp says no one will be able to go into those two cities for a thousand years. MacArthur's people are playing it safe right now until experts on the ground can settle it."

"That's a huge difference," Janet said.

"Yeah, well, Los Alamos is saying that the confusion is being caused by the Trinity test. That bomb was relatively close to the ground, as compared to a B-29 dropping from tactical altitude, and, yes, that site is terribly hot. And there's radioactive materials that went walkabout after the blast. Indian reservations downwind are turning up a lot of sick people. But there's also some pretty horrifying numbers coming out from the Japanese. Somewhere near seventy-five thousand were killed outright when the Bomb went off in *Hiroshima* from blast and radiation. Some of our medical scientists are predicting three to four times that number once the radiation sickness comes into proper focus. Big politics in that issue, as you might imagine."

"We've been tasked to go to both *Hiroshima* and *Nagasaki*," I said.

"Lucky you," Billy said. "Our medical world is still trying to figure out how to do that safely, if that's even possible. Fortunately, the big medical effort is taking place beyond the city limits and not down near ground zero."

"Why is that?" Janet asked.

"Because that's where the people who 'survived' the initial blast went. There are only a few people left alive in those two cities. The survivors who could, fled. What's left is thousands of dead or grievously ill people. It's a hideous mess, when there's no wind. And when there is wind, whole precincts downwind get dosed."

We sat there, trying to absorb everything he'd been saying. He gave us a moment.

"Look," he said. "I'll gen up a list of what you'll need to get from *Tokyo* down to *Hiroshima*, and from there to *Nagasaki*. I'll include a place to stay in *Tokyo*. There are US Navy ships in *Hiroshima* harbor, probably down closer to *Kure*. I suspect there are some near *Nagasaki*, too. That's where you'll stay, aboard US Navy ships. Then you'll need transportation into or at least as near the cities as you can safely get. Lots of unknowns in both target areas, none of them good. Now: who speaks Japanese?"

Janet explained her qualifications. He brightened at that. "Great," he said. "Try to downplay all that when you're around American authorities. They'll shanghai you in a heartbeat. Just communicating with the Japanese is a *huge* problem."

"From what we've been told," I said, "neither MacArthur nor Van Rensselaer are going to be happy when we show up."

"Have no fear," he said with a grin. "I'll prep the message in Leahy-speak. No one fucks with him. No one."

This was all good, I thought. Except, the Japanese army and navy had perpetrated war crimes and barbarous behavior throughout Asia. China. Korea. Java. Singapore. Malaysia. Indonesia. Thailand. Guadalcanal. Borneo. The Philippines. The list was sadly long. A humanitarian effort in all those conquered places made sense. But, in my opinion, we ought to leave the Japanese islands to experience a few years of societal die-off for what they had done. Instead, it looked like we were now going all out to raise them from the ruins of their own making. I wasn't comfortable with that. I'd faced their torpedoes and guns at sea.

"How should *I* act?" I asked, remembering Janet's plan. The *daimyo*. The fearsome, American giant. Aloof. Impatient. Imperious. Silent. Capable of—what?

"What do *you* think?" Billy asked Janet. "You know their culture, their language. I don't. I'm a number cruncher. I think the Japanese will look to the captain here, not you, which means they'll never see you coming."

She laughed at that and then asked me to stand up.

I did. Billy was fit and strong. I was also fit and strong, but much bigger than he was. He got the point immediately.

"If we dress him up right," she said, "I think he'll intimidate *any* Japanese he meets. That's when I, the oh-so-subservient woman assistant, the lowly interpreter, will begin probing."

"Why would they be the least bit interested in becoming our ally?" Billy asked.

"Because the captain here," she replied, "will make some deliberately ambiguous pronouncements about the atomic bomb, Russia, and the rise of communism right next door. If there's anything the Japanese respect, it's raw power. We'll be talking to small fry, but trust me, word of these encounters will get back to whoever's left in the Japanese bureaucratic aristocracy, assuming they survive the war crimes tribunals. Plus, they're gonna be invaded after all, by legions of American expert delegations, showboating politicians, and sneaky diplomats."

Billy nodded. "I get it," he said. "Give me a day to draft up your requirements." He paused for a second, then grinned. "I'd love to see Van Rensselaer's face when he receives the message."

"Not popular here in the EOB?" I asked.

Billy became serious. "He had an impossible job, considering the scale of the Manhattan Project. I think he pulled off his part of it. I personally resented his imperious manner, and I'm not alone in that. Besides, guys who have a 'van' or a 'von' in front of their names tend to raise American hackles, you know?"

TWENTY-SEVEN
NEW WAYS

For all the war years the word "*Tokyo*" had represented the place where the horrors of the Pacific war originated. I'd never formed a picture in my mind of the actual city until late in the war, when I saw the newsreel pictures taken through Norden bombsights as the B-29s plastered the fuzzy streets and blocks two miles below with bright bomb flashes and clouds of smoke. The smoke and fires were all gone as we descended over *Tokyo* Bay in our DC-3 transport, but there were swaths of utter destruction clearly visible. Nothing left but the veinlike canal networks surrounding blackened squares, the same canals into which terrified Japanese had plunged during the firestorms, only to be boiled alive five minutes later. As we flew over the city center, we could see much less due to the smoggy haze hovering over the city. Even Mount *Fuji*, normally a prominent feature visible from *Tokyo*, was invisible.

Haneda airport had no passenger terminal. We were told to stay in our seats as the plane taxied noisily down to one end of the field where there were American vehicles and planes parked around a complex of large

US Army tents. I hadn't seen those since Guadalcanal. An American flag hung limply in the still air on a temporary flagpole. A few hundred yards away several US Army trucks were being loaded. They were lined up in a road convoy formation, with a couple of armored personnel carriers at each end of the convoy. We were both extremely tired, having endured the by now familiar (to me, anyway) endless slog across thousands of miles of Pacific Ocean.

The plan was for us to go downtown to MacArthur's headquarters, where we expected to be assigned rooms in one of the expropriated hotels in the embassy district. We'd stay there for two days and nights, and only then go see Van Rensselaer and possibly the General at the headquarters building. Apparently, headquarters had learned there was no point in even talking to arriving visitors from the States until they'd had two days to recuperate from the ordeal of a trans-Pacific crossing.

There was a Navy lieutenant waiting for us when we debarked from the DC-3. He introduced himself and I immediately forgot his name. He had a staff car waiting nearby, and we were soon on our way toward the city center. The roads were in tolerably good shape but only because there were mounds of burned debris on either side, looking like black snow after a big storm. Some of the suburban areas we went through were thoroughly demolished, with no people or even animals in sight. And no trees, either. The silence as we drove along with the windows open was disturbing. There were no people out on the streets and almost zero vehicle traffic. It was as if the entire area was still stunned from what had happened, and the population—the surviving population, I reminded myself—was probably still in hiding. I turned to Janet to say something but she was asleep. Smart girl. I asked the lieutenant, who was driving, how the Japanese were acting around Americans.

"When we first got here there were people out along the roads and streets," he said. "Women mostly, some children, the occasional older male. As our convoy drove into the city center, toward the imperial palace, they all turned their backs as the convoy drew abreast. We thought they were being hostile, but later found out that they were so ashamed that Japan had surrendered they turned their backs so we wouldn't have to see their shameful faces. That's how different things are here."

"Are they lurking around, trying to kill Americans?"

"Not at all, and our new chief of staff, who's something of an Asian specialist, told us why. The Japanese army headquarters staff was totally against surrender. They wanted a fight to the death for all Japanese. It was the emperor who saw the light, presumably after the A-bombs. He was the one who sent the surrender message, not the military government, and he also got on the national radio, for the first time ever, and told the people of Japan to basically knock it off—it was his imperial will that the war was over."

"Yeah, and?"

"To the Japanese, that meant that they were no longer allowed to *do* anything to harm the occupying Americans when they came ashore. That order was coming directly from a god. And, that's pretty much what's happened. They've been cooperative. They do what we tell them to do. It hasn't hurt that each day of the occupation brings in more food, medicine, and other stuff. We're sure there's some die-hard *bushido* types out there, but, perversely, their friends and neighbors are telling these guys, well, if that's how you feel, you have a perfectly honorable and traditional way to solve your dilemma."

"You mean suicide."

"Yes, sir. You know the US Marines have this motto: death before dishonor. That shit originated right here in Japan."

Amazing, I thought. But it had to be true. It was good to know that once we left the capital and went to the two cities that there wouldn't be hostile crowds wanting to kill us both.

"One more question," I said. "We're going to *Hiroshima* and *Nagasaki*. That deal still hold in those cities?"

He hesitated. "Sir, I can't guarantee that. Supposedly, more people got killed here by the firestorms in the *Tokyo* region than did down there. But we're hearing strange shit. Our battalion commander went down there. He came back saying the survivors had this awful look about them. Living dead, he called them. They've seen something so bad that they're not entirely there anymore. I'll tell you this—there are more US security troops around *Hiroshima* and *Nagasaki* than there are here in the capital region. One major who was down there with the CO said he couldn't tell who was more scared—our security troops or the Japanese who'd lived through it."

"And the cities? What did they say about the cities?"

"Gone, Captain," he said, grimly. "Just fucking gone, excuse my French."

We were met downtown by a Navy commander, who immediately took us over to a nearby hotel. He gave us a written guide for new American arrivals in occupied Japan. We were each assigned a room on the second floor and were given printed English instructions regarding the hotel's baths, bar, restaurant, and curfew regulations. There was a scary paragraph about what to do in case of an earthquake, which were not uncommon. I had taken precautions when packing to include a bottle of good Scotch deep in my sea bag, which seemed to have survived the trip. I made sure by fixing a drink as soon as I got to my room. Janet's room was right next door. I looked for a connecting door; no such luck.

The room was small, maybe ten feet by fifteen. There was a single window, but no glass. Instead, there was a parchment roll that could be pulled down for privacy. The bed was practically down on the floor, with a standing lamp on either side of the bed. The room was neither heated nor air-conditioned. The rooms had bathrooms containing a toilet fixture, but not showers or bathtubs as Western hotels did. There were towels but no soap. If you wanted to wash away a trans-Pacific odyssey, you went down into the basement to the baths. You walked to the stairway wearing a thin, mid-thigh-length robe and sandal-style slippers. Everywhere you went in the hotel there were people in sight, mostly elderly women—outside your room, in the hallways, the stairwells— whose mission was to give you directions, attend to service requests, or even escort you to different areas in the hotel.

The baths were interesting. Once there you first took a hot shower and then were escorted by tiny Japanese matrons to the actual hot bath and shown how to get in. There was no soap provided in the shower, and no clothing, slippers, or towels were ever allowed in the hot bath area. The water was more than hot, and the headquarters instructions pamphlet said to stay no more than three minutes until you had become accustomed to using Japanese baths. It took me almost three minutes to fully submerge and when I got back out a few minutes later, the steamy atmosphere of the room felt a little chilly. More escorts as I went back up to my room, where the door was being held open for me when I arrived.

After lots of bowing, I got to be alone in my room. I looked for a room phone, but there wasn't one. If you wanted to communicate with, say, the front desk or another room, you stuck your head out the door and sent one of the ubiquitous women off with your requirements. I'd wanted to call Janet, but gave it up. I was pretty sure she was long asleep. Relaxed after the hot bath, I gingerly got into the bed, and was gone in sixty seconds.

I slept into the late morning. As soon as I started making noises in the room, there was some tentative tapping on the door and then two maids scuttled in to open the window shades and bring a tray of tea and the smallest biscuits I'd ever seen. I was standing there in my skivvies but, after lots of bowing, they still made no eye contact. Apparently, they were supposed to be invisible, and you, the guest, were supposed to behave as if they were. Okay, I thought. I was hungry by then and wondering if the dining room was open. I got dressed in wash khakis and headed downstairs, accompanied by much twittering along the hallway. I approached the desk and was given a sealed envelope. I took a seat in the lobby. The note was from headquarters, which explained that I needed to tell the front desk to call them whenever I woke up. They would then send a car that would take me to the American Embassy, where there'd be food.

Idiot, I thought. Of course there wouldn't be food or drink in the hotel. The whole damned city was on the verge of starvation, with many thousands of people being kept alive by generous deliveries of staples from the dreaded Occupying Power. As if to emphasize that fact, a convoy of US Army canvas-backed trucks came rumbling down the street out in front, led by an armored personnel carrier and then a jeep with an Army driver, an American officer in the back seat, and a Japanese civilian up front.

One of the front desk ladies came to tell me in halting English that a car was en route. Where's Janet? I wondered, but then she came down from upstairs, looking much refreshed. She sat down next to me and said something in rapid-fire Japanese to the air, which resulted in more tea and some kind of tiny cakes. The Japanese staff was extremely deferential to her, but I noticed they wouldn't even look directly at me.

"They don't dare," she explained after we'd had some tea. "Your sheer size has them in awe. I'm starving."

"Me, too, but there's no food here. I guess we have to go to the embassy to get a meal. You okay?"

She said yes, still tired but much better than yesterday. I told her about going to the baths and she groaned. "I would love to do that," she said. "But I just collapsed on that bed and that was that."

"There seem to be a lot of rules about the baths," I said. "And maybe we can get some soap at the embassy?"

She smiled. "You're about to find out just how alien this country is compared to the West," she said. "Etiquette is everything. So, the best thing for you to do is to maintain an aloof silence, oh *Daimyo*, which is what they expect. Get yourself in character. That way they'll know how to behave. Imperious, powerful, man of few words, and curt when talking to me. Don't ask—demand. I'll do my bit."

"Well," I said. "Being a mere woman, you must know your place."

She stifled a grin, but managed a swift kick to my left ankle nonetheless. Then I had to smother a grin. I was suddenly glad she was there. I said so in a low voice.

"None of that, superior male species," she said through clenched lips. "Remember—*kabuki* is the term of art."

I muttered a small profanity. I'd looked up the word back in the States. There were many meanings.

Then an Army corporal came into the lobby. Our car was ready. I stood up and smoothed down my uniform. When I looked up, every Japanese in the lobby was bowing.

Daimyo, I thought. I glared at everybody, which they seemed to expect. Janet gave me the high sign: go to the damned car, please. I took a deep breath to swell my chest, and then tromped to the front doors. Nobody in the entire lobby moved until I went through the door. Damn!

TWENTY-EIGHT
EL SUPREMO

Meeting General MacArthur was a treat. He was extremely courteous and yet, in person, he was bigger than life. "Everybody" knew that he was imperious, vain, often irascible, demanding, and impatient. We saw none of that during our five-minute courtesy call. He gave us a small lecture on what he was trying to accomplish here in occupied Japan. "My job is to work myself out of this job," he said, "and leave behind the foundations for a democratic-style government on its way to becoming an important player among the other industrialized nations. I tell every American not to do or say anything to screw that up while they're here. Given our cultural differences and the atomic bombs, this will be no walk in the park, for either of us. Before you go back to Washington, I'd appreciate a debrief."

That was it. I promised we would see him before we left. There were no questions about why we were there or what we'd be doing. He either already knew or was pretending that he did. Admiral Leahy had probably told him that we were on a private mission for the president, and, since that came from Leahy, that was enough for MacArthur and every-body who worked for him. One of his aides took us to Van Rensselaer's office. We had to wait for about five minutes before being ushered in. I told Janet that he was making sure we understood that he was much more important than we were. She just rolled her eyes. The aide reap-peared, gesturing for us to go in.

Van Rensselaer acted like nothing had happened between us. He handed each of us an itinerary for our trip to the two cities, a set of cre-dentials in both English and *kanji* Japanese, a radiation counter similar to what we'd worn at Los Alamos, a one-page letter signed and sealed by MacArthur himself, requesting every American command in Japa-nese territory to render all aid and assistance to the bearer, and, finally, a two-page directory of the Occupying Authority staff showing who was responsible for what throughout Japan. There were no phone numbers because none of the nation's phone systems worked.

"There are six delegations expected to arrive from the States and the UK within the next ten days," he said, "to carry out medical and technical research at the bombing sites. Concurrently, American hospital ships will arrive at both *Hiroshima* and *Nagasaki* to provide aid for the indigenous population and medical services for any American organizations conduct-ing postwar research. If you begin to feel sick, your credentials and that letter will get you priority medical attention. At the moment both cities are sealed off from entry; people trying to leave the cities are given a brief medical exam and then allowed to leave if they pose no danger to others. Pay attention to your OSL radiation recorders—if you experience a spike, report in to the military police compound immediately. They'll get you to the hospital ship for further treatment. Understand that we don't *know* what the radiation situation is in those cities. Lots of theories, but, so far, not much actual data. Except that a lot of people are dying, weeks after the Bomb.

"Finally, I propose to send an Army officer with you on your—excursion. His job will be to keep our headquarters here informed as to where you go, to whom you talk, and any conclusions you reach attending to your tasking from the White House. You'll find him useful if you run into problems, and the General feels that he needs to know what you're doing here and whether or not you turn over some interesting rocks."

I felt Janet beginning to bristle but I quickly intervened. "Good," I said. "We're all venturing into *terra incognita*. The General's need to know is perfectly reasonable."

He seemed to relax. I think he'd expected a hell, no reaction from me, but in fact, it did make perfect sense. We could report to the president as we liked, but the General needed to keep his fingers on the pulse of Japan, especially if there were signs of an incipient popular revolt against the emperor's embarrassing surrender. MacArthur was nothing if not a superb bureaucrat.

"When do you want to leave?" he asked. "We normally give people two days, but if you're ready to proceed, we can have you on an airplane tomorrow morning."

I looked at Janet, who nodded. "Tomorrow morning will be fine," I said. I paused for a moment. "What happens to the Manhattan Project now that we've revealed the Bomb to the entire world?" I asked.

It was his turn to pause, as if thinking about what he was allowed to say. The habit of extreme security died hard. "It changes gears," he said. "We have working designs and now we need to build inventory. That's a very different effort. And, for what it's worth, some of the senior scientists think there's a way to make a much, much bigger bomb. Something they're calling a *hydrogen* bomb. A hundred times more powerful than Fat Man and Little Boy. It remains an open question."

I nodded. The American way. Does that thing work? Yup. Can you make it bigger and more powerful?

"Neither one of us looks forward to going into these cities," I said. "President Truman came to Janet's house to convince us to take on the mission."

His eyebrows rose. "Did he indeed," he mused. Then he sighed. "I think this whole thing—atomic weapons—is the most terrible genie to ever have been coaxed out of its bottle. It did its job convincing the Japanese emperor to just outright quit. But now what? I think the next war could wipe out everyone on earth. I hope I'm wrong."

"How long will you be here in Japan?" Janet asked.

"Not much longer," he said. "I haven't had leave for three years. I'm weary. I have a home on the Hudson, which I think will be a perfect place to erase the past three years from my mind. I'm going to retire, I think. How about you two?"

That question caught us off guard. We'd been growing closer and closer during the time with each other back in the States, but we were both taking it one day at a time. I was at a sudden loss for words. Van Rensselaer grinned. "I believe the term of art was screw you," he chuckled. I think I blushed. Janet was busy staring at her shoes.

"Look," he said. "The war's over. You'll probably make flag after what you've done. Or put your papers in and run off into the sunset with the lovely commander here. Anyway, enough personal intrusion. You're all set for your, um, visit. I must warn you; it'll be the most unpleasant thing you will ever, ever do."

TWENTY-NINE
GONE

V an Rensselaer's words at the end of that suddenly awkward meeting didn't begin to cover what we saw when we were driven into the remains of *Hiroshima*. Janet actually wept. She'd spent months here a long time ago when it had been a beautiful seaside town. Now, I was reminded of those glassy desert sands at Alamogordo. The city was bathed in a strange ambient light, as if a stunned atmosphere was still trying to recover. There were a thousand still-smoldering piles of God knows what lining each street as the car took us through at a crawl. Streetlamps looked like blackened candles that had melted down to their bases. Our escort told us there had been thousands and thousands of people abroad in the streets when what the Japanese were calling the second sun had bloomed in the early morning sky over *Hiroshima*. The stench of death was still discernible even though weeks had passed. A narrow river ran through the center of town and two bridges formed a T intersection at one point. Our escort said that if you got out and walked over the junction of those two bridges you could see the silhouettes of humans burned into the concrete pavement. Everywhere we looked, we saw small clumps of carbon and tiny pieces of scorched rags on the sidewalks and in the blackened doorways. No small birds, or any other animals.

There were no able-bodied people visible, either. We'd seen small clumps of tattered Japanese queuing for food and medical help on the outskirts of the city, but that was it. The only buildings still standing were the ones that had been made of reinforced concrete, and they were burned-out shells. Their rectangular windows had blackened edges framed in stalactites of molten glass that had dripped down the walls. There were smoldering windrows of carbonized trees piled up against the hillsides and the concrete walls of some of the buildings. What few automobiles we saw were burned out and mostly upside down on the sidewalks. We had our windows rolled up tight to keep any radioactive dust and the pervasive smell of death out of the car, but the silence outside was almost tangible. There was something wrong with the sky.

Out in the river there were several long, black sandbars made up of wreckage. Scores of offshore seagulls covered most of them as they searched for food. I didn't want to think about what they were scavenging, or what would happen to the birds after their foray into the city. Our escort said the Japanese had pushed hundreds if not thousands of unrecognizable human remains into the river after the bombing. This part of the river was tidal, which meant that twice a day there was a flush of human and other sad detritus out into the bay.

Up on the side of one low hill was a large complex of buildings that our escort told us had been a hospital, which for some reason didn't seem too badly damaged. But since hundreds of walking wounded had gone there after the blast, carrying particulate radiation with them, the buildings were now badly contaminated and the hospital unusable. The car took us by the ruins of *Hiroshima* Castle, from which the ancient *daimyos* had ruled. I'd seen pictures of it, but it was now unrecognizable. We then went down to the waterfront, where there had been shipyards, dry docks, and other naval facilities. The buildings there were made of steel, so they had pretty much survived, but it was clear that any people had not. There were large mounds of dirt and sand on the approach streets that our escort said were mass graves. Then he looked at his watch.

"Time's up," he announced. We'd been in the city for about forty-five minutes, which was the maximum time allowed due to the uncertainty about the residual radiation. We looked at our OSLs and saw that, yes, the readings had moved from where we'd started our tour. Even inside a steel staff car with the windows shut, we'd accumulated some radiation. It was probably nowhere near enough to be a lethal dose, but it was substantially more than our OSLs had recorded at the Trinity test.

We were driven down to a landing in the harbor, where a Navy launch was waiting. Janet and I were then taken out into the harbor to an American destroyer anchored three miles offshore. As our launch approached the ship, I was struck at how bad she looked. She was a Gearing class, three twin-barreled five-inch guns, torpedo tubes, lots of AA guns, and two radars, one surface, one air-search. She was weather worn, rust-streaked, her side paint faded, and there was clear evidence of field-repaired battle damage. I told Janet that she was obviously a veteran of the *Okinawa* campaign, where destroyers had paid a heavy and bloody price to unceasing suicide attacks.

The ship's captain met us at the top of the accommodation ladder and welcomed us aboard. He was distressingly thin and I couldn't guess his age. The crew as we passed through the ship looked pretty much the same—prematurely aged nineteen-year-olds with bags under their eyes and taut faces. *Okinawa*, I thought. Definitely *Okinawa*. The ships off *Okinawa* had lost more men than the combined army and marine divisions ashore, courtesy of the dreaded *kamikaze* squadrons. The captain told us that I'd be berthed in the unit commander's cabin, and Janet in his inport cabin. He'd moved up to his sea cabin. We had a late lunch in the UC cabin, where we had a chance to talk. I asked him why there were destroyers in the *Hiroshima* harbor.

"It's over," he said, wearily. "But the word 'Japan' is synonymous with 'treachery,' so there are destroyers and cruisers in every major port. There's a carrier offshore providing CAP stations along the entire coast."

"Any signs of trouble?" Janet asked.

"No," he said. "It's been totally quiet. My XO keeps saying that it's the kinda quiet before a hundred Comanche come over the ridge, whooping and screaming. I keep Combat and two gun-mounts fully manned and ready at all times."

"Wow," I said.

"It's a little scary here, Captain," he continued. "There's no activity. No fishing boats at sea. No lights ashore. Nothing moving in the city. No radio intercepts. No planes. No ships. No people, as far as we can see on the big eyes. A strange glow that shows up after dark up in the hills above the city. And that's not the worst of it."

"What is?" Janet asked.

"Every tide that comes out of those three river channels over there brings out so many bodies that we have to set Circle William in the ship and get the entire crew inside the house because of the stench. I'm talking hundreds, if not thousands. It's like the city is flushing all its cemeteries at once. And dead animals, too. Dead fish, horses, mules, cattle, small birds, and even seagulls. Whatever they're scavenging now is probably killing them."

"Radiation," Janet said.

"So we're being told," he said. "We pay close attention to the relative wind. If it gets upwind of us, we button up."

"This food is pretty damned good," I said. "How's that possible?"

"We get resupply ships weekly," he said. "Reefers, oilers, mostly. We're doing okay. They told us to take nothing from the city. Is this radiation stuff true?"

I told him that the occupying forces weren't sure, so they were being careful about stay-time in the city itself. He asked if I knew what an atomic bomb was, how it worked, and why the city couldn't recover.

Janet took that moment to declare she was exhausted and retired to the captain's cabin across the passageway. I asked the CO if he had any whiskey. He grinned and said hell, yes. So for the next hour I told him all about the Manhattan Project and what an atomic bomb was all about.

He'd become so absorbed that he failed to finish his whiskey. I didn't have that problem. I was drinking more and enjoying it more, as the saying went. When I was finished, he asked what we two were doing here. I explained that to him as well, along with who'd sent us.

He could only shake his head. "We beat the bastards," he said. "I still want them all to die, and if anyone told me to, I'd empty my magazines into the countryside. We lost—"

He stopped, overtaken by emotions forged in too many gunfights against crazed Japanese pilots slamming bomb-laden aircraft into the picket destroyers off *Okinawa*, killing and maiming Americans by the hundreds.

"I understand," I said. "I was a tin can CO and then a cruiser CO, from Guadalcanal through Bougainville. But this new bomb has changed the equation forever. Believe it or not, we're gonna need the Japanese as allies in the Far East one day. China's going communist. The Russians will soon have the Bomb—their spies stole it from us. We either convince Japan that we're their only hope to maintain their civilization and identity out here in Asia, or they'll disappear."

"What's wrong with that?" he asked. "Good riddance, I mean. Jesus *Christ!*"

"Because that will leave the western Pacific to the bad guys, and, eventually, they'll head east to take what we've got. It's better that they get stopped out here, with allies, than along the West Coast, don't you think?"

He shook his head. "Dead," he said. "That's what I want. All of them *dead*. For what they did. For all the men, women, and children they slaughtered. Americans, Chinese, Koreans, British, Indonesians, Guamanians, Malayans, Filipinos, every POW they captured, everywhere they goddamn went. I want them all dead, burned, buried, and forgotten. Ask anyone aboard. I've got lookouts posted all day, hoping and praying for some deranged bastard to shoot at us so I can unload with five-inch."

Man, I thought. This alliance effort is going to be really hard these next few years.

I told him as gently as I could that I was tired, and that we'd need to go back ashore first thing in the morning. He nodded, sighed, and apologized for lashing out. I said I understood completely, and that I'd stood over too many burials at sea in the first three years of the war.

"Haven't we all," he muttered.

"Except, when the president of the United States comes to your house and asks you to go to Japan, and then explains why it's important that we convert the Japanese from dire enemies to allies, that's called the Big Picture. The one way above your pay grade and mine. So, no shooting, okay?"

He just stared at me for a moment, as if he couldn't grasp what I was saying. Then he nodded. "Yes, sir," he said. "Anything you need."

"Thanks, Captain," I said. "Good night. And I apologize for sounding soft on the Japanese. I feel like you do. But feelings are no longer the currency of the realm."

After he left, I thought about going down the passageway to the in-port cabin. But this was a small ship. Senior officers moving about on a destroyer could never do so without somebody noticing. Fact of life. It was still early, but I decided to turn in. I had no idea how we were going to fulfill our mission tomorrow. I hoped that Janet did.

THIRTY

THE GROUND TRUTH

I slept well. The long familiar motion of a warship at sea, with all its night sounds: bells for the time, the sounds of the watch-change on the bridge right next door, the howl of the forced draft blowers spooling up to blow tubes after midnight—those were comforting sounds. Everything was as it should be. It was when the blowers suddenly wound down, or there was a rush of bitch-box communications, that you knew something had gone off the tracks. It wasn't my ship, but I was programmed after years of command at sea to hear it. Warships never slept; a third or a fourth of the crew were always awake and on watch, creating a deeply familiar susurration of footsteps, hatches closing, muted voices and commands, the humming sounds from the boiler rooms, the slap of a seaway against the hull were a captain's lullaby. It's when something changed, like a sudden spooling up of the blowers, that you sat up in your rack and looked for your sea boots as the phone began to ring, as you knew it would.

You, sir, are so far out of your depth, I kept reminding myself. I dreamed that night of the Trinity test, re-experiencing the brain-searing flash and then that fiery, mile-wide, bellowing incubus blazing into the dawn air as it devoured the air and the very ground from which it had sprung. Along with images from *Hiroshima*. I suddenly realized what was so different about that city—everything was in black and white. There was no color, anywhere. Color implied life. There was nothing left alive in that cremated city. Not even insects.

Janet arrived in the unit commander's cabin the next morning a half hour after reveille, followed by a steward with coffee and some cinnamon rolls. She was dressed in the WAVE version of working khaki—slacks and a short-sleeved blouse. She looked refreshed if a little hollow-eyed, as if perhaps she had entertained some of the same dreams I had. The captain checked in a few minutes later, informing us that breakfast would be brought up in a half hour. He had an interesting question for us.

"The whole crew wants to know who you are, Captain," he said. "And why you're here. What can I tell them?"

Janet saw my hesitation and stepped in. "*We* work directly for the president," she replied. "I speak fluent Japanese. We're here to assess the impact of the atomic bomb on regular Japanese citizens. Not public officials or the military leaders, but regular civilians, people who lived and worked here. And who lost friends and relatives here."

"I would think that's something that could just be assumed," the captain said.

"You don't know the Japanese as I do," she replied. "The A-bomb represents power at an insurmountable level. The Japanese respect power. If someone A-bombed an American city, Americans would hate them until the end of time. The Japanese are different. I think they'll absorb what happened here and in *Nagasaki* and say: let's not mess with these people *ever* again. In fact, if they'll have us, let's join them as allies, if only so they'll *never* come do this to us again."

The captain was at a loss for words. Janet let him off the hook.

"We could be wrong about that, of course," she said. "This bomb changes everything about warfare and that's why the captain and I are here. To test those waters. To see if the usual Japanese pragmatism re-asserts itself—or not. It's an important question."

The captain started to say something but then decided not to. He simply nodded and then backed out of the cabin, probably thinking we were nuts.

The boat ride back to the dockyard complex was medium horrible. The rivers were cleansing themselves again and the atmosphere just offshore was nauseating. The bosun driving the launch kindly gave us handkerchiefs anointed with diesel oil. I kept my eyes in the boat for the whole trip, trying to ignore the heavier thumps as the boat made its way through the mess streaming out to sea. We were met at the dockyard by an Army colonel in full formal greens with medical insignia who told us he was taking us to the site of the biggest hospital in *Hiroshima*, where there were hundreds of people awaiting medical treatment. He explained as we made our way carefully across the atomic wasteland that the top two stories of the hospital were gone, but the bottom half had been shielded from the direct blast wave by a ridge between the building and the city center.

"Even so, the hospital is contaminated," he said. "So we've brought in tents for the docs to work in. They're making the sickest patients take showers and dispose of clothing before they approach the treatment tents. They're handing out chemical suits to the most contaminated people. We have a couple DC-3s coming in later today with supplies, but the scene is pretty depressing."

"Burns?" Janet asked.

"Yes, burns, contusions, concussions, and undefined internal injuries. A lot of hemorrhaging from just about every human orifice. Blindness is common. The victims' hair is falling out in clumps. The lines are long, but the people are patient and orderly. Some of them have relatives helping them. As I walk toward the treatment tents, all I can see are trembling arms reaching out to me for help. It's all I can do not to look at them."

"We want to talk to some of them," Janet said.

The colonel shook his head vigorously. He paused, taking a deep breath before speaking. "They're mostly walking dead," he said finally. "And I'd guess they know it. The Japanese docs know it, but they do their best. Some of the victims die in the waiting line. The kids go first, of course. You'll see a lot of small, covered bundles behind the benches. The docs have organized some people to walk the lines and recover the dead. I don't know where they're taking them. But they're busy, I'll tell you that."

I watched the colonel's face up there in the right front seat. He was trying mightily to display the professionally emotionless visage of an infantry commander hearing the butcher's bill after a tough engagement. Stone-faced, thin-lipped, but betrayed by the rapid blinking of his eyes. The driver was an older Japanese, who I hoped did not understand much English and decide to drive us into a tree.

We stopped asking questions. This was going to be a bust, I thought. Looking over at Janet, I could see that she'd reached the same conclusion. And yet, I thought, we needed to see this, firsthand. The bureaucrats would spare the president most of the horror. He wanted us to tell him like it was.

See it we did. The line—actually there were two lines, on either side of a road leading up toward the hospital. There were ten US Army tents arrayed in what had been the front parking lot. The hospital building was bigger than I'd expected and yet part and parcel of the city's destruction. The top half had been sheared right off by the invisible hand of the blast wave that had come howling out of the city center. The rest of the building had the by now familiar look of the concrete buildings in the city center. Standing, but bruised, with blackened windows and patches of bright orange rebar showing through the front sections of the building. The hill above the building had been swept clean of what had probably been a wooded hillside.

The approach road to the hospital was lined on both sides with injured people. The car stopped at the hospital complex's main gate. Janet and I then got out and began to walk up the sloping driveway. The colonel came with us. There were hundreds, if not more, Japanese on either side of the road. They stared at us as if we were aliens from outer space. I could under-stand: a white American woman in uniform, escorted by what looked to them like an American giant, also in uniform. I was certainly no giant, but compared to the diminutive Japanese on either side of the road, I probably looked like one. It was as if we'd stepped into a valley of pain and desper-ation. The crowd was made up mostly of women, whose anguish radiated from every burned pore. I had to remind myself to breathe and I dared not look at Janet's face. Even scarier, there was no sound escaping this mortally wounded crowd. No one said anything. No cries of anger. No pleading for help. They simply were right *there,* squatting in stoic silence by the side of the driveway, united I'm sure by the knowledge that death was within them. Their faces were fascinating—I'd seen Japanese woodcuts where the exaggerated Asian features seemed otherworldly. And yet, there they were. Except now they were mostly bald, with half their faces burned so red that it hurt to see them. I stopped looking.

Janet called it off. "Keep going," she said to the colonel. "We can't bother these people."

"Thank you," the colonel replied. "There's another place. It's a coal mine where they'd used POWs. Out of the direct path of that radiation cloud. We're using it as a food distribution center. Able-bodied family members are coming there. Lots of them are contaminated, so we put our guys and the food supplies in the entrance to the mine, which is still clean. Want to try that?"

I said yes and asked if there were surviving buildings there. The colo-nel said yes, several, including the POW barracks.

"Let's try for one of those," I said. "You have interpreters there, I pre-sume?"

"Yes," he said. "They're not great, but good enough to explain the handout process to the people. The Japanese are painfully waiting for anything—there's been no food getting into *Hiroshima* for days now and now they are afraid to eat fish or rice from paddies near the city."

We went back to the car and then drove up to the mine works, where another great crowd was waiting. We got to the POW building and went into the dining room, which contained three long tables with wooden benches and some chairs at the head. There were some windows but they were covered with bamboo shades and bars. The room reeked of coal dust, smoke, and death.

I took up the head of the table with Janet sitting on my right side with her notebook. The colonel, accompanied by two armed soldiers, brought in two middle-aged Japanese men and one elderly woman. They looked frightened, their eyes darting around, probably expecting an execution squad. I stood up in front of my chair and all three visibly quailed and dropped onto their knees and then into impossibly deep bows. Janet started speaking to them in rapid-fire Japanese after which they slowly, uncertainly stood back up, making sure not to look at me. I sat down and nodded to Janet, as if I was giving her permission to continue. They sat side by side on the nearest bench, keeping their eyes down as if their lives depended on it. Janet took a seat on the opposite bench and began talking to them. I assumed my role at the head of the table as the duty ogre in the room, staring straight ahead with my best court-martial face on. The colonel and his men withdrew to the farthest table and pretended not to care about anything at all.

Janet finally coaxed them to start talking and even I could immediately tell the difference between her Japanese and that of our "guests." I had heard Japanese only in wartime movies, where they spoke to each other in a rapid and harsh tone, which sounded like they were about to draw swords and go at it at any moment. Janet's tone was not harsh but definitely superior and I could make out individual syllables; the three Japanese answered in short, respectful guttural bursts, bowing their heads each time they spoke, signaling total subservience every time. It was obvious they were scared to death.

At one point Janet told me in English that she was getting somewhere. Staying in character, I grunted without looking at her and then nodded. She bowed her head in in my direction and went back at it with the three civilians. I caught the colonel nodding approvingly from his distant table as if he understood what he was seeing, that we were role-playing.

She "interviewed" four more sets of people, all of them equally scared until Janet reassured them that I had been fed recently and did not plan to eat them. I was suddenly thirsty when the second group was brought in, and I knew if I was thirsty, those Japanese must have been positively dehydrated. I turned to the colonel and said the words "water, please" in my best *daimyo* voice. The colonel nodded and sent his two men to get some clean water. They came back with canteens and a stack of paper cups. I got the first cup, naturally, Janet the second, and then the Japanese were each given water. Their hands were trembling so badly that I'm not sure how much they got but it was clear they were desperately thirsty. God only knew how long they'd been in line on that dusty industrial road leading into the mine complex. The soldiers gave them refills, which disappeared in seconds. Then Janet began again.

THIRTY-ONE
STAYING THE COURSE

After four sets I could see that Janet was getting tired, so I stood up. The Japanese stood up immediately and went into deep bows. I told the colonel we were done for the day and asked if they could get these people back into their place in line. Janet assured me that the Japanese in the line would see to that. Once they left the room to go back to the main tunnel entrance, we could relax. I apologized to the colonel for talking to him like he was a dog, but he grinned.

"I savvied how you two were playing it," he said. "No offense at all. With your permission, my lord, I'd like to go to the mine and see how the supplies are holding up. We have some C rations there for our troops; I'll see if I can bring some back for you. Not promising, mind you."

We thanked him and he and his crew tramped out. Then Janet and I conferred. "Is this working?" I asked.

"Sort of," she said. "You deserve an Academy Award, by the way; you were intimidating *me*."

"These people have lived under a regime of militarist monsters since the late nineteen thirties," I said. "I suspect anyone in a foreign uniform would scare them, especially an American who shows up after an atomic bomb."

"They've been living like that a lot longer than that," she said. "Those people in line at the mine are mostly simple fishermen and rice farmers. They were too old to be drafted and they were providing food, which became increasingly important once our subs went to work. Many of them have relatives at home who are in a bad way because they were in the city. There was nowhere to go, so they went home."

"How do they view the Bomb?" I asked.

"An act of God," she said, simply. "An angry, very displeased god. Who brought the sun down from the heavens to punish them. The sun is a centrally important entity to the Japanese. Japan, or *Nihon* as they call it: *Nihon* translates roughly as the land of the rising sun. Japan is east of China, so they see the sun first. They don't know what to do next. Everything's gone—fresh water, food, the roads, the harbor. Interestingly, they revere the emperor for stopping the war! In their view he was placating the sun god from whom he is descended, who appeared in the heavens to burn down the entire nation. Every one of them have relatives or neighbors who are simply gone. One man said that when they are in their homes and villages after dark, everyone weeps."

"Is the fact that we're feeding them and offering medical assistance making any impact?"

"They might one day be grateful, but right now I think they're in extended, communal shock. I'm not entirely sure they've connected the Americans to what happened. They will eventually, of course. You saw them. We're alien beings who arrived after the sun-bomb—that *is* what they're calling it, by the way—and offered to help. These are uneducated people. I even had to simplify my language so they could understand me. They've been subject to Japanese army propaganda since the invasion of China. I think they're too stunned to figure it all out."

"Will they figure it out?" I asked.

"They'll remember," she said. "Once they put the Bomb and the

Americans together, they'll also remember who came to feed them, and that it wasn't their government in *Tokyo*. One thing I did learn—for every individual we saw at that hospital, there are ten more suffering out in the countryside with their families at their sides as they die of invisible radiation poisoning or blast injuries. These were shipyard workers, street cleaners, food stall workers, deliverymen, the layer of menial people in every city who make things run. Those people out there at the mine aren't young people—the young men have all gone for soldiers, and most never came back. Those are their parents, sisters, or grandparents. Japan lost an entire generation in this war."

"Only because *they* set out to conquer all of Southeast Asia," I reminded her. "And did a damned brutal job of it, too. The Japanese aren't the only ones who lost a whole generation of young men, are they. Plus, they started it—everywhere."

She nodded. "I know that," she said. "But I'm not sure *they*"—she gestured toward the mine works just visible through the shuttered windows, where desperate crowds of old people waited patiently for anything at all—"understand all that. Obedience to authority is a big part of Japanese character and always has been. The man-god in the palace told them the war was necessary, a mandate from heaven. That was echoed all the way down the line, with a liberal dose of *bushido* thrown in. You know: 'war is a once-in-a-lifetime opportunity to die with honor.' And *this* is how it ended."

"Did you ask the question?"

"Yes, I did. Who brought this calamity down on your heads? The Americans, most said. Then I asked why. Embarrassed silence. Everybody looking down. Then I told them it was because their government, not the emperor, started a war against America at Pearl Harbor. A war with China. A war with Korea. Singapore. The Dutch East Indies. The Philippines. Australia. Do you remember anyone asking you if you were in favor of doing all this war?"

"And?"

"They were clearly afraid to say. Germany wasn't the only country with an SS. But then I told them that the American general in *Tokyo* now ruled Japan. Then I asked if they wanted a voice in what happens to Japan from here on out. What happens to them. Many didn't understand the question, but some of the women did. The ones whose sons had never come back. I told them that this was the one opportunity they would ever have to prevent calamities like this, because in America, the people have a voice."

"They understand that proposition?"

"Honestly, I'm not sure. But they'll go home to their villages, and people will want to know what the Americans told them. I told one woman, who was a schoolteacher for rising teenagers, that the emperor may have said he was in agreement about going to war, but that the world was full of emperors and kings whose palaces were surrounded by warlords. Sometimes an emperor has to say what they want in order to remain emperor. She taught history, and she got the allusion immediately. With any luck, the seeds will have been planted."

I waited for more. She sighed, a painful sound. "I'm exhausted," she said, finally. "Just looking into their eyes hurts. The only good thing is that I think I now know what to tell Mr. Truman."

"Well, that's good," I said. "Because I'm lost for words. I agree: this is beyond terrible. And we've got *Nagasaki* to go."

She looked at me and shook her head. "I don't want to see any more of this," she said. "Rivers and harbors choked with dead babies. Legions of hairless, skinless walking dead. The smell of starvation in the air. Silhouettes of human beings burned into the concrete. The whole city seen in black and white. Stories about the rain turning black for three days. And this thundering, accusing silence. No. I'm done."

Truth be told I was relieved to hear her say that. Besides, without her, there was nothing I could do—I was mostly a prop and I was as sick of what we'd been seeing as she was. Part of my brain kept telling me: remember, these bastards would *not* surrender. We were going to lose thousands upon thousands of *our* young men carrying out an invasion, where we'd be opposed by every living, breathing Japanese man, woman, and child in the country.

But I had a problem now, having seen firsthand the ghastly results of dropping an atomic bomb on a city, an act to which I had personally contributed. My conscience no longer was speaking to me. I'd also heard that the *Nagasaki* bomb had been even more powerful than this one. I was with Janet—I did *not* want to see the results of that. I'm sure many of those scientists at Los Alamos were probably proud of their work and how it had ended the war. Except for Oppenheimer, perhaps. "You won't understand what you've created until you use it," he'd prophesied. Amen, Jesus.

We sat there in silence as the afternoon sun began to set. The colonel returned with just one of his men.

"They've run out of everything at the mine," he said. "The guys handing out food even gave away their own rations. There's another convoy en route from *Yokohama*, but it won't get here until midnight or so. I suggest you go back to your ship for tonight, and then I can get you to *Nagasaki* in the morning in one of the empty food trucks."

"That makes great sense," I said, jumping in before Janet could tell him of our change in plans. "We may have new orders by then—the ship has communications with Pearl and the States."

Janet started to say something but then I think she understood what I was trying to do. The colonel said he'd get the car and pick us up right here.

The ride back through the city was even more depressing as Janet told me more about what the people had told her. The litany of injuries was unending, but worse was the rumor going around that all of Japan now looked like *Hiroshima*. They'd gotten a taste of mass destruction after the firestorm bombing of *Tokyo* five months earlier. Some of them had gone to the capital city to see how bad it was, and then come back to the countryside with hair-raising tales. Now this. They don't know what

to think, she said, and that's amplified by the fact that none of the officials who had ruled their lives with military determination and generous
amounts of cruelty were in evidence anymore. They'd heard rumors that
a group of militarist firebrands had tried to assassinate the emperor himself. To them, the emperor embodied the spirit of the entire country. Kill
him, you killed *Nihon* itself. No wonder the sun-god had blazed in fury
over their city. Insane stuff like that.

We got back to the ship and retired to our respective cabins to shower
and change uniforms. Our khakis were sent to the ship's laundry with
instructions to wash them twice to make sure they got every particle of
sand or dirt that might be radioactive. Even our cap-covers were to be
washed. Our uniform shoes, which had triggered their onboard dosimeter, were steam cleaned in the one operating fireroom. We met with
the captain in the unit commander's cabin at eighteen hundred for a
much needed meal. We were sitting around the table after supper, telling
him what we'd seen and heard that day, when a radioman knocked and
brought in a personal-for message for me from Washington. It was classified top secret, and the precedence was Operational Immediate.

The first thing I checked was the signature line. Van Rensselaer. Wait
a minute, I thought. He was in *Tokyo*. The radioman had said Washington. Then I read the text:

> XXX HST concerned about rising Allied and national criticism
> of city A—bombings. First medical and scientific delegations in
> both cities painting appalling pictures. Efforts to plan postwar
> alliances in jeopardy. D.MAC requesting instructions. HST needs
> your report on both cities ASAP. Submit direct to WH: (COSWH)
> after final visit. Crucial: info no other addees. FADM Leahy
> sends. Acknowledge. VanR. XXX

I showed the text to Janet. She bit her lower lip but nodded. I asked the
radioman for a message blank.

"This is a reply to the sender," I said. "One word: wilco. OpImmediate precedence."

"Yessir," the radioman said and then left in a hurry. Wilco was Navy speak for "will comply." On a ship, only the captain could say wilco. He would know that came from me.

I sat there for a moment and then asked the captain if he had any more whiskey. He shook his head. Then I remembered my sea bag stash. I thanked him for dinner and his ship's hospitality. Once he graciously left, I went rummaging and produced my bottle of Scotch. I poured us both a generous measure. I lifted my glass toward her and took a mighty draft. So did she. I was being selfish, but I thought our need was greater than his.

"Now we know why Truman wanted us to come out here," I said. "Remember all those comments about personal and organizational agendas? Looks like that shit's begun."

"Can you blame them?" she said. "Most of those scientists and doctors have never seen what real war looks like. If *Hiroshima* and *Nagasaki* are their first exposure, there must have been a lot of puke-stops for their bus."

"We *have* to go on," I said. "And it may be worse—the *Nagasaki* bomb had a greater yield than this one here."

"The president's order to send us here," she argued, "was aimed at determining the chances that we might persuade the Japanese people to join us going forward. I told you I thought I had the answer to that, and it's this: the Japanese people right now, after these bombs, are a blank sheet of hot, malleable metal. If we play it right, and play it right now, we can bring them aboard. I don't need to go to *Nagasaki* to confirm that."

"We need to go to *Nagasaki* to bolster *our* credentials to tell Truman that. I agree with you, but if opposition is rising, someone will use our failure to visit both cities against the president. We've got to go. That's what our mission was."

"You gonna order me to go, Captain?"

"My dear Janet, I'm going to order *both* of us to go. As long as we do, no one in Washington or anywhere else can contradict anything we say. And—this is probably unfair—between the two of us we convinced Harry Truman to cry havoc and let slip the dogs of atomic war. *We* can't stop short now. *We* simply can't."

She seemed to crumple a little bit. I got up and went around the table to hug her. I wanted her to stay with me for the night but that wasn't possible aboard a destroyer with hundreds of prying eyes. I realized I was falling in love with her and had the sense, for once in my life, to tell her.

Good move, that, if I say so myself.

THIRTY-TWO
NAGASAKI

Nagasaki was different. I'd sat in on a preliminary briefing at the Manhattan Project headquarters in Washington just before we left for Japan. The Bomb dropped on *Hiroshima* hit the aim point. The *Nagasaki* bomb missed the city center aim point because of heavy cloud cover over the city. *Hiroshima* was built on the delta of the *Ota* River, which was essentially a flat plain transected by seven river-delta channels. That fact allowed the blast wave unimpeded movement. *Nagasaki* was mostly nestled in a valley, which confined the explosion somewhat. The *Hiroshima* bomb (known as Little Boy and weighing in at ten tons) was a gun-type uranium design, in which the scientists had great confidence because of its simplicity. Only about a quarter of the fissionable material achieved fission before the Bomb blew itself apart, but even that resulted in a twelve to fifteen kiloton yield. The *Nagasaki* bomb (known as Fat Man) was an implosion device using plutonium, most of which did achieve fission. It ended up creating a twenty-two thousand kiloton blast. The affected area in *Nagasaki* was smaller than in *Hiroshima*, but where the Fat Man took effect, the damage was much more severe, as was the radiation.

The quickest way for us to get to *Nagasaki* was for our destroyer to get underway and sail there overnight, arriving midday. Both *Hiroshima* and *Nagasaki* were port cities, but there were more port facilities still standing in *Nagasaki*. The ship nosed carefully alongside the least damaged pier when we arrived. The US Army had established refugee centers at the northern and southern ends of the city, and a truck had been waiting for the ship's boat to bring us into the port and alongside a pier. Whatever we might think about Van Rensselaer, he had absolutely organized everything we might need. The truck was a covered deuce and a half similar to the food trucks we'd seen in *Hiroshima*. Janet and I squeezed into the right side of the bench seat while our driver, a master sergeant, drove. The windows were rolled up tight and there was some kind of cheesecloth stretched over the two vents, with an OSL dosimeter attached to each vent.

The master sergeant told us that the industrial heart of *Nagasaki* extended up a valley northwest of the downtown. Anything that had been in the valley was gone, totally. Anything on the other side of the two hills that formed the valley was relatively undamaged, except where fires had gone up and over the hills and down into dense neighborhoods constructed of wooden buildings. There'd been two major weapons plants in the valley, the *Mitsubishi* torpedo factory and an even larger *Kawasaki* military ordnance plant. Big industrial complexes, he told us, both now nothing more than radioactive dirt. All working in the plants that morning had been consumed by the fireball. I remembered the trees in *Hiroshima*, denuded of any branches or greenery. Here there were only black stumps about six inches high, if that.

As best we could tell, he said, there was little residual radiation. The scientists told us that the main radiation pulse came at the ignition of the Bomb, and if you were in the way of that, you were, literally, toast. He chuckled at that analogy. He'd been on *Okinawa*, we learned. We button up because so much of the dust still contains radioactive particles, he continued, and there's a hell of a lot of dust in this city that used to be God knows what—buildings, people, animals, trees, bridges, *Shinto* shrines.

"What do the survivors look like?" Janet asked.

"Burns," he said. "Horrible burns. And there's another thing—the ordinary people in Japan were for the most part already starving. Food was severely rationed and people were run-down by months of no real food. The big fishing fleets that used to go out of here had been gunned down by American submarines. They went out at night to fish with light. The subs would surface out of nowhere and shoot them up with their deck guns. Nothing much got back to port. After a while there weren't any boats left, either, or any fishermen who'd be willing to go out. If boats did bring in fish, it went to the army. Same thing with rice. What farmers did produce was appropriated by the army and sent to their garrisons overseas. A lot of farmers simply gave up."

"Where did you learn all this?" I asked as we made our way through distressingly familiar swaths of total destruction and empty, buckled streets.

"There was a medical school here," he said. "Not all that damaged in the bombing. The Army sent some of our docs there to start providing medical aid. One of them told me all that. The Japanese doctors and nurses went out to attend to the wounded but then they became contaminated because of all the hot dust. I guess they breathed in radioactive stuff and then their lungs started bleeding and then they died. If they'd worn surgical masks, many would have made it. But no one knew about the radiation. Then it rained, a scary black rain, according to witnesses. The rain was hot, too. The water and power systems were all down, so people collected rainwater . . ."

"*We're* supposed to talk to survivors," Janet said. "Where can we do that?"

"At the refugee centers," he said. "Biggest one is up at that hospital. Do you two speak Japanese?"

"I do," Janet said. "Is the Army distributing food?"

"We are," the sergeant said. "But we've had trouble getting stuff in so it's hit or miss. They come in the hundreds. It's tough to watch. As much as I hated their army, these are old people, women, children. Their goddamned army is nowhere to be seen. No surprise there, the cowardly bastards."

The food distribution center in *Hiroshima* had been set up in a coal-mine complex that had been shielded from the direct blast. The one here in *Nagasaki* was a tent city in front of a four-story concrete hospital building, which was not structurally damaged except that all the windows were blown out. Now the main entrance was barricaded. Once again there was a long line of people on one side of the approach street. Four tents marked with large wartime red crosses were in one parking lot. The food tents had been put up on the brown lawn in front of the main hospital building. There were teams of American medics, each accompanied by a Japanese doctor if their white coats were any indication. There were a dozen Army deuce and a half trucks parked nearby. Our truck drove past the line and then went behind the perimeter surrounding the food tents. We could see people pointing at the truck, probably anticipating a resupply.

"You got food back there?" I asked, indicating the cargo area of the truck.

"No, sir," the sergeant said. "The Navy's got a stores ship coming in tomorrow. Supposing it does show up we'll be back in business. Problem is there's nowhere in the city to store it, so we'll do a truck convoy back up here and probably store it in the hospital building."

"I thought that was contaminated."

"They had a big pathology lab in the basement; nobody went there after the Bomb hit. Our docs don't think the building is all that contaminated, but the people won't accept the food if they think it came from the hospital. We'll have to sneak it out of the basement into some trucks parked behind and then drive it around, so it looks like it came from the port."

Damn, I thought. The power of a rumor. The sergeant parked the truck and went to find the major running the refugee operation. When he came back, he said that one of the medical tents was being used for storage and that we could set up in that. As we got out of the truck, the major came trotting up and saluted, a gesture not missed by the crowd of injured Japanese, who went silent and assumed respectful attitudes. The major was maybe five foot six in his shoes, so there was a marked contrast between us, both in size and height. I think the crowd was also amazed to see a woman in uniform accompanying me. Almost every woman standing in the line put both of her hands over her mouth when they got a look at the two of us. The men averted their eyes so as not to be seen staring at us. Staring was impolite.

Janet told the major we'd need some drinking water, someplace for us and the people brought in for her to interview to sit, if possible, and a small security detail.

"Yes, sir, Commander," he said immediately. "We got word from General MacArthur's HQ in *Tokyo* to get whatever you'd need. We washed down some tables and chairs from the hospital offices; they're already in the stores tent. Our OSLs show they're not hot. We brought a water buffalo in with us; your water will be in lab glassware from the hospital. Also thoroughly washed."

"Great job, Major," I said. "Let's get set up."

He saluted again and then we headed for the tent.

For the next four hours we repeated the experience we'd had at *Hiroshima*. I sat there like a stone Buddha, saying nothing, while the Japanese tried not to stare at me. It was the same mix of people, and Janet would spend the first few minutes assuring them that the *daimyo*—I heard her use that word—would not hurt them. The women were more willing to talk than the men, which Janet had said was because they were ashamed for their country. They didn't seem to be angry at Americans for having set loose a sun-bomb on them. It was as if they recognized that they were simply victims of war and that calamity, even a sun-bomb, was to be expected. They, too, were very thin and for the most part, malnourished. They were grateful for some fresh water. Apparently, all water had become suspect, especially after that black rain had put so many people into the ground.

I kept an eye on Janet, and by six o'clock it was evident that she was flagging. We stopped having people come in; that brought the major. He asked how it had gone and Janet told him very well and thanked him for setting everything up so well. He hesitated and then said there was one more man we might be interested in.

"He claims to have been a senior professor from *Tokyo* Imperial University. He's rather—arrogant, as if he had been someone important in the country, and indicated that he was not being showed proper respect. He's not injured, but he's plenty angry about what's happened here— with the Bomb, I mean. Little guy, maybe sixty, and full of himself. Not military, but said he'd worked for both the army and the navy. One of the intel guys interviewed him in English, which he speaks pretty well. Claims to speak German as well. I don't know, but if the commander here speaks real Japanese, it might be interesting."

"Was he here for the Bomb?"

"He was, but several miles away at his family's home. He came with members of his family to get food, probably claiming he had an 'in' and could get them preference. Wears a European suit that's seen some wear and tear. Said he'd come back home from an assignment in Korea."

That piqued my immediate interest. "Where in Korea?" I asked.

"He didn't reveal that," the major replied. "Just said he was a professor of physics and that he had been working in Korea."

"Bring him over, immediately," I said in my best *daimyo* voice. "*I* want to talk to him."

Fifteen minutes later an MP brought in a small, older Japanese man who strode in like a puffed-up functionary, looking imperiously around the room and then directly at us. I think he expected us to stand up, but when we failed the first basic etiquette test, he visibly stiffened. Janet offered him a seat but he refused it. Said he wanted to stand. The major remained behind, sitting in a corner. He obviously wanted to know more.

"Tell him *I* said to sit down," I said in an unmistakably authoritarian voice. He hesitated, but then took a seat, suddenly looking a little more apprehensive.

"Janet," I said. "I'm going to question this guy. I need you to act as a straightforward interpreter. If this is who or what I think he is, this is now intel business."

She nodded respectfully, staying in character, although I'd probably hear about it later.

"What is your full name?" I asked. Janet translated.

He drew himself up to his full height, even sitting in his chair, and gave his name in Japanese. Janet carefully wrote it down and showed it to me.

"What was your role in Japan's atomic bomb project in Hungnam?" I growled, while giving him my angry *daimyo* glare.

He literally gasped, his eyes widening in shock. He swallowed several times before being able to speak. I could see the major's jaw drop when I asked that question. Janet began to translate, but the professor waved her off.

"How do you know about this?" he asked, in heavily accented English.

"I was there for the test, Professor," I said. "Out in those small islands off the Hungnam shore."

"That is not possible," he hissed. "No one was out there."

"I was on an American submarine. I was sent by my president to witness the test. We had intelligence that it was coming. We knew about your program, Professor. We knew all along. The Germans told us everything when they knew they had lost the war."

"No!" he yelled. "They would *never* do that!"

"But they did," I said. "And when we captured that submarine bringing you uranium, we knew it was true. What was your role?"

He seemed to collapse in place. He closed his eyes. "This cannot be! Can*not* be," he cried. "We invented the fission process, back in 1939. Japan invented the atomic pile."

"That's news to me," I said. "I thought Professor Fermi cranked up the first nuclear pile, under the stadium in Chicago."

"No, that was just American propaganda."

He paused to take a breath. It was pretty clear that he believed all this crap. I got up and went over to his chair. He had to strain his neck to see my face. The crowd took a collective breath, probably anticipating I was going to cut his head off with my invisible sword. "What was your role in Hungnam?" I asked, again, amping up the menace in my voice.

"Director of enriching the uranium," he said softly.

"Takes time, does it not," I said, as if I, too, was a professor of physics and knew all about it. "What concentrations did you achieve?"

He looked down and just shook his head.

"Good enough for a test, though, correct? Even a little one."

That seemed to anger him. "Good enough, yes," he bristled. "And it was not so little. The water is shallow there. The crater on the bottom afterward was thirty meters deep and two hundred meters in diameter."

"Was that your production model?"

"Yes," he said. "And we were so close to actual production. But the test was incomplete—not enough uranium. Then *Hiroshima*. And right after, the Russians came. Our army fought them, three regiments. But they had two *divisions*. We destroyed as much equipment as we could and dumped our uranium stocks into the sea."

"We were told you were getting uranium ore from near Shanghai. Pitchblende."

"That was all a great secret. You could *not* have known."

"The Russians had spies in your program at *Tokyo* Imperial University," I said. "Japanese nationals, in fact. They were present in the university *before* you moved to Korea. The Russians also knew what you were doing there in Hungnam. They wanted your materials and equipment for themselves, for *their* atomic program. They knew that the Nazis were sending you materials, first by air routes over southern Russia, then by submarine. They knew about the Chosin Reservoir power stream, all going to Hungnam. They knew about the centrifuges. The industrialist who built all those facilities in Korea for your program had an engineer who was on the Soviet payroll."

I paused for a moment to let that all sink in before going on. His face was quivering with all this bad news.

"If it makes you feel any better, the Russians also knew all about *our* program. They waited for us to test one and then drop one, and that's when they declared war on Japan. When you conducted that test off Hungnam, they finally knew *you* had the Bomb. Just like we finally knew you had the Bomb. When I reported the test, my president was then convinced to use the Bomb on cities in Japan. *Hiroshima, Nagasaki.* What I am telling you, Professor, is that it was your test off Hungnam that set in motion the bombings of *Hiroshima* and *Nagasaki.*"

There was a look of growing horror on his face as I went through this lit-any of espionage and betrayal. Some of it I was plain making up, of course. The Soviets *had*, of course, penetrated our program at several levels, so it made sense to me that they would have had assets at Hungnam, probably Korean, whom the Japanese had impressed into slave labor. But it was sat-isfying to see this smug professor starting to come apart at the seams.

"Where is the rest of your development team?" I asked.

He clamped his mouth shut, unwilling to talk anymore. I suspected he didn't want to hear any more, either.

"I'll bet the Soviets have them," I said. His eyes went wide again, and then he nodded, still unwilling to say it.

Janet tapped my arm. "We should turn this guy over to MacArthur's people," she whispered. She was, of course, right. The pitiful remains of the Japanese government were shrilly denying any sort of Japanese research into atomic weapons to our intel people, protesting that they were the victims of incredible American cruelty. That was rich, seeing as the word "Japanese" had become a synonym worldwide for the word "cruelty" for too many years.

I called the major over and told him quietly to take this man into custody immediately and hold him until MacArthur's headquarters sent down instructions. Make sure he doesn't get ahold of the means to com-mit suicide, I told him, remembering Portsmouth. Within minutes five MPs came through the door and hustled the professor out of the tent. I then told the major we needed to get back to our host ship as soon as possible.

Once back aboard, after another sobering trip through an atomic wasteland, masks and everything, I told the CO that I had an op-immediate message for General MacArthur with info to Admiral Leahy. In that message I informed them about the professor's claims and statements, and that he was in custody here in *Nagasaki*. Van Rensselaer came back within one hour with a message to the Army commander responsible for the *Nagasaki* area, info to me, directing him to hold the professor in strictest secrecy and reiterating my instructions about suicide prevention. We knew we wouldn't hear from Leahy until the next day due to the time differences.

Over dinner, Janet asked me if I thought this guy was who he said he was. I shrugged and asked what was bothering her. "His name translates roughly to the Japanese version of John Doe," she said, referring to her notebook.

"Well, it looks like *Tokyo* HQ will soon find out," I said. "Once they get him up there, that is. Of course, there are two possible reasons they may want him ASAP."

"Two?" she asked.

"One, there's probably a commission somewhere who wants to know all about their program and how close they got before the Russians rolled them all up over there in Korea."

"And two?"

"If Mr. Truman is going to sell the idea that Japan should transform itself from our mortal enemy to our new ally, there may be a serious effort already underway to bury even the idea that these bastards almost had an A-bomb of their own."

She whistled softly. I changed subjects.

"What did you get from the Japanese you interviewed this time?"

"Pretty much the same as from *Hiroshima*," she replied. "War is war. Calamity is to be expected. Whatever we as ordinary people thought about the war, we had no real say. To speak against the war was an invitation for the *Kempeitai* to come see you. After that happened, no one would ever see you again. That was understood. The only thing the sun-bomb did *for* us was to make it clear that the war was coming to an end. What the sun-bomb did *to* us was to wreck everything."

"Do they appreciate the fact that we're now feeding them?"

She laughed. "Half of them are deeply grateful," she said. "But the older men wonder if there's an ulterior motive, as in, fatten them up and *then* eat them."

"Aw, c'mon. Seriously?"

She shrugged. "We're *gaijin*," she said. "Foreigners, or, in another translation, aliens. With a sun-bomb."

I closed my eyes for a moment. The gulf between what we as Westerners thought and felt, and what the Japanese thought and felt, seemed unsurmountable. She sensed my thought.

"Look, my dear *daimyo*, we've done what Mr. Truman asked us to do. Let's go back and let all those brilliant people at State, the National Security Council, and the White House figure this mess out. Most importantly, let's go home, too. I am more than ready to blow this particular pop stand."

Damn the woman, I thought. She always makes such sense and is able to read my mind. I, too, wanted out of Japan. I called the CO again and said I had another message to send.

THIRTY-THREE
WHAT TO SAY

Within forty minutes of my sending it, General MacArthur's office came back and told us to return to *Tokyo* to give him a personal briefing. The CO came in with the radio messenger and informed us that he was going to take us up to the capital city; all the cargo planes in the area of occupation were busy moving food supplies throughout the country. To prove the point, he showed us the crowds assembling on the pier. A rumor had gotten loose that his ship was bringing in food supplies, since no American warships had docked in the city in memory.

It was now four thirty; *Tokyo* was some six hundred miles northeast of here. The captain said he was almost at 50 percent fuel, so he'd have to go at his most economical speed, sixteen knots, to conserve fuel. That would put us in *Yokohama* at five or so in the morning the day after to-morrow. His lordship the General would just have to wait, I thought. The possibility of crapping out for the next thirty-six hours broke my heart, but we'd just have to endure. Janet gave a sigh of relief, and went to get cleaned up before dinner. We'd have to put together a briefing of sorts for the General, and also for the president. Maybe one would do it for both of them, I thought, but then realized that the one for Mr. Truman had to address some issues that MacArthur might not yet be privy to, and deliberately so. I smiled to myself, remembering the old Navy saying—when the elephants dance, the mousies take cover.

After dinner Janet and I enjoyed the last of my Scotch as the ship pointed out into the Pacific Ocean for the run north to *Yokohama*. We talked about what to put into the two different briefings. I suggested she give the briefing to MacArthur because she was the one who'd talked to the survivors. She was fine with that. I would talk about my interview with the so-called professor, because I'd seen the actual test off Hungnam.

"I think I'll tell him what we talked about in terms of confirming they had a program," I said. "I don't know where the Army will take him, but I suspect there's already an intelligence group forming up to investigate whether or not Japan even had a program."

"And I suspect that our good friend Van Rensselaer will have some thoughts about what we say or don't say to MacArthur," she said. "He's a senior member of the occupation headquarters staff, but everybody knows he works for Leahy."

"MacArthur will certainly know that, too," I said. "He spent most of the war fighting the Japanese *and* the accursed United States Navy."

She laughed at that. Suddenly we both became aware that our destroyer had rounded *Kagoshima* and encountered a deep ocean swell. The ship began to pitch and roll a bit. To me it was a comfortable motion, one that had put me to sleep more than once on my own destroyer, and later, my cruiser. Janet, on the other hand, had an anxious expression on her face.

"Why don't you go hit the sack," I said, helpfully. "There'll be straps on the bunk. Strap in. If you think you're gonna get seasick, keep a trash can handy by the bunk."

She gave me a look that said thanks for mentioning seasickness, but retired hastily from my cabin for the captain's inport cabin. The CO stuck his head in fifteen minutes later and said there was a storm several hundred miles east of Japan that was kicking up some big swells. We'd be broadside to them for a good part of the run north to *Yokohama*.

Great, I thought. I now knew that I was going to be writing up the briefings all on my lonesome, that was for damn sure. I got up to secure some of the loose items in the cabin as the rolling became more pronounced. Then I hit the sack and let the mesmerizing movements of the ship—up, up, up, hold, then a heady swoop down into the oncoming sea, a moment's shuddering as green water poured over the bow, a deep roll to starboard, then back up again, together with a gentle roll to port, then back to starboard. Better than any sleeping pill ever invented.

Like everyone else in the US Navy in the Pacific, I still hated the goddamned Japanese, falling back, as we all did, on the eternal premise that they started this shit at Pearl Harbor. Not to mention the Rape of Nanking, their army's treatment of POWs, their civilian massacres throughout Southeast Asia, their enslavement of Korea, and other atrocities too numerous to mention. Beasts. Barbarians. Monsters. Murderers. Having met the maimed populations of *Hiroshima* and *Nagasaki*, I was now a little bit torn between sympathy for them and utter hatred of their armed forces and the warlords who'd set them in motion. Including their precious emperor, who for some strange reason was being held blameless.

Poor Janet, I thought as I drifted off to sleep, relaxing in the familiar and gentle arms of the deep, secure in the knowledge that there'd be no enemy subs, aircraft, or any other threats to disturb my sleep. No sound-powered phone calls from the bridge. No urgent calls from Main Control about a sudden engineering problem down below. Yes, we were transiting in Japanese waters. Except they were now American waters, by God. About goddamned time, I thought, ignoring the tugs of my conscience about what I'd seen in those two sun-blasted cities. It was easy to dispel the scenes ashore with memories of steaming into Pearl Harbor a week after the attack. Tugboats had been still creeping through the remains of Battleship Row, picking up bodies. Two badly blasted battlewagons still had their church pennants flying under their national ensigns. Search parties were still scrambling along the overturned hull of *Oklahoma*, banging on the hull plates to see if any personnel trapped inside would respond. Welding teams cutting through the ship's bottom in a race against time and dwindling air. Treacherous bastards whose ambassadors were negotiating in Washington while their carrier groups were descending from the far north Pacific under cover of December weather.

Now, almost four years later, at grievous cost in ships, men, and material, America had loomed up out of the western Pacific skies like some vengeful specter to crush the tattered remains of the blood-soaked Japanese Empire in atomic fire. Goddamned right, too. I was sorry for the starving old ladies at the centers. I was sorrier for the wives and children who'd emerged from makeshift trenches out on Ford Island to watch their husbands' ships burn, and the families up at Schofield Barracks prostrate in the government quarters while Japanese planes strafed the housing area. For fun. Killing kids. Dogs. For fun.

The president now had to figure out how to deal with this thing called communism that was sweeping through China and points south. Korea was prostrate after years of Japanese occupation. It might well be that *our* news about finding a Japanese atomic scientist would be suppressed in favor of developing the Japanese as our allies—probably our only allies—in East Asia. Above my pay grade. I was just one more surplus Navy captain, and I realized I was perfectly willing to submerge into the historical ooze if that's what my country needed right now.

THIRTY-FOUR
PLANNING THE BRIEF

The next day the seas calmed down, allowing Janet and me to begin to work up our briefings to General MacArthur on what we—she, mostly—had learned from our sorrowful tours of *Hiroshima* and *Nagasaki*. I told her about my conflicting views on A-bombing Japanese cities and my enduring hate and contempt for the things the Japanese had done in Asia.

"I was an intelligence official in Washington," she said. "The things you're talking about were well known, of course, and there are probably some we don't yet know about. But once we recognized that the Japanese were doomed, the people we worked for began looking ahead—what happens after we win this thing? What's the postwar world gonna look like? How do we prevent something like this from ever happening again? And then the atomic bomb exploded onto the world stage and changed everything."

"Okay," I said. "So, here's my question: do we brief the A-bomb results to General Douglas MacArthur, who has personally experienced the brutish power of Japan, their atrocities—like the Bataan Death March, and all the rest of it—as the logical conclusion of total war? Or as an opportunity to sweep Japan and its people into our orbit going forward against the Soviets and their own imperial ambitions?"

She smiled. Oh, shit, I thought.

"You're overthinking this, my dear *daimyo,*" she said. "Let's do this: I conducted the interviews with the survivors. I'll tell it like it was. How they were being treated during the war. How they'd been starved into submission. What happened if someone failed to toe the imperial line. All set within the context of what the A-bombs did. How they are desperately dependent on our refugee centers for the most basic necessities. Then I'll turn it over to you to tell them about their own atomic bomb project. How close it came. What would have happened if we'd staged the invasion fleet offshore and they'd had one of those. He'll have his staff there. They'll challenge you, some itinerant Navy captain talking about affairs of state, and you can then flatten them with what you know, what you've seen, first at Trinity, and then in Korea."

I nodded, but not happily.

"The elephant in the room is this," she went on. "If the United States wants to bring the Japanese into our postwar orbit, how do we address their own atomic bomb program? And that, dear heart, is an issue *way* above our pay grade. If either of us gets a question like that, we simply say that the president told us not to speculate on that."

"General MacArthur will see right through that," I said.

"Good for him," she said. "But he can't challenge *us* on that issue, right? He'll have to take that up with his boss, Harry S. Truman, won't he?"

I fell silent. You are way out of your depth, I told myself. On the other hand, Janet seemed to be fully capable of dealing with this situation. How was this possible? I finally asked her.

She laughed. "I spent more than two years in Japan as a young graduate student," she said. "This is a game the Japanese would instantly recognize. All of their board games relate to power. That's what I have to tell Truman. If he wants them to join us in the postwar great power game, it's his to lose. And he's no dope, is he? We've done our job. Now we need to get home and talk to the president. MacArthur will not be happy with our access. So: in *Tokyo*, we will be polite, very respectful, full of admiration for himself, and dismissive of any notions that we're at all significant when we brief the president."

"*Jesus,* Janet," I said. "Really?"

"He'll buy it," she said. "I guarantee it. This is a guy, five stars or not, who believes his own bullshit. And, he has the track record to prove it. He'll think our protestations of insignificance will give him full play when he talks to Truman. The trick is for us to get home *before* he talks to the president."

"And how do we do that?" I asked, somewhat in wonder at this woman's ability to see the game in progress.

"We get Leahy to demand that we come home. Right now."

"How?" I asked again. There's an echo in here, I thought.

"Van Rensselaer," she said, triumphantly. "Why do you think Leahy sent him here in the first place?"

I sighed. That night, that out-of-my-depth feeling descended on my tired brain. It was the lack of Scotch, I told myself. Had to be. My *daimyo* persona was in tatters, I realized. The ship took a particularly heavy roll out of absolutely nowhere. Now *that* I understood. I wedged pillows where they had to be and went off to sleep.

THIRTY-FIVE
EL SUPREMO

*T*okyo Bay had blackened coastlines. The atmosphere was somewhat charged as we made our way carefully into *Yokohama* Bay. We were headed for the *Yokosuka* naval base, which had been treated to repeat B-29 missions, but was now being rehabilitated to accommodate the US Navy ships servicing the occupation forces, including MacArthur's headquarters downtown. We'd been told the B-29s had left the imperial palace alone, along with the *Chiyoda* diplomatic district of embassies and consulates. But once the Japanese had dispersed most of their military industrial facilities into the suburbs of the city and beyond, anything outside of the *Chiyoda* district became fair game, the weapon of choice being incendiary bombs. The destruction along both shorelines was total and looked a lot like what we'd seen down south.

To get to the actual base at *Yokosuka*, we had to drive up and around a point of land and then back down into the military harbor. It was slow going, due to the CO's concern about mines and also a plethora of wrecks, some small, some the size of battleships and cruisers, capsized in the shallows. Once we rounded *Agatsuma* Island, we found several large US Navy Service Force ships at anchor. Two fleet oilers, two hospital ships, one troop transport, three cargo ships, including one so-called reefer with frozen food stores. There were also mine-sweepers, a couple of destroyer escorts, and one of the old battleships that had been raised from the bloody mud of Pearl Harbor. A two-star flag flew from her foremast. Our tin can exchanged flashing-light call signs messages with the USS *California* and then we were assigned an anchorage among the supply ships. As soon as we were anchored, a launch headed in our direction from the battlewagon, so Janet and I mustered on the quarterdeck, our sea bags in hand. We thanked our CO for his hospitality and wished him and his ship well. I apologized for all the taxi-service runs.

"Hell," he said, with a reassuring grin. "No problem. At least one of these Service Force ships is bound to have ice cream."

"I see you're keeping your priorities in order," I said with a grin of my own.

There were more people in evidence as we made our way by car up to the city and then into the *Chiyoda* diplomatic district. Many of the streets and roads had been cleared and there were lots of Japanese carrying off building wreckage and other debris—in baskets. Occasionally we'd come to small mountains of debris, and there were some bulldozers loading stuff into Japanese army trucks, although no one working was wearing uniforms of any kind. Once again, the hand of American fire had been deathly thorough. There were no trees or any sort of greenery in sight, even in areas that had obviously been parks.

By midmorning we were ensconced in the same small hotel we'd been billeted in upon arriving in Japan. Our Army officer escort waited while we checked back in to the same rooms we'd had before, and then we were off to MacArthur's headquarters. Our uniforms were reasonably clean and pressed, courtesy of our host destroyer. That said, our escort had scanned us with radiation detectors upon entering the lobby of the undamaged corporate headquarters of the *Dai Ichi* Mutual Life Insurance Company because we'd been to the A-bomb sites. To our surprise, both of us registered on the detectors. This produced a quick conference among the security people, who summoned a doctor. He checked the readings and decided the radiation levels were acceptable. We would have to make sure we sat as far away from the General as possible in his office. He had not been to the sites, and was not inclined to go. Dugout Doug to the end, I thought irreverently.

MacArthur was still instantly recognizable due to the war-long efforts of his extensive public relations staff. What we'd missed before was that he was in his mid-sixties, with all the stress lines in his face that high command and almost four years of combatant command could engrave on a man of his age. One of his aides, a full colonel, brought us in and then left, closing the door behind him. We sat in two armchairs facing his enormous desk, far enough from him that I could just make out the glittering circle of five stars on his shirt collars.

"Tell me about the professor," he began, without further ado. His voice projected clearly, reminding us what a notable orator he was.

I described my interview, keeping it to five minutes.

"How did you know what to ask?"

I then gave him my background, starting with the Portsmouth encounter with the U-boats and the two Japanese engineers, and then with the Manhattan Project and Van Rensselaer. I left out my OpNav assignment as not being relevant to the discussion. But he thought otherwise.

"It says here," he said, picking up a piece of paper, "that you worked directly for Admiral King. Is that correct?"

"Yes, sir, I did."

"In what capacity?"

"I solved problems that seemed to evade the Navy headquarters staff's ability to solve."

He nodded. He'd been chief of staff of the Army, so he knew exactly the kind of problems that tended to evade the Army headquarters staff's ability to solve. I would have loved to see what else was on that briefing sheet about me.

"And you were the one who witnessed the Japanese test explosion of a nuclear device off Korea?"

"Yes, sir, I did. From a submarine."

A thin smile appeared on his face. "That must have been quite a ride, I imagine."

I nodded. "It was, General," I said. "But the main thing was that I'd also witnessed the Trinity test and knew what an atomic bomb looked like, as opposed to what happens when, say, an ammunition ship blows up."

He nodded again. "Do you think that this professor was genuine, in terms of his being associated with their program?"

"Yes, sir, I do. He even went so far as to declare that Japan, not America, actually invented the controlled fission reaction."

"Really," he said, reaching for his familiar pipe.

"Well," I said, "in the thirties, as I've learned, research into atomic science was a worldwide endeavor. The Brits, Germans, Japanese, Italians, French, Russians, Scandinavians, and Americans—physicists, chemists, mathematicians, Nobel Prize winners—shared all their discoveries through the medium of scientific papers, which were available worldwide. Once Hitler began to take shape as the monster he was, the sharing tended to stop as the possibility of another world war began to materialize."

"And I thought the Bomb was all our doing," he said.

"The science was truly an international endeavor," I said. "The first so-called atomic pile, a term for a controlled nuclear reaction, was accomplished by an Italian scientist, Enrico Fermi, working at the University of Chicago, anecdotally under the university's stadium. In those days state boundaries were transparent to exchanges of high-level science. They were actually looking for a way to make an endless source of heat, not a bomb. With heat, you could boil water, make steam and thus electricity. They were calling it atomic *power*."

"Who thought up the Bomb, then?"

"Any physicist who knew how a chain reaction worked knew that it could be turned into a devastating bomb. Nuclear power envisioned a controlled reaction. A bomb was simply an *un*controlled nuclear reaction. The trick was to keep the nuclear material together long enough for a full, unrestrained, and comprehensive chain reaction to take place. We're talking nanoseconds."

"And where did you learn all of this?" he asked.

"From Captain Van Rensselaer," I said. "He's been inside the Manhattan Project since the beginning. I blundered into the project when we got inside that U-boat and found uranium."

"I rather doubt you tend to blunder into anything, Captain," he said.

"With respect, General, I certainly did with this hairball."

He turned his attention to Janet, who'd been sitting there keeping her face entirely neutral. "Commander, I understand you are fluent in Japanese and lived here for some years. You work for Naval Intelligence?"

"Yes, sir," she replied. "Or, I did. I've been seconded to the White House staff."

His eyes narrowed. Mention of the White House staff had caught his immediate attention. I held my breath. Unless I was wrong, President Truman did not want General MacArthur to know exactly why we were here.

"And you interviewed refugees from *Hiroshima* and *Nagasaki*," he went on. "On your recent expedition to the islands of *Kyushu* and southwest *Honshu*."

She nodded. "I did," she said. "I wouldn't call them refugees, however. Stunned survivors is more like it. They're calling the Bomb the sun-bomb. They said a second sun blazed in the heavens and then their city was gone, along with thousands of people. Strangers, relatives, their doctors, their universities, their markets—all gone in one flash."

He nodded again, his face truly sober now. He puffed away on that ridiculous corncob pipe for a long moment. "My title," he said, finally, "is the Supreme Commander for the Allied Powers in Japan. Abbreviated SCAP. Isn't that lovely? I have direct and absolute authority over all the Japanese people *and* their emperor. My orders are to demobilize and disarm Japan, bring their war criminals to justice, and then reconstitute Japan as a constitutional democracy. I may just be here for a while."

We both nodded. It was a simply enough stated mission, while clearly a Herculean task.

"Commander," he said, staring imperiously at Janet, "did you in the course of your interviews with the atomic bomb survivors discern a deep-seated antipathy toward America for using the atomic bomb?"

Wow, I thought. Talk about seeing right through to the heart of the matter! It was as if he knew exactly why we were there. My friendly little voice pointed out that I shouldn't have been surprised. This was Douglas MacArthur we were talking to, but Janet handled it beautifully.

"The Japanese are a stoic people," she said. "I think that they accept the use of the atomic bomb as yet another inevitable consequence of war. Like the firebombing of *Tokyo*. Or the starvation caused by American submarines. And the sheer numbers of young men who went away to war and never returned—and never will. So, it wasn't like they were doing all that well in the previous months and years."

"There's a commission coming in a month or two," MacArthur said. "To track down where, when, and how, and possibly if, the Japanese attempted to build a bomb. I'm trying to decide how to manage that. The Japanese army generals we have in custody claim that there might have been a navy project. Their senior navy people say there may have been an army project. Both claim it got nowhere, as far as they know, for lack of funds and materials."

I didn't say anything, not wanting to confirm his suspicions about our purpose. He looked at Janet, who shook her head. "I didn't even know about an *American* project until I got pulled in at the last moment," she said.

MacArthur appeared to give up. "Well, let's see what they come up with. My question is that, if they did succeed, are there more Japanese A-bombs hidden somewhere? Not everyone in Japan was happy with the surrender, you know. One extremist military group almost succeeded in assassinating *Hirohito*, so he couldn't surrender to the Allies. He beat them to the punch by telling the country it was all over. On public radio.

It was the first time any of his people had ever heard his voice. I'm told the entire population stood up and bowed to their radios while he was speaking."

"A damned close-run thing, then, General," I commented, quoting Wellington.

He nodded. "And then there's to be a war-crimes tribunal," he said. "Judges from all the Allied countries. A staff of hundreds. And then a staff of Japanese lawyers for the accused. There are many accused. They wanted me to preside. I pointed out that I had other things to do just now. The president relented, thank God, but I know that I will be dragged in, one way or another. But my biggest job right now is to turn the lights back on throughout Japan. The roads, the railroads, all the bridges, housing, the rice paddies, the steel mills, the coal mines, and the resumption of raw materials imports, which is how this mess began in the first place. Oil, metal ores, wood, wire, meat, rice—the lists are endless, and these things have to come from countries Japan recently wrecked. That's going to be a tough sell. You see my problem, Captain?"

I closed my eyes for a moment. "I fought, too, General," I said. "Guadalcanal, Bougainville, and some of the island campaigns. I am not sympathetic to Japan's needs."

"Neither am I, Captain," he said forcefully. "But I have my orders, and I think I understand why, even though the president has not shared his inner thoughts with me. But looking at the world stage, it is clear that China is lost to communism, and that communist Russia intends to dominate Europe now that they have occupied a great part of it. But that world stage belongs to the president, not to any generals. When you brief the president, please do me the favor of telling him that I know my place."

"I'm not expecting the president to ask either of us to assess you, sir," I said. "We are just messengers."

"Nevertheless," he said. "Make that point, please."

"Yes, sir. Assuming he cares to hear our opinion on anything like that. We are pretty insignificant individuals."

"If that were true," he said softly, "we wouldn't be speaking, and you two wouldn't be here. In other words, don't try to bullshit a professional bullshitter, Captain."

I had to grin, and to my relief, he did, too. It was time to go.

"May we speak with Captain Van Rensselaer?" Janet asked.

MacArthur shook his head. "No. He went back to Washington three days ago, at my request, I might add. He and I had a small disagreement as to his role in this command."

Janet looked surprised. MacArthur saved her. "Brigadier General Walters will arrange for your return to Washington," he said. "I'm presuming you got what you came for?"

"Yessir," I said immediately. "And thank you for the outstanding logistical support. It was most helpful."

He stared down at his desk for a moment, as if he had one more thing to say, but then shook his head. His office door opened, the aide beckoned, and off we went. Much impressed.

THIRTY-SIX
HEADING HOME

As our car started off for the short drive to the hotel, I asked our escorting officer, yet another Army major, where I could get a bottle of Scotch. He said something to our driver, an Army sergeant, who then took us to the American embassy building. He was young for a major, and wearing a West Point ring. Not tall, a bit swarthy, with big shoulders and a martial arts confidence to him. I saw him glance at my build with recognition. He was reserved when we met and I introduced him to Janet; I almost thought he was about to bow. Interesting guy.

There were no formal diplomatic relations yet in place, and thus no US ambassador, but the building had been reoccupied by the Occupation forces and there were several low-level American diplomats already in place. There were also armed guards prominently arrayed around the building. The senior official there was an ex-consul, who had no official duties other than to supervise the rehabilitation of the premises and prepare for the eventual reestablishment of full diplomatic relations. Unofficially he was busy locating the threads of eventual diplomatic relations with the Palace, the National Diet, and their version of a Foreign Office. The major easily talked our way through the main gates and then went inside the rather imposing but obviously somewhat run-down building.

He came back in ten minutes with a wrapped package under his arm, and then we went on to the hotel. I reimbursed him with some greenbacks that I still had in my wallet. I asked him how it was that there was whiskey at the still unofficial embassy building. He grinned.

"Legend has it that the General told the State Department cookie pushers that there could be no food reliably supplied unless there was reasonable compensation for the Supreme Allied Commander's special efforts. The acting consul, without batting an eye, had replied: Scotch or bourbon? MacArthur had said, simply: yes, thank you."

"God bless the General," Janet remarked. "Where should we go for food tonight?"

"You have any more of those US dollars?" he asked. "If you do, privately offer the hotel manager twenty greenback dollars and ask if he can provide a traditional Japanese meal for your personal experience before you leave. So that you can then sing the praises of Japanese cuisine and his hotel back in America. You'll be amazed. Do not ask *what* anything is—just experience it."

"And our travel back to the States?"

"There'll be a car here at around eleven tomorrow. You're to fly to Manila, and from there I don't know, but someone at GHQ in Manila will know. Captain Van Rensselaer set all that up before he went back."

"What happened between the General and Van Rensselaer?" I asked.

"I think it was more of a personality conflict than anything else. Van Rensselaer could be—pushy—at times, and 'pushy' from a subordinate does not sit well with the General."

I nodded. "So, the old rule still applies—personality conflict. The five-star Army general had a personality; the Navy O-6 had a conflict."

He grinned. "As always, Captain. Nothing ever changes in that regard, does it? Enjoy your dinner. When they mean to impress you, it's downright amazing."

"It almost sounds as if, here in *Tokyo*, the war never happened when it comes to doing business," Janet observed.

"Oh, it happened all right," he said. "Just look around this city. And out around the base at *Yokosuka*. I grew up here, in Japan. My father was prewar State Department. That's why I'm on MacArthur's direct headquarters staff now. Language-wise, with a little makeup I can disappear in this town. They're nothing if not practical; they know a flood of non-warriors are coming. What's done is done. For the 'players' in *Tokyo*, there's recovery money to be made."

THIRTY-SEVEN
BRIEFING THE PRESIDENT

We left *Tokyo* at around noon the next day and flew to the *Kadena* Army Air Force base on *Okinawa* to refuel. We ended up spending the night on the base for an unexpected engine change, and left the next morning early, arriving in Manila late that afternoon. *Kadena* had been undergoing a major expansion, which meant that a horde of imported construction commands and companies from the States were going around the clock to extend and repave the runways, build fuel farms, control towers, and even hangars. It was a noisy night.

In Manila we were assigned berths aboard a Navy troop transport that was stationed in Manila harbor to receive any Allied POWs who might still be out there in the wilds of Luzon Island and elsewhere. There were a disturbing number of them still being brought in from distant camps, and in terrible shape, too. The bulk of the Allied prisoners had already been recovered and sent back to Pearl for extensive medical treatment and some time to recover from being starved for years by their Japanese torturers. We each received a cabin in the officers' quarters aboard the transport ship, a converted passenger liner.

The inner parts of Manila were still in ruins, courtesy of the Japanese scorched-earth policy when they finally were driven out of the shattered brick, stone, and mortar ruins of the occupied city. We were driven through the city from the airfield, and I was saddened by what I saw. As a Pacific Fleet sailor, I'd been there often. Seeing Manila recovering took some of the sting out of seeing *Hiroshima* and *Nagasaki*. The A-bomb was the least we could do, I told Janet bitterly. The Filipinos we encountered were battered but not defeated. They are a resilient people, and, unfortunately, too used to being occupied by foreign conquerors, including the United States. But they'd kept their honor, resisting the Japanese throughout the war, often at great cost.

We had to wait a day in Manila, which we spent aboard the ship. There was no point in going ashore, with misery everywhere. And rising disease. We spent some time rehearsing what we were going to report to Mr. Truman when we got back, while our memories were still fresh. We each regretted not having had a cameraman with us in the A-bomb cities. But then Janet realized that any pictures would show mostly nothing. There'd be time for photos once the commissions got going, and besides, if a cameraman had passed a radiation hot spot, the film would have been ruined.

There were all sorts of people aboard that ship, ranging from barely surviving soldiers down on the ship's hospital deck to American civilians who'd been hidden in the city trying to get back to the States. The ship's main dining deck had been turned into an all-hands situation, where civilians, troops, diplomats, businessmen, important Filipino refugees, Allied soldiers, and officers mingled indiscriminately without any of the social barriers that would most certainly have been there prewar. Some genius had made sure the ship came out from Pearl with booze, so it was kinda fun, now that the war was over. Janet and I retired to my cabin for the night and tried to make up for lost time.

The next day we boarded the Pan Am Clipper in Manila harbor with a priority pass for the long, long trip back to the States. I must say, Van

Rensselaer had been thorough in arranging our trip home, literally half-way across the globe. Fortunately, we physically arrived in Washington on a Friday, which meant we could both submerge into the comforting quiet of a Washington weekend before having to rise back up and attend to business. I called Admiral Leahy's office Friday night to say we were back. One of his staff said the admiral and the president were away for the weekend and to check back Monday, and then said, actually, Tuesday. Monday's gonna be a bear, he sighed.

I chose to go to Janet's home rather than bother my friend up in Chevy Chase. We slept through the weekend, and the change to Tuesday was a godsend—even by Sunday night, we weren't ready. Monday turned into a logistics day. Janet had to reconnect with Naval Intelligence, and I had to show my face in OpNav. And then uniforms, back pay, food in the house, bills and other mail, and by that evening we had a drink, skipped dinner, and went back to bed, still trying to accommodate to a new time zone. Janet pointed out that if we could drill a hole right through the center of the earth from Washington, we'd probably pop out in a *Tokyo* suburb. Where they'd kill us, I remarked. As a favor, she said, her eyes still blurry from the trip.

I tried to call Leahy's office the next morning, but ran into a righteous White House palace guard stone wall. For a moment I thought about trying to impress them with our presidential mission orders, but settled for a message to the admiral that we were back and ready to report. They reluctantly took the message, noting that my message would be one of hundreds, just so I'd know. I told the surly secretary that this concerned the atomic bomb, and if she lost the message, President Truman himself would fire her. Then I hung up.

Mention of the A-bomb must have worked. That afternoon, a much more polite White House staffer called back and said we'd be tentatively meeting with the president himself tomorrow afternoon, time to be confirmed. Janet was eavesdropping on an extension and told the staffer that the president would be welcome to come to her riverside home if his schedule permitted. The staffer just couldn't help himself and told her that the president of the United States did not come to other people, but rather they came to him. She said simply, he's been here before. Get the word to him that the invite is open. He'll be pissed if you don't. Really. We'll come there, of course, if that's necessary, but do tell him.

Then we both hung up. I couldn't imagine what that poor guy thought about this development, but I told Janet he'd be squirming until someone senior told him what to do. I need to check the bourbon supply, was all she said.

I got her to drive me to my old gym. I desperately needed to work out. She went shopping and then came back in an hour. I dragged myself into her car, my body a mass of aches and pains. Weight lifting is an effort best done regularly, I'd discovered. Again. She was less than sympathetic. There are other, more pleasant ways to relieve stress, she said, helpfully. I think I groaned out loud. It was a lovely offer and also entirely out of the question. I managed a long, hot shower and then an even longer nap before dinner. Janet had set up the "river room," as she called it, for visitors.

"You think he'll come?" she asked.

"Somebody will," I said. "He took such pleasure at getting out of the White House the last time."

"Hope so," she said. "I upped my game with regard to the bourbon. Got some Old Forester."

By eight thirty we'd both about given up. I'd tried some of the more expensive bourbon and still didn't much care for it. Once a Scotch man, always . . . etc. Then there they were: a flare of headlights in the driveway again, and we both grinned at each other. I was still a little stiff and achy, but Janet had applied some warpaint and perfume and looked delectable. The usual Secret Service mob came in and spread out through the house looking for lurking assassins, and then there he was, HST himself, with those big glasses and an even bigger grin when he saw the bottle of bourbon. He thanked Janet effusively as she handed him a libation and then we sat down and exchanged a few pleasantries. He looked a little bit older and also a bit worn down. The end of the war had brought a whole host of new problems and an even larger host of people banging on his door for solutions, social access, pork barrel favors, the daily international crisis. Then Janet turned to the issue at hand. The president settled back to listen. One of the Secret Service men looked different from the rest as he sat nearby in a hall chair. He was older, no sunglasses, and not as in-shape as the rest. I assumed he was a bit more than just a palace guard, but that was okay with me.

She briefly described our trip and then the horrors we'd seen in the two cities. She talked about what a huge undertaking it would be to even feed Japan in the near future, and what a good job the Army was doing about it. The soldiers, she said, had probably arrived full of hate for the Japanese, but once they saw the result of the A-bombs, and then the starving people who were, as politely as they could, begging for just the basics while shedding skin and hair as they waited, they were no longer the enemy but just people, mostly older, women, and children, whose eyes were still wide at what they'd witnessed on The Day. She took some time to describe her interviews and the conclusions she'd drawn from just talking to these people. She reminded the president that stoicism, obedience to authority, acceptance of whatever Fate brought, and absolute trust in the emperor had been ingrained in them since the dawn of time in Japan.

"What was their opinion of the Bomb?" he asked.

"Yet another manifestation of the catastrophes that can come when war breaks out," she said. "Just like the fact that an entire generation of promising and beloved sons went away to war and never came back."

The president opened his mouth to speak but then stopped. "I was about to say they started it," he said, "but somehow, given what you've been describing, that seems a bit inadequate now."

"I don't think that the surviving general population, the farmers, fishermen, industrial workers, clerks in corporate Japan, shopkeepers, had any idea that they started it, as we all like to say. It wasn't what they were told by their all-powerful government—for years."

He nodded. "And Captain?" he said. "What's your take?"

"Janet took the deep pulse, Mr. President. She could speak to them in their own language, at which they seemed absolutely amazed. And from a foreign woman, of all things. Unbelievable. I think I mostly intimidated them, because of my size."

"I believe that, Captain," the president said. His glass was empty and Janet quietly took care of that problem.

"I think the most important thing I discovered was that their military had been exploring atomic power since well before the war. I interviewed one professor who claimed that Japan had discovered the possibility that the atom could be split to produce energy. He confirmed that Japan and Germany had been collaborating since before the war. I fed him a wee bit of BS about how we'd known all, and that the Russians had known all along, and that I'd witnessed their pathetic test. I thought he was about to cry. But when I asked where the rest of their team was, he shut down. MacArthur's people may have better luck."

"Where's this professor now?" he asked.

"General MacArthur's people have him."

"I see," the president said. "How is the good General?"

"Working hard to rise to the occasion, I would say," I replied. "He has a sure grasp of what's going to be required to reconstitute Japan and how long it might take."

"As *shoguns* go," Janet offered, "he's about perfect. Immense political authority, a great sense of diplomatic majesty, an aura of total command, and from what we saw, he is assembling a first-class staff of specialist people to make it happen."

"Diplomatic majesty," the president murmured. "Got that right."

"Plus," I said. "Someone here has told him that we are going to try to bring Japan into our geopolitical orbit."

Truman raised his head. "Is that so?" he asked rhetorically.

"We had an audience with the General before we left," I said. "At his request. It was impressive just being in the room with him, and then he proceeded to demonstrate a grasp of what he faced in the coming years, and was kind enough to share that with us. He was most interested in the professor because he had a commission inbound to study just that whole issue."

Truman nodded. "I think that's going to take five or six years to accomplish, but from what you're telling me, I need to do a better job of cutting the General into the interagency process that's gearing up to build the postwar world to our liking."

"I got the impression he's pretty well informed about what's happening here in Washington, sir," I said. "That said, I could well be mistaken."

Truman gave me a frosty grin. "I sincerely doubt that, Captain, *and* Commander. You two have been very helpful to me, not so much in telling me stuff I may not know, but confirming what I've been told with dependable, agenda-free ground truth, as the expression goes. So: you think the idea of getting Japan to be an ally is feasible?"

I turned to Janet. She was the one who'd talked to real people.

"Yes, Mr. President, but not until we have reconstituted Japan as a modern industrial society. They will want to feel that they're in charge of their own destiny. Whoever ends up in charge of their new government will be determined not to become some vassal state. I think you'd succeed if you kept them from becoming socialist, or worse, a communist state. The Japanese are hardworking people who value intelligence and compete for jobs and schools on the basis of national examinations. The people who get put in charge of this effort will have to be at least as smart and hardworking as they are. In my humble opinion, Japan and its people are at a junction where clever people can mold them into what we need. They in turn will mold us back to do that in a Japanese way."

Truman smiled. "I think I understand that, but if I don't entirely, I have people who will," he said. "By the way, you guys want a job?" We laughed.

Truman stood up and thanked us again for our hospitality and the good job we'd done going out to Japan at such a difficult time. He told us that he might ask us, as a team, to do similar tasks in the future, depending on what the Navy had in store for us. And if you need some support in that regard, he said, know that you have a friend in the White House. Don't hesitate to ask, okay?

We thanked him and then the security mob coalesced as if by magic in the foyer, surrounded their peppery charge, and then were gone.

THIRTY-EIGHT
VAN RENSSELAER'S FAREWELL

The next morning Janet was called into her office. Subject not revealed, but she was pretty sure they wanted to know where she'd been, what she'd been doing, and where her travel-expense form was. Important stuff.

"Someone gonna give you trouble?" I asked over morning coffee.

"Better not," she said. "If anyone gets snotty, I'll just tell them Harry Truman paid us a visit last night and the number crunchers can check with the White House. That oughta do it."

I laughed. God, yes. That absolutely would do it. At least she had an "owner" who cared. I didn't think I did. Admiral King was still the CNO, but that was surely about to change now that the war was over. I doubted that he or anyone else in the Navy was thinking: whatever happened to dear old Wolfe Bowen? I went upstairs, took a morning shower, and then got dressed in dress khakis, as if I might have somewhere official to go.

Then the phone rang. It was a staff guy from Admiral Leahy's office.

Fleet Admiral Leahy, I reminded myself. Five stars, not just some pedestrian four-star. Can you come now?

"Absolutely," I said. "On my way."

"Thank you, sir. Admiral Leahy said to tell you: well done. The president was pleased with your report."

"Thanks, Commander. It was a pleasure to have him visit again. Oh, I don't have a car available. Would it be possible—"

"Yes, sir. What's your current address?"

I gave it to him and he said it would be a few minutes.

Ten minutes later a black sedan arrived and off we went, not to the White House but to the Bethesda National Naval Medical Center in northeast Washington. FDR himself had drawn the first crude design drawing of Bethesda years ago, with its tall tower and expansive grounds. I asked the driver why Bethesda, and he told me that Captain Van Rensselaer had had an apparent heart attack. I lapsed into silence. When we got there, I asked the driver to wait and then went inside. I was directed to the fourth floor, where the cardiac recovery unit was. I was met there by a cardiologist who said the White House had called and that I was expected. Well, knock me over with a feather, I thought, but at least there was no need for a "who are you and why are you here" conversation.

"How is he?" I asked right away.

"On borrowed time, I'm afraid," the doctor said. "He's a tall man, and his heart has simply given out. Stress, smoking, general exhaustion, and what we're starting to call time-zone fatigue. He only just returned from Japan. Are you a close friend?"

"Close enough," I said. "He was heavily involved in the atomic bomb project since 1942. Stress does not adequately describe that effort or his part in it."

The doctor blinked in surprise. "I see," he said. "Well, he needs oxygen to speak. Keep it short."

"Why," I asked, "if he's going to die anyway?"

The doctor stared at me as if I were some kind of heartless monster, but then relented and nodded. "Okay," he said. "Actually, I think he wants to talk to somebody."

He took me to Van Rensselaer's room. "Be prepared," he said. "He doesn't exactly look—good."

I thanked him and went in. Not looking good was the understatement of the year. Van Rensselaer was almost cadaverous, except for those piercing eyes. His imposing frame was much diminished and there were no traces of his previous *hauteur* and general superiority. It was a dismal sight. There were IVs in each arm and an oxygen line to his nostrils. His eyes were closed, and his breathing was labored. I pulled up a chair as quietly as I could. He stirred and opened his eyes.

"You," he whispered, and then tried to clear his throat.

"In person," I replied. "And you . . ."

"I know," he said in a stronger voice. "Shot at and missed . . ."

I grinned at him. "Did MacArthur do this?"

His lips twitched as he tried to smile. There was a stainless-steel cup with a straw on the night table that I assumed was ice water. I offered it to him and he took some, but I had to hold on to the cup.

"MacArthur and I did not get along, it turned out," he said.

"I heard," I said. "One of his staffers said that you could be—pushy, at times. I told him I was astonished, hearing that."

Another attempt at a smile. "Don't ever underestimate his hatred for all things Navy," he said. "According to him, he could have beaten the Japanese in eighteen months if the goddamned Navy hadn't gotten in the way."

"I'll bet he didn't hate that Navy PT boat skipper who extracted him from Corregidor," I said. "While he left his entire Army behind, destined for the Bataan Death March and points north."

"He said that Chester Nimitz fought him at every turn," he whispered. "Until he at last prevailed upon the Joint Chiefs to let him invade the Philippines. He got so mad telling me off that his corncob pipe caught fire. Amazing how an illustrious family whelped such a phony. Dugout Doug to the end."

He was spooling up. I decided to change the subject. I told him about encountering the Japanese professor at *Nagasaki*, and how he claimed that they'd invented atomic fission.

He snorted and managed to dislodge his oxygen line, of course just as a nurse came in to check on us. She dealt with that issue while giving me a dirty look.

"We screwed that up," he said, once she left. "All eyes on the Germans, especially once Einstein sent that letter to FDR. That's what all the pressure was about, right from the beginning. Einstein said the Nazis were on the verge of harnessing nuclear fission to make a superbomb. Even the Brits echoed that assertion, getting their intel wrong, as usual. The Nazis were further along than we were right from the beginning of the Manhattan Project. But it's hard to do good science when you're getting bombed every night. Even so, none of us, from Oppenheimer on down, *ever* even entertained the notion that the Japanese had a program. Once the B-29s got going, anyone who'd seen Oak Ridge would have laughed at the very idea that they were working on one. Our photo guys would have seen it immediately."

"Until Portsmouth," I said.

"Until Portsmouth," he repeated. "That was a shock, and I felt more than a little responsible."

"That was certainly *not* the case," I said. "That's the thing about using submarines to do stuff. You can't see them. Your problem was that you took the weight of the whole damn program on your shoulders."

"Somebody had to," he said. "Groves couldn't do it all, and I had the president of the United States asking me every single day when we'd get one. It was hard. It was slow. It was frightening, way-out-there science. Maybe burn up the atmosphere. Maybe make human life extinct. Loose the power of the sun on all our heads. Besides, can you imagine how many GIs we could have saved if we'd had it before *Iwo* or *Okinawa*?"

"The good thing was that we—you—got it before Operation Olympic. That's something to be very proud of. They were predicting a million casualties. Instead it was two, three hundred thousand casualties—all theirs."

"Yeah, okay, now look at me." His voice was stronger.

"I am looking at you," I said as sympathetically as I could. "Where's your family?"

He sighed. "My parents are gone," he said. "I have an older brother and a sister, both in their fifties, who are selling off parts of the estate to maintain their lords-of-the-manor lifestyle. I was the youngest, and thus inherited only some small acreage on the Hudson, essentially nothing. Primogeniture, the European model, you know. The Van Rensselaers are effectively gone. The Roosevelts, the important ones, are gone. Truman is probably overwhelmed as the country shifts gears. Leahy's beyond tired. He did come out to visit, by the way, God bless him. But with two aides who were continuously taking calls from the White House on a phone circuit they'd set up especially for him here in Bethesda. He finally apologized and said he had to get back."

"And Groves? Does he know you're ill?"

"Probably not," he said. "And he's circling the wagons now that the effects of the Bomb are starting to leak out. But he brought the thing home and ended the war. Guys like me were always in the shadows, part of FDR's secret mafia. A powerful, exhilarating deep secret game. But now the Congress is finding out about the Russian spies in the program, so Oppenheimer and his friends are coming under fire. MacArthur is, happily, ten thousand miles away, but there's talk about putting him up to run for president one day. Against Truman. It's a new day in America, and probably time for us dragons to go back into our caves. I've had a most interesting run, so this heart thing does not much dismay me."

"I'd been hoping you'd write a book, you know, about being the ultimate inside man in the Manhattan Project. Even in the little time I saw you in action, you must have some fascinating stories to tell."

"That would be the problem," he said with a wry smile. 'They' would never let me publish it. If nothing else because the Bomb itself is becoming controversial. That was one of the reasons Truman asked you to go back—he wanted to hear from somebody *he* trusted just how bad it was and how the Japanese themselves felt about it."

I told him of our debrief at Janet's house, and what we'd learned. I spared no details about the damage and destruction. "People were say-ing that the big firebombing raids on *Tokyo* had done almost as much damage, but I must say, they're wrong about that. *Tokyo* was beginning to come back to life by the time of our second trip; in my opinion, those other two cities won't come back for years, if ever."

He closed his eyes. I wished for a moment that Janet had come along. She had a lot more people skills than I ever would.

"Don't let the lovely commander get away," he said, as if he'd read my mind. "That was my life's second big mistake. Too much me and no room for anyone else. I pretty much knew I was going to be a lifelong bachelor after going to my first dance at the academy. The girls were all scared of me because of my height."

"But you obviously loved what you were doing," I said, trying to re-assure him. "The bureaucratic power, the pressure, the way that bureau-crats and even senior officers were scared of you. I still remember the look on King's face that day you walked out. You had to love all that."

"I did indeed," he admitted. "I absolutely loved being one of FDR's horsemen of the apocalypse, so I cannot complain that I am now alone. I appreciate your coming to visit, Captain Wolfe Bowen. You will make a good admiral, I think."

"I don't know about that," I said, still not allowing myself to use his first name. I thought about explaining the hump boards, and the coming fleet-wide cull of the captain herd, but he was clearly weary and then one of his monitors began chirping. That nurse was back in a flash, gesturing that my time was up.

"Been good to know you, Captain," I said as I was getting up, aware now that more than one monitor was getting upset.

He nodded. "My best wishes to the commander," he croaked as more medical staff came in. "And to you. Thank you again for everything."

By the time I got back into the staff car, I wondered if he'd already gone.

THIRTY-NINE
BRAND-NEW WORLD

The following day I received a summons to the CNO's office. They told me to report by 1100 in service dress uniform, which now, as fall began, would be service dress blues. Janet had already left for some more interviews at the Naval Intelligence headquarters. I looked forward to it because Fleet Admiral Chester Nimitz had just relieved Fleet Admiral E. J. King as CNO. A summons from Ernie "Jesus" King was always fraught with professional peril. Nimitz, on the other hand, was known to be a pleasant, reasonable, and reserved officer, who'd commanded in the Pacific with quiet, almost majestic authority and with none of the bombast attributed to some of his contemporaries, such as MacArthur or King. King had always been feared; Nimitz was universally revered. I couldn't imagine why he'd want to see me. They said they'd send a car.

As it turned out, it was an in-office awards ceremony, with Nimitz presenting me a Legion of Merit medal. His executive assistant and a couple of aides were also present.

"Well, done, Captain," he said. "The president himself directed this award, and did so in a manner reflecting his sincere appreciation for your services regarding the atomic bomb project and especially its aftermath."

I saluted him, and then thanked him, although I was still somewhat bewildered why Janet Waring wasn't here getting the same award. I did, for once, have the sense not to ask any questions.

"I wish I could say that I knew all about this," Nimitz said, "but Admiral Leahy called me last night and told me that this is what the president wanted. You must have rung a bell over there, Captain, because this is somewhat unprecedented, as you may realize. But just because I don't know exactly what you did doesn't detract from the award or your remarkable service to the president."

"Were you briefed on the atomic bomb before we dropped it, Admiral?" I said. "If I may ask, that is?"

"The first I personally knew about anything about it," he replied, "was when President Truman called me at my headquarters in Guam on the transpacific cable and told me that a top secret mission would launch from Tinian the next day and that, if it worked, the war would soon be over."

"Wow," I said. "That's amazing to me."

"Me, too, once I learned what all that meant," he said with a smile.

"Well, sir, if it's any consolation, Mr. Truman himself didn't know anything about the thing until after FDR died. I was there when he was first briefed on it. He was not happy with having been kept out of the loop as vice president."

"So I have heard, Captain," he said. "That was about as big a secret as one could imagine, wasn't it? And you were privy to it. I'm impressed, sir."

"Yes, sir, it was." Then I took a chance, but if anyone deserved to know, it was C. W. Nimitz. "There was only one greater secret, Admiral, which probably accounts for this medal."

"What was that, Captain?" Nimitz asked, patiently. Aides were waiting, impatiently.

"That the Japanese had one, too."

The color drained out of his face. For a moment he was speechless. I could see the shock in the faces of his EA, the rear admiral, and two other horse-holders present for the impromptu awards ceremony. *What?!*

He took a breath and then said: "One day, Captain, I would love to hear about your part in this."

"Absolutely, sir," I said. "One fine day."

He smiled again, knowing exactly what I meant. As in, if they ever let me tell it, and we both knew they never would.

I took my leave. On the ride back to Janet's home, I was trying to figure out how to tell her I got a medal and she did not. It just wasn't right. She had done as much as anything I had done, if not more. I wondered if I should go see Leahy and get this straightened out. But as I arrived back at the river house, it occurred to me that my role—our role—in this adventure had just come to an end. Van Rensselaer was dying if not already gone. Probably the latter. Our good friend the president was certainly immersed in the immense problems of state, which by now probably made the atomic bomb project something of an afterthought. The Bomb would now take on a life of its own in the world; the people who created it would soon be relegated to the sidelines of world affairs. They might even one day feel the collective opprobrium of the world's nations once the world got a good look at what Janet and I had seen. America could take the sting out of that by revealing that the Japanese had been creating the same thing, and for the same reasons. I wondered if that would ever happen, though. That revelation might undo our overarching strategic objective of bringing them into the fold of the free world.

Janet got home at five that evening and we had our customary drinks in the river room.

"So how was your day, dear," she quipped in a parody of wifely interest.

"Just great," I replied, going with it. "Chester Nimitz gave me a medal, the Legion of Merit. I'm not sure he understood what it was for, but I suspect that the White House had a hand in it. How was your day?"

She tried to stay in character but couldn't manage it. "Really? Chester Nimitz himself?"

"In the flesh," I said. "I wanted to ask him where your medal was but couldn't summon up the courage."

She laughed. "Mine was at the DNI's office," she announced. "Same kinda reaction—here's the Legion of Merit, with an 'I'm sure this is merited but not sure what for' expression on the DNI's face."

"Well, I'm glad to hear it, my dearest Commander," I said. "For a moment there I thought I'd have to hide it from you."

"Because I'm a woman, no doubt," she said. "And a WAVES to boot. Do you even know what WAVES stands for?"

"Um," I began.

"Right," she said. "Women Accepted for Volunteer Emergency Service. WAVES. Not to be confused with real naval officers, and certainly not to be taken seriously in other than an administrative capacity."

"Quite right, too," I said with as straight a face as I could manage.

"Bastard," she muttered.

"Bastard, aye," I said. "Will you marry me?"

"Hell, no," she grumped.

"How about tomorrow?"

"Well," she said. "Tomorrow's another day. You'll have to un-bastard."

"Yikes," I said. "Change my spots and everything?"

"Yup."

"What if I decide to stay in?" I asked. "Take Mr. Truman up on his offer to put in a word with the hump board? Become an admiral of the ocean sea and everything?"

"You're not gonna do that."

I sighed. "No, I guess not," I admitted. "The hump board ALNAV is out, by the way. The numbers are pretty staggering."

"How's it gonna work?" she asked.

"They'll invite probably half of the serving O-6 grade naval officers to consider retirement from active duty. That's before the board convenes. They'll waive the twenty years of service requirement to qualify for retired pay. There are quite a few captains who made grade early just by surviving. Guys with eighteen, nineteen years of service. So that's only fair."

"How many years do you have in?" she asked.

"Coming on twenty-two. The basic rule is you get two and a half percent of your current base pay as retired pay, which is pretty generous."

"But still," she pointed out. "All these guys who get 'plucked' are gonna have their income cut. And everyone's predicting a recession. Jobs are gonna be tough to find."

"Yes, jobs will be few and far between. Truman alluded to that, didn't he? That's why you have to marry me, Commander with active duty pay."

She laughed. "I'll think about it, soon-to-be ex-Captain. But you're gonna have to be really nice to me, right? And I'm going to be the senior one, right? Lots of respect. Maybe even some groveling."

"Absolutely," I said. "Want a demonstration?"

"Right now?"

"Well," I said.

Then the phone rang.

I started to get up but then subsided. Respect, she'd said. Her house, her phone. Her problem, whatever it was. With respect came responsibility. I grinned at her and nodded at the phone. She laughed and went to get it.

Admiral Leahy's office calling, she reported. We're sending a car. Need the both of you to come in, please. Now would be nice.

I asked for the phone. "If this concerns a trip to Japan the answer is no," I growled.

"Hello, Captain," the nice young lady said. "I have no idea of why he wants to see you. He usually doesn't share. Get me Captain Bowen and that ONI commander. It's Fleet Admiral Leahy—that usually does it."

"Don't care—no more goddamn excursions to Japan," I said.

"Oh, Captain," the aide said. "Don't be that way. He's an old man. He wouldn't know what to do if you refused to come when called. He might even send the Marines."

Janet frowned and relieved me of the phone. "We'll be ready when the car shows up," she said, sweetly, and hung up.

We waited for ten minutes outside Leahy's office. A pretty young civilian secretary finally beckoned us in. I tried to glare at her, but it was hard when she blew us a kiss as we went through the office door. We assumed the customary standing position in front of the Great Man's desk.

"The president has a job for you both," he began. "He's standing up something called an Atomic Energy Commission. The underlying idea is to deflect all the current hostile press and general disapproval for using the Bomb on helpless Japanese civilians by changing the focus of our atomic program onto the peaceful uses of atomic energy. Unlimited electrical power. Clean, nonpolluting power stations. Not to mention the medical uses of atomic isotopes to detect and cure cancer. The possibility of developing atomic power plants for ships and large airplanes, which would never have to be refueled. He wants to call it Atoms for Peace. Make everyone look forward to the possibilities of nuclear fission for the benefit of all mankind, instead of backward to the destruction of two Japanese cities."

I couldn't think of anything to say, and neither could Janet.

"He wants you two to be accredited to this commission as White House technical representatives. With duties to be specified by the president. That way everyone knows you're Truman's people, just like everyone knew who Roosevelt's people were, and why they were there. You both have seen firsthand what the Bomb could do. No one in this commission can claim that experience. Commander, your knowledge of Japanese will be invaluable to the members of the commission when they start asking questions about the dangers of using atomic power without careful supervision."

"And what's my role, if I may ask?" I said.

He looked up at me, and for the first and only time in my life, I saw him smile. "Your role is to protect her, Captain," he said. "An election is coming. There will necessarily be people on this commission who are not friends of the president. You have credentials. You were the man who confirmed the Japanese program. You were also there to debrief the Japanese victims in *Hiroshima* and *Nagasaki*. And, last but not least, you're the biggest Navy captain I've ever seen. Somebody starts browbeating

Commander Waring here, I would expect you to loom to good effect. The commission will be made up of senior academics, bureaucrats, and political operatives from both parties, who will have no experience with, what did the president call it, hired muscle. That's how they'll perceive you after the first incident, whatever it is, which means they'll never see you coming when it's time to report to the president."

"*Kabuki*," I muttered.

"Just so, Captain. Enjoy. And thank you again for all you two have done."

He turned back to his paperwork and we obligingly left.

"You think this is a paying job?" I asked Janet after we were safely in the car.

"Oh, yes," she said. "Why?"

"Well, then, maybe you don't have to marry me after all."

She grinned. "Sayeth the fly, to the spider, perhaps?"

I tried to keep a straight face, but, boy, it was hard.

AUTHOR'S THOUGHTS

Well, the obvious question: did the Japanese government try for an atomic weapon during World War II? I am convinced they did. But not the way the American government did. The Japanese government was an aggregation of factions. The army. The navy. The barons. The imperial court. The emperor himself. It is clear from the records that the Japanese army and navy both had nuclear programs. It is equally clear that neither one knew anything about the other's program. The army and the navy were competing factions in Japan. Competing for budget money, bureaucratic power, approval at court, and influence within the bureaucracy. They did not speak to each other. To speak to each other as equals would have meant a distinct loss of face for both of them. Simply not done.

In the earliest years of the twentieth century the fundamental science of atomic energy was an international endeavor. Individual scientists would make discoveries and then share them with all the other physicists working in that area—worldwide. So it's not like the Japanese would have been starting from scratch in the field. Their top mathematicians and physicists were part of the international network and well known to their European counterparts.

Adding to my conviction is the effort made by the US government to suppress any evidence that Japan had a bomb project in motion. The sources I used to dig out this story all complain about how other sources and information they needed and knew existed were firmly withdrawn from access. There could only be one reason for that: Japan was a vitally needed ally in the postwar decade of rising communism in China and the growing realization that the Soviet empire was bent on the destruction of American ideals for world peace. The Japanese were happy to oblige by assuming the cloak of nuclear victims, a pose they could not sustain if the facts of their own nuclear program ever spilled out.

On balance, I think the American government was right. Smother the actual history. And today's strong strategic alignment with the United States proves that: Japan is now the primary bulwark against the imperial ambitions of China in Asia. No other country in Asia is capable of doing this. The atomic bombings of two Japanese cities were tragic, as was the entire war. Equally tragic, in my opinion, is the enslavement of China and Russia under the rubric of communism, which has resulted in far more deaths than were experienced in those two cities.

I can't imagine the angst produced by the decisions to reconstitute Japan as the industrial giant of Asia and an ally of the United States, given the savagery of the war in terms of how many Americans died or never came home. My father, who went out to the western Pacific in 1942 and came back in 1946, would not speak to a Japanese person for the rest of his life, even when he became a vice admiral. Senior American politicians would explain the move to bring Japan into the American orbit in terms of the Japanese people, who never really got a vote in the original decision for Japan to start a war with the United States. It was bad guys in the Japanese government who started the war, not the Japanese people. I can just hear a grieving mother whose son never came back saying: that's a distinction without a difference.

Truman's decision was, however, the essence of statecraft. Having watched FDR rule, he knew that the big picture, in every sense of that expression, comes first. The Atoms for Peace program didn't happen under Truman. Eisenhower made the original speech in 1953, but for the reasons I cited.

ACKNOWLEDGMENTS

The bibliography of the atomic bomb project during WWII is beyond huge. The book that got me interested in the story of Japan's atomic project was a book about Germany's involvement in Japan's project, called *Germany's Last Mission to Japan: The Failed Voyage of U-234,* by Joseph Mark Scalia. That led to the book *Japan's Secret War: How Japan's Race to Build Its Own Atomic Bomb Provided the Groundwork for North Korea's Nuclear Program,* by Robert K. Wilcox, which describes how North Korea jump-started its current nuclear weapons program by building on the remains of the Japanese works on its east coast. *The Apocalypse Factory: Plutonium and the Making of the Atomic Age,* by Steve Olson, describes the development of plutonium, and *Dark Sun: The Making of the Hydrogen Bomb,* by Richard Rhodes, details the making of the hydrogen bomb. The bibliography section of *Dark Sun* consists of twelve pages of small, single-spaced listings. As always, I consulted many other sources, assisted by daily searches on Google.

The question remains: did the Japanese put together an A-bomb and test it? Just for the hell of it, I consulted some obscure charts of the sea area off *Hungnam,* near the group of islands one researcher said was the location of their test. Contemporary charts don't show this, but one from 1952 showed a deformity in the sea bottom just off those islands some three hundred feet deep and a quarter mile in diameter. There are no other such deformations within one hundred miles of *Hungnam*, up or down the Korean coast.

I lived through the decade when Japanese superiority in manufacturing, education, quality assurance, precise attention to technical detail, and technical innovation burst upon the American industrial scene. It took more than a decade for American manufacturing to catch on and then catch up. In 1964, my destroyer, USS *Morton* (DD-948), went into the Japanese naval shipyard in *Yokosuka*. *Morton* was a main-engineering basket case. Nothing worked as it should. One morning, I was surprised to see down on the pier a line of over a hundred Japanese women, all dressed in white uniforms, and each carrying a basket. They came aboard, went down into the firerooms and engine rooms, and proceeded to dismantle every one of our main machinery pumps and motors. Each woman carried away parts of things like main feed pumps, generators, vent fans, and really big steam valves in their straw baskets.

Four days later, they were all back and reinstalling the parts and pieces they had taken. When we lit the plant off, everything worked. Everything was running so smoothly and quietly that you couldn't be sure that the plant was even lit off. No steam leaks. No roaring noises from the main feed pumps. No vibrating pipes. The valve handles could be turned with one hand. This was mechanical engineering at its finest. The women thought nothing of it. Business as usual. The machine, whatever it was, large or small, had a plan of specifications. Do what you have to do to return the machine to its own specifications. Of course it will work. Is this news, gentlemen? Um . . . could those guys have fashioned an atomic bomb? Yes, I think they could. And probably have, by now.

ABOUT THE AUTHOR

Cynthia Brann

P. T. Deutermann is the noted author of many previous novels based both on his experiences as a senior staff officer in Washington, DC, and at sea as a navy captain and, later, as a commodore of destroyers. His World War II works include *Iwo, 26 Charlie; The Last Paladin;* and *Pacific Glory,* all of which won the W. Y. Boyd Literary Award for Excellence in Military Fiction, as well as *The Hooligans, The Nugget, Sentinels of Fire, The Commodore, Trial by Fire, Ghosts of Bungo Suido,* and *The Iceman.* He lives in North Carolina with his wife of fifty-five years.